Go ahead and scream.

No one can hear you.

You're no longer in the safe world you know.

You've taken a terrifying step . . .
into the darkest corners of your imagination.

You've opened the door to . . .

THE NIGHTMARE ROOM

OTHER BOOKS BY R.L. STINE

THE NIGHTMARE ROOM, BOOKS 1-2-3
THE NIGHTMARE BEGINS!

DANGEROUS GIRLS

DANGEROUS GIRLS 2
THE TASTE OF NIGHT

BEWARE!
R.L. STINE PICKS HIS FAVORITE SCARY STORIES

THE HAUNTING HOUR
CHILLS IN THE DEAD OF NIGHT

NIGHTMARE HOUR
TIME FOR TERROR

R.L. STINE

THE NIGHTMARE ROOM

THE NIGHTMARE CONTINUES!
BOOKS 4-5-6

◭ AVON BOOKS

An Imprint of HarperCollins*Publishers*

A Parachute Press Book

THE NIGHTMARE ROOM
LIAR LIAR

CHAPTER 1

When I was little, a kid told me that everyone has an exact double somewhere in the world. I told the kid he was crazy.

I'm twelve now. And I just saw my exact double. Of course, I didn't believe my eyes. He didn't just look like me—he was me!

I wasn't staring into a mirror. I was staring at a boy with my face—my straight, brown hair, my blue eyes, my sort-of crooked smile. My FACE! My BODY! I was staring at ME! ME!

I know, I know. I sound a little crazed.

But you'd be crazed too if you had an exact double, and you didn't know who he was or where he came from.

I'm going to take a deep breath. That's what my dad always tells me to do. "Take a deep breath, Ross," he says.

My dad is a studio exec—one of the bosses at Mango Pictures. He spends his day arguing with movie producers, directors, and movie stars. He says he takes about a million deep breaths a day. It helps keep him calm.

So, I'm going to take a deep breath. And I'm going to start my story at the beginning. Or maybe a little before the beginning.

By the way, I lied about the blue eyes.

I don't have blue eyes. Actually, they're dark gray. Which is almost blue—right?

I guess I'll start my story at school. I go to Beverly Hills Middle School, which is only a few blocks from my house.

I know what you're thinking. I'm so lucky to have a dad in the movie business and live in a big house in Beverly Hills with a swimming pool and a tennis court, and our own screening room in the basement.

You're right. It's lucky. I'm very lucky. But I still have problems. Lots of problems.

The other morning Cindy Matson was my problem. I ran into Cindy in the hall between classes, and I could see she was really steamed. Her face was red, and she kept tugging at her black bangs, then clenching and unclenching her fists. Tense. Extremely tense.

"Ross—where were you?" she asked, blocking my way.

Cindy is taller than I am. She's at least seven or eight feet tall. And she works out. She could be a stuntwoman for *Xena*: *Warrior Princess*. So I try to stay on her good side.

"Uh . . . where was I?" I thought it might be safe to repeat the question.

But Cindy exploded anyway. "Remember? You were going to meet me? We were going to Urban Outfitters together yesterday afternoon?"

"Yes, I know," I said. "But you see . . . " I had to think quickly. "My tennis lesson got switched. Because my regular instructor hurt his hand. He was trying to open one of those cans of tennis balls. And his hand got stuck, and he sprained his wrist. Really. So my lesson got moved. And my racket was being restrung. So I had to go to the tennis shop on Wilshire and get a loaner."

I stopped to breathe. Was she buying that excuse? No.

"Ross, that is *so* not true," Cindy said, rolling her eyes. "Your tennis lessons are on Saturday. Can't you ever just tell the truth? You forgot about me—right? You just forgot."

"No way," I insisted. "Actually, what happened was . . . the truth. The total truth. My dog got sick, and Mom asked me to help take him to the vet. And so I—"

"When did you get a dog?" Cindy interrupted.

"Huh?" I stared at the floor, thinking hard. She was right. We don't have a dog.

Sometimes I work so hard on these stories, I mess up some of the details.

Cindy rolled her eyes for about the thousandth time. "You do remember that you're going with me to Max's pool party Friday night—don't you?"

I had completely forgotten.

"Of course," I said. "No way I'd forget that."

The bell rang. We were both late for class.

We turned and jogged off in different directions. I turned a corner—and bumped into Sharma Gregory.

Sharma is tiny and blond and speaks in a mousy whisper. She is the anti-Cindy. She's very pretty, and she's a true brainiac. Last April she won a trip to Washington, D.C., because of an essay she wrote. (But she didn't go because she was invited to a really cool Oscar party.)

"Hey, Ross—" She pointed at me. "Max's party Friday night—right?"

I grinned at her. "Yeah. For sure."

"Should I meet you there, or do you want to come over to my house first?"

Oh, wow. I'd also asked Sharma to go with me to the party!

Why did I invite her? She'd let me copy off her chemistry test. So I thought I'd give her a break.

"Uh . . . I'll meet you there," I said. I flashed her a thumbs-up and hurried into English class.

I closed the classroom door carefully behind me and tiptoed to my seat. I hoped Miss Douglas wouldn't notice I was late. Luckily, my seat is in the back row, so it's easy to sneak in and out.

"Ross, you're late," Miss Douglas called.

"Uh . . . yeah," I said, tugging my notebook from my backpack. Think fast, Ross. "I had to stay late in Mr. Harrison's class and . . . uh . . . help him return some books to the library. Mr. Harrison meant to give me a late pass, but he forgot."

Miss Douglas nodded. I think she believed me.

"If you will all take out your essays," she said, straightening the books on her desk. She's always lining up the things on her desk, making them perfectly straight.

"I'd like for some of you to share your essays with the class. Why don't we start with you, Ross?" She flashed me a toothy grin. Her gums show when she smiles.

"Uh . . . share my essay?" I had to stall for time. Had to think fast.

I started the essay last night. Well, actually, I started to think about starting the essay. But then *WWF Smackdown* came on. And by the time it was over, it was time to go to bed.

Miss Douglas's grin faded. "Do you have your essay, Ross?"

"Well, I wrote it," I told her. "But it's still in my computer. Because we had some kind of electrical backup or something at my house. And my printer blew up! Smoke was pouring out of it like a toaster. So I couldn't print what I wrote. But I'm getting a new printer after school. So I'll bring it in tomorrow."

Good one, huh?

At least, I thought it was good. But before I knew it, Miss Douglas swept down the aisle until she stood right over me.

She gazed down at me sternly through her red-rimmed glasses. "Ross," she said through gritted teeth. "Listen to me. Be careful. If you keep this up, you may fail this course."

I stared back at her. "Keep what up?" I asked.

CHAPTER 2

I hurried to my locker after school. Some guys wanted to hang out, but I couldn't. I knew my dad was waiting outside to drive me to my acting class.

Dad isn't thrilled about my acting lessons. But Jerry Nadler, my teacher, is an old friend of Dad's. And Jerry says I have talent. He says I look like a young Tom Cruise. And he thinks my crooked smile will make people remember me.

I know I don't have much chance of being a big movie star. A lot of movie stars come to my house, and they're really awesome people. But I wouldn't mind maybe acting in some commercials and making a lot of money.

I started to toss stuff into my locker. But then I stopped and let out a groan. A brown envelope stuck out from the pile of books on the floor. My dad had asked me to mail it for him two days ago, but I forgot.

I'll mail it tomorrow, I decided. I slammed the locker shut and clicked the combination lock. I saw Cindy waving to me down the hall. But I shouted that I was late.

"Where are you going?" she called.

"Uh . . . got to help my mom do some charity work," I called back. "Collecting candles for the homeless!"

Why did I say that?

Why didn't I just tell her the truth? Sometimes I don't know why I make up these stories. I guess I do it because I can!

I flashed her a thumbs-up and made my way out the front door.

Dad's black Mercedes was parked right across the street. It was a sunny day, bright blue skies, hot as summer even though it was late autumn. The sun made the car sparkle like a big, black jewel.

"Yo yo yo!" Dad greeted me. "What up, Ross? What up, dude?" He thinks it's funny to talk really dumb, ancient rap talk. Mom says if we just ignore it, maybe he'll stop.

"Hi, Dad," I said. I slid onto the black leather passenger seat. "Ow." It was burning hot from the sun.

Dad checked himself out in the rearview mirror. He patted down the sides of his hair.

Dad is very young looking, and he's proud of it. He has straight brown hair and dark gray eyes, just like me. I see him check out his hair every time he passes a mirror, making sure he isn't losing any.

He's always tanned. He says it's part of the job. He always wears the same thing—black pants and a black T-shirt under an open sports jacket. He says it's the company uniform. Just like the black Mercedes is the company car.

Dad is always making fun of the movie business. But I know he loves being a studio big shot.

He checked the mirror again, then pulled the car away from the curb. I leaned forward and turned the air-conditioning to high.

"I've got to stop at the Universe Films lot and see a producer I'm trying to sign up," Dad said. "Then I'll take you to Jerry. How are you and Jerry getting along? Is he teaching you anything?"

"Yeah," I said. "It's good. We've mainly been reading scripts. You know. Out loud."

Dad snickered. "You ready for your screen test?"

I laughed, too. "Not yet."

The car phone rang. He pressed the phone button on the steering wheel and talked to his secretary about some budget mixups.

Palm trees rolled past us on both sides. Dad turned to me. "You mailed that envelope, right? It had very important contracts inside."

"Yeah. I mailed it," I said. A white lie. I knew I'd mail it tomorrow.

"Whew. That's good." Dad sighed. "If it's late, they'll nail my hide to the wall."

"No problem," I replied.

"I've been out of the 'hood, on location so long, we haven't had a chance to rap much," Dad said. "How's school?"

"Great!" I told him. "Miss Douglas said today I'll probably make the honor roll."

"Hey—all right!" Dad slapped me a high five and nearly drove off the road.

The phone rang again. Dad talked until we pulled into the Universe lot. The guard waved us through.

I'd been here with him before. We drove past the long, low white buildings until Dad found a parking space.

He ushered me into a big room that looked more like a living room than an office. It had two long, red leather couches, facing each other on a thick, white pile carpet, red drapes that matched the couches, three TV sets, a black-and-chrome bar, and bookshelves all around.

No desk.

"This is Mort's office," Dad said. "You wait here. I'll only be five minutes. This is really important to me. I've got to sign Mort on the dotted line."

He gestured to the tall shelves cluttered with framed photos, award statues, plaques, vases, and other junk. "Look around. But be careful, Ross. Don't touch anything. Mort is a nut about his collections. He goes berserk if he finds a fingerprint on anything!"

"No problem," I said.

"I've got to get this guy on my side," Dad said. Then he vanished out the door.

I settled onto one of the red couches. I sank

about two feet into the cushion! It was the softest couch I'd ever sat on in my life!

After a minute or two I got bored. I walked over to the shelves and began to check out all of the photos and awards.

I saw a framed photo of Mort and the President of the United States, grinning together on a golf course. It was signed by the President.

And there were dozens of other photos of Mort with movie stars and important-looking people.

One shelf held a knight's helmet and a gleaming silver sword. Probably props from a movie.

The next shelf was filled with award statuettes and plaques. I stopped in front of a familiar gold statue. An Academy Award! An Oscar!

I rubbed my hand over its smooth, shiny head. I realized I'd never touched an Oscar before.

"Totally cool!" I said out loud.

I couldn't stop myself. I had to hold it. I had to see how heavy it was, and what it felt like to actually hold an Oscar in my hand.

It was a lot heavier than I thought. I gripped it tightly in both hands. It was so smooth. The gold gleamed under the ceiling lights.

Holding it around the middle, I raised it high over my head. "Thank you!" I shouted to an imaginary audience. "Thank you for this award! I love it and I really deserve it!"

I raised the statuette higher—
—and it slipped from my hand.
I fumbled for it. Made a wild stab.
Missed.
And watched it crash to the floor.

It made such a heavy thud as it landed on its side. And then a horrible craaaack! I knew I'd never forget that sick sound.

I dropped to my knees to pick it up.

"Please be okay. . . . Please be okay!"

No. It wasn't okay.

The Oscar's round head had broken off.

I held the statue's body in one hand, the head in the other.

And then, still on my knees, I heard the rapid click of footsteps.

Someone was stepping into the office!

CHAPTER 3

I froze in panic. My heart raced in my chest. I could hear the rasp of my rapid breaths.

I dived to the couch and frantically stuffed the Oscar—both pieces of it—under the couch.

I glanced up to see Dad enter the room. "Ross? What are you doing down on the floor?"

"Oh. I . . . dropped my chewing gum," I said. "But I got it back." I climbed shakily to my feet.

Dad eyed me curiously. "I thought I heard a crash in here. Is everything okay?"

I shrugged. "A crash? I didn't hear anything."

He studied me for a long moment. "Well . . . what did you do with the chewing gum?"

"Swallowed it," I said.

That struck him as funny. He laughed. "It went great with Mort. I think I won him over. Come on. Let's get you to Jerry's. You're late."

My knees were still shaking as we walked to the car. That was such a close one, I thought. But I should be okay now.

Of course, I was wrong.

• • •

We got home just before dinnertime. Hannah, our cook, was already bringing dishes to the table. Dad went into the den to make some phone calls.

I dropped my backpack in my room. Then turned to see my eight-year-old brother, Jake, walk in. "Hey—Jake the Snake!" I greeted him. I raised my hand. "Give me six!"

"I don't have six fingers!" Jake whined. "And stop calling me that!"

"Okay. How about Jake the Jerk?"

"Don't call me that, either!" My little brother is the Whining King of Beverly Hills.

You've probably already guessed that we don't get along. The problem is, Jake and I just don't have anything in common. He doesn't have a sense of humor. He isn't fast thinking.

He doesn't even look like me. He looks like Mom's side of the family—curly, carrot-colored hair, pale white skin, green eyes, a narrow rat face with his front teeth poking out.

"Hey, Rat Face!" I said. "What are you doing in my room?"

"I want my comic books back," he whined. Jake has a huge collection of Japanese comic books.

"Comic books? I don't read comic books," I said.

"You borrowed them!" Jake cried. "You borrowed them last week. You said you'd return them!"

"I never borrowed any comic books. Get lost," I said.

Why do I torture Jake like that? I don't know. I had the comic books in my bottom desk drawer. I could just hand them back to him. But I wanted to make him work for them.

He deserves it. He's such a whiner. And he never helps me out.

Last week I wanted to go hang out with some guys at the Planet Hollywood over on Wilshire. I begged Jake to tell Mom and Dad that I went to Sharma's house to study chemistry.

But he wouldn't do it. "I can't tell a lie!" he said.

"Why not?" I asked him.

"Because it's not right."

That's why I enjoy torturing him.

"I know where the comics are," he said. He dived past me and pulled open the bottom desk drawer. "There!"

I started to protest when I heard Dad's voice from downstairs. "Ross—get down here!"

Uh-oh. He sounded angry. Really angry.

I picked up the stack of comics and heaved them at Jake. Then I slowly made my way downstairs. "You called me?" I asked in a tiny voice.

Dad had his cell phone gripped tightly in one hand. "I have Mort on the phone," he said, scowling at me. "Mort says he changed his mind about working with me. He found the broken Oscar."

My mouth dropped open. "Oscar? What Oscar?"

"Ross, I told you not to touch anything. I told you

what a nut Mort is about his stuff. He found the Oscar pieces shoved under the couch."

"But . . . I sat on the couch the whole time," I said, my heart leaping around in my chest, my mouth suddenly dry. "I never saw any Oscar."

Dad said something into the phone, then clicked it off. He glared angrily at me. "You were the only one in the office."

"No," I replied. "Actually, a cleaning lady came in. Uh . . . two cleaning ladies, and I saw them dusting the shelves. I—"

Mom came in, carrying a load of shopping bags. "What's going on?"

"Ross is standing here, dissing me. He's lying to my face," Dad said, shaking his head. "Lying to my face!"

Mom sighed and let the bags drop to the carpet. "Ross," she whispered. "You're making up stories again?"

"No—" I started.

"Punish him!" Jake cried from the top of the stairs. "Punish him!"

"This is serious, Ross," Dad said, rolling the cell phone in his hand. "Very serious. You may have just lost me millions of dollars. You do have to be punished for this."

"Cut off his hand!" Jake shouted.

Mom gasped. "Jake! Where did you get a horrible idea like that?"

16

"It's what they do to liars," Jake said. "In some country somewhere. I learned it in school. Cut off his hand!"

Mom shook her head. "Well, we're not going to do that."

"No, we're not," Dad said. "We're going to do something much worse."

CHAPTER 4

"You're grounded," Dad said.

He slapped the cell phone against his palm as if it was a policeman's club. "You've got to stop being so dishonest all the time."

"But I'm not!" I protested. "I—"

"You're grounded until I say you're not," Dad said sharply. Slap slap slap. The phone against his hand.

I swallowed hard. "But—what about Max's swim party Friday night? A lot of people are counting on me!" (Mainly the two girls I asked to go with me!)

"Sorry, Ross," Mom said softly. "You'll just have to miss it."

"But—I've learned my lesson!" I cried. "I'll never lie again. I swear!"

"He's lying." Jake walked into the room.

"Shut up!" I screamed at him. I turned back to Mom and Dad. "Really. I promise. I'll never tell another lie as long as I live."

"That's no good, Ross," Dad said firmly. "You have to prove yourself."

"I'll prove myself after Max's party," I said. "Please—?"

Mom and Dad both shook their heads. "No more arguing. You're grounded."

"Don't ground him. Cut off his hand!" Jake insisted.

Dad turned to Jake. "Jake, they cut off a hand for stealing—not for lying," Dad said.

"Oh," Jake replied. "Then cut off his lips!"

Mom and Dad burst out laughing.

I didn't think it was funny. With a growl I stomped up the stairs.

I deliberately bumped Jake into the wall. Swinging my fists, I raged into my room.

I was so furious, I thought I'd explode. "I hate my parents!" I screamed. And I kicked the wall with all my strength.

"Oh, wow."

My sneaker went right through the wall! Plaster crumbled to the floor. I had kicked a big hole in the wall!

"Ross? What was that?" Dad shouted.

"Uh . . . nothing," I called. "Nothing."

Friday night. Party night. And where was I?

In my brother's room, playing a stupid Nintendo wrestling game with Jake the Jerk.

Jake loves this game because it gives him a

chance to beat me up. On the screen, he pounds me and knocks me to the canvas. Then he jumps up and down on me for half an hour. Then he lifts me over his head and heaves me to the canvas a hundred times.

He goes nuts, furiously pushing the controller, beating me to a pulp.

It's a thrill for him.

But I wasn't thrilled. Stuck at home watching Jake while all my friends were partying. And Cindy and Sharma were there waiting for me, getting angrier and angrier.

Maybe I should have called them and told them I'd been grounded.

But I couldn't. It was too embarrassing.

Dad was thousands of miles away, in the Philippines, shooting a kung fu movie. Mom was visiting the Lamberts, friends of ours in Malibu.

The game ended. Jake pumped his fists above his head and did a victory dance.

Loud music floated in through the open window. Max's house was just down the block.

I leaned on the windowsill and peered out. I could see the lights from Max's pool. I heard kids shouting and laughing.

"I should be there," I muttered.

I turned to my brother. "Here's the deal," I said.

He shoved a game controller at me. "Come on. Let's go. Round Twelve."

"Here's the deal," I repeated. "I'm going to let you watch a DVD in my room."

That's usually a big deal to Jake. Because he doesn't have a DVD player in his room. And I have all the best movies.

But he frowned at me. "And where are you going?"

"Out," I said. "Just for a short while. Just for an hour. Then I'll be right back."

"I'll tell," Jake said.

I made a fist. "No, you won't."

"You're grounded, Ross," he said. "You're not allowed to go out. I'll tell."

"You can watch any movie you want," I said. "And you can eat a whole bag of M&M's. You don't have to share or save any for later."

A few minutes later I crept out of the house. I'd changed into a baggy, black swimsuit and a cool black-and-red Hawaiian shirt, my party shirt. And I packed a towel and a spare swimsuit into a plastic bag.

"Ross—!" Jake called from my bedroom window. "Ross—you'll be sorry!"

I just laughed.

CHAPTER 5

"Party time!" I declared, taking my usual shortcut through the tall hedges, onto the terrace in Max's backyard. It was bright as day, and the teardrop-shaped pool sparkled. Dance music blasted from the big speakers on the roof of the pool house.

In the center of the terrace a man in a white jacket stood behind a table, making tacos. I glimpsed Max's parents sitting with some other adults away from everyone near the back of the house.

Wild splashing. Shouts. Loud laughter.

I saw a vicious splashing battle at one end of the pool. Some poor guy was being splashed by four or five girls, who were really into it.

Across from them a pool noodle war was taking place. Guys were smashing each other with pool noodles, beating each other, slapping backs and shoulders and heads. *Thwack. Thwaaack. Smaaaack.*

Two pool noodles cracked in half, and everyone laughed like crazy.

"Hey, Ross!" Max came hurrying over, carrying a

can of soda in one hand and a taco in the other.

Max is big. Big arms, big chest. He looks like a jock, but he isn't into sports at all.

He has short, spiky brown hair, and big brown eyes, and a grin that spreads over his entire face. And the girls all think he's one big puppy dog.

He was dripping wet. He'd just climbed out of the pool. He was wearing denim cutoffs, soaked to his skin. He had spilled some taco meat on his chest.

"Ross, I didn't think you were coming, man." He tried to flash me a thumbs-up and nearly dropped his taco.

"Hey, it's a party—right?" I replied. "So I'm here."

He chewed off a hunk of taco. "I heard you were grounded for life or something."

"No way!" I protested.

"That's what your brother said."

"He's crazy," I told Max. "Why would I be grounded?"

I saw Cindy jump up from a chair at the edge of the pool. She wore a white two-piece swimsuit. Her black hair bobbed behind her as she ran across the terrace toward me. "Hey, Ross—where were you?"

"Hi," I flashed her my best smile. "How's it going?"

"You're an hour late," she boomed, crossing her arms in front of her. "What happened?"

"Well . . ." I thought hard.

"It was my brother," I said. "Jake wasn't feeling

well. He was kind of sick. So I wanted to stay home and cheer him up. You know. Read him a few books. Play some games. I guess I lost track of the time."

Cindy's stern expression faded. "That was really nice of you," she said softly.

"Well, he's my only brother, you know. I try to take good care of him."

Over Cindy's shoulder, I saw Sharma waving frantically to me from the deep end of the pool.

"I'm starving," Cindy said. "Those tacos look really good. But I waited for you to get here." She started pulling me towards the food table.

"Uh . . . go get yourself one," I said. "I'll meet you over there in a sec. I just want to drop my bag somewhere."

She hurried to the taco guy, and I jogged around the pool to Sharma. "Hey—what's up?"

She narrowed her eyes at me. "Where have you been?"

I told her the same story about staying home to cheer up my brother. She ate it up, too.

"What were you talking to Cindy about?" she asked.

A Frisbee came flying out of the pool. I grabbed it and tossed it back. "Oh. Just something about school," I said.

"Want to get some tacos?" Sharma asked.

I looked across the pool and saw Cindy waiting for me by the taco table.

"Uh . . . not right now," I told Sharma. "I really need a swim. That water looks awesome, doesn't it? Why don't you get in, and I'll meet you in a sec?"

I spun away and hurried back to Cindy.

I'm going to be running back and forth between the two girls all night, I realized. This is like a totally bad TV sitcom. Only, it's my life!

"Here. I got you a taco," Cindy said, handing it to me. "What were you talking to Sharma about?"

"Just a school thing," I said. "She had a question about some homework."

Cindy stared at me suspiciously.

I turned and saw Sharma waving to me from the deep end of the pool.

How long did it take Cindy and Sharma to figure out the truth?

Not long.

Somehow, a few minutes later, all three of us found ourselves standing together at the edge of the pool. Cindy looked at Sharma. Sharma looked at Cindy.

"Are you here with Ross?" Cindy asked.

"Yes," Sharma replied. "You, too?"

"I can explain," I said.

They didn't give me a chance.

Cindy grabbed me around the waist. Sharma grabbed my legs. They picked me up—and heaved me into the pool.

I splashed hard.

The cold, clear water rose around me.

I bobbed to the surface. And felt hands grab my hair. And shove me back down.

"Hey—help!" I sputtered.

But they pushed me underwater. Held my head down.

I wrestled and thrashed my arms. I burst free. Shot up to the top, gasping and choking.

I saw them both laughing, both excited. They thought it was so funny.

They shoved me under again. And held me down.

I squirmed and kicked. But I couldn't pull free.

I could hear them laughing above me. They were paying me back. Having their revenge. Enjoying it so much.

They pushed my shoulders down. Pressed down on my head.

Too long . . . I thought. Too long!

I felt panic tighten my chest. I swallowed some water and started to choke.

Hey—I'm drowning! I realized.

Let me up! Too long! You're DROWNING me!

CHAPTER 6

My chest ached. I swallowed more water.

Didn't they realize what they were doing?

Not funny! You're DROWNING me!

Lights flashed in the water. Blue. White. Blue. White.

I . . . can't . . . breathe . . .

And then—finally—I broke free.

The hands lifted. The weight vanished.

I shot up hard. And broke the surface, coughing and sputtering.

I sucked in breath after breath, my chest still aching. The lights flashed in my eyes.

The pool sparkled so brightly. . . . So painfully bright.

I shut my eyes and plunged back into the water.

I dived underwater and started to swim away from the two girls. Moving smoothly now, taking slow, steady strokes. I opened my eyes and swam, feeling my body start to relax.

I was nearing the deep end when I saw the figure

swimming toward me.

He was underwater, too, and taking the same slow strokes. He stared through the clear water at me.

At first I thought I was gazing at my reflection.

Did Max's parents put a mirror in the pool?

But no.

I was staring at another boy. Another boy swimming straight at me. A boy with my hair, my eyes, my face.

Closer . . .

The water was so clear . . . so bright and clear.

I stopped my swim strokes. I let my arms float to my sides. And I stared through the water . . . stared at a boy who looked exactly like me!

CHAPTER 7

We both stopped and stared wide-eyed at each other. Lights shimmered and flashed in the water, making it seem unreal, like in a dream.

He seemed to be just as surprised to see me!

This isn't happening, I thought. He's a total twin. He's even wearing a baggy black swimsuit.

No. No way.

I swam closer.

His eyes grew wider. His expression changed. Now he looked angry. Upset.

Air bubbled from his open mouth.

And then he formed two words with his lips.

What was he saying? I struggled to understand.

Floating in place, I stared harder.

Go away.

That's what I thought he was saying.

More air bubbles escaped his open mouth, and he formed the words again:

Go away.

Why was he saying that? Why did he appear so angry?

Who was he? What was he doing here? I wanted to ask a dozen questions.

But my chest felt about to burst again.

I had to get air, had to breathe.

I raised my arms and kicked, and pulled myself up to the surface. Again, I took in breath after breath.

And then I waited for the other boy to surface.

He had to breathe, too—right?

I treaded water and waited, brushing water from my eyes, sweeping back my dark hair with one hand.

Where was he?

He didn't surface.

I swam slowly in his direction, my eyes searching the water.

I did a breast stroke, moving a few inches at a time, ducking my head under the surface, peering into the shimmering, blue light.

No.

No sign of him.

I reached the wall at the deep end, turned and floated back. I dived under, down to the pool floor, then back up to the top.

He was gone. Vanished.

But—how?

Who was he? Why did he look so much like me? Why did he tell me to go away?

Questions, questions.

I climbed out of the pool. Shook myself like a dog trying to get dry. I grabbed my towel and wrapped it around my shoulders.

Cindy and Sharma were still at the edge of the pool. They were laughing and dancing to the music blasting from the pool house.

I ran to them, waving frantically, my bare feet slapping the stone terrace. "Did you see that guy?"

They didn't stop dancing.

"Did you see him? The boy in the pool who looks like me?" I asked.

They ignored me. I guess they were still angry.

"I—I think I have a twin," I said.

Sharma scowled at me and rolled her eyes. "One of you is enough," she snapped.

"You really didn't see him?" I asked.

They kept dancing.

I suddenly realized it was getting late. "What time is it?" I asked.

They talked to each other as they danced and pretended I didn't exist.

I ran across the terrace to Max. He was kidding around with three girls from our class.

I slapped him on the back with a wet towel to get his attention.

"Got to run," I said. "I have to pick Jake up at a friend's house. Awesome party!"

"It's just starting!" he protested.

But I gave him a thumbs-up and took off. I stopped at the hedge and turned back.

Shielding my eyes from the bright lights, I

searched for the boy who looked so much like me.

No sign of him.

Cindy and Sharma were laughing hard about something. A boy did a bellyflop into the pool, sending up a high wave that drenched both of them.

I ducked through the crack in the hedge and began to jog across backyards toward my house. I knew I had to get home before Mom returned.

Jake the Snake would never lie for me. He'd love it if Mom got home first so he could tell her I sneaked off to Max's party.

I stopped at the bottom of the driveway and gazed up at the house. "Oh no," I moaned.

The lights were on in the front rooms. Mom's Jaguar was in the driveway.

No. No. No.

When did she get home? I wondered. Does she know that I'm not there?

Has Jake already squealed on me?

Keeping in the shadows, I made my way around to the side of the house.

The gardener planted a row of olive trees there a few years ago. The trees are short, but one of them is tall enough for me to stand on a branch and reach my bedroom window.

I only use it for emergencies.

And this was definitely an emergency.

If Mom found out that I left Jake by himself and sneaked out to Max's party, I'd be grounded until I was at least sixty years old!

I had to climb through the upstairs window into my bedroom, then walk downstairs as if I had been there all along.

If Jake said I went out, I'd tell Mom he was crazy.

I stopped a few feet from the olive tree. I gazed up at my dark bedroom window.

An easy climb.

No problem.

I reached for the bottom tree limb. Started to hoist myself up.

And two hands wrapped around my waist, grabbed me hard, and pulled me down.

CHAPTER 8

As I fell back, I heard a high-pitched giggle in my ear.

I tumbled to the ground. Spun around quickly. Jumped to my feet.

And stared angrily at Jake.

"What are you doing out here?" I cried. My voice cracked.

That made Jake giggle even harder. His eyes flashed excitedly in the dim light. He loves scaring me. It's a total thrill for him to sneak up behind me and grab me or shout, "Boo!"

"What are you doing outside?" I repeated, grabbing him by the shoulders.

His grin grew wider. "I saw you coming."

I squeezed his tiny shoulders harder. "When did Mom get home? Does she know I went out?"

"Maybe," he replied. "Maybe I told her. Or maybe I didn't."

"Which is it?" I demanded.

"Maybe you have to find out," he said.

I loosened my grip. I smoothed the front of his T-shirt. "Listen, Jake, help me out here. I—"

The dining room window slid open. Mom poked her head out. "There you are, Rosssss."

I could tell by the way she hissed my name that she was totally angry.

"Get in here," she said. "Both of you. Right now." She slammed the window so hard, the glass panes shook.

She was waiting for us in the kitchen, hands pressed tightly against her waist. "Where were you, Rosssss?"

"Uh . . . nowhere," I said.

"You were nowhere?"

"Yeah," I said.

Jake laughed.

Mom's eyes burned into mine. "You weren't home when I got here. Were you?"

"Well . . . it's not what you're thinking," I said. "I mean, I didn't go to Max's party."

"Yes, you did!" Jake chimed in.

"Then where did you go?" Mom asked. "Why are you wearing a bathing suit? And why is it wet?"

"Uh . . . You see, Jake was watching a video. And I was so hot . . . I just went outside to cool off. I took a swim in our pool. Really. I knew I was grounded. So I just hung around the pool."

Jake laughed.

"Shut up, Jake!" I shouted. I spun away from

him. "He just wants to get me in trouble, Mom. I was in the backyard. Really."

Mom scrunched up her face as she studied me. I could tell she was trying to decide whether or not to believe me.

The phone rang.

Mom punched the button on the speakerphone. "Hello?"

"Oh, hi. Mrs. Arthur?"

I recognized Max's voice. I could hear the party going on in the background.

"Yes, Max. Did you want to speak to Ross?"

"No," Max replied. "I was just calling to tell him he left his towel and his extra suit at my house."

I slumped onto a kitchen stool. Caught again.

Mom thanked Max and clicked off the speakerphone. When she turned back to me, she did not have her friendly face on. In fact, she was bright red.

"I'm really worried about you, Ross," she said in a whisper.

"Huh? Worried?"

"I don't think you know how to tell the truth anymore."

"Sure, I do," I said. "I just—"

Mom shook her head. "No. Really, Ross. I don't think you know the difference between the truth and a lie."

I jumped off the stool. "I can tell the truth!" I protested. "I swear I can. Sometimes I make up things because . . . because I don't want to get in trouble."

"Ross, I don't think you can stop making up things," Mom said softly. "When your father gets back from his shoot, we need to have a family meeting. We need to talk about this problem."

I stared at the floor. "Okay," I replied.

And then I suddenly remembered the boy in the pool. And I had to ask.

"Mom, can I ask you a strange question? Do I have a twin?"

She narrowed her eyes at me for a long moment. Then her answer totally shocked me. "Yes," she said. "Yes, you do."

CHAPTER 9

I gasped. "Huh?"

Mom nodded. "There's a good twin and a bad twin. You're the bad twin." She laughed.

"Ha ha," I said, rolling my eyes. "Good joke, Mom."

Mom squeezed my shoulder. "Why would I want two of you?"

"I want a twin!" Jake cried. "Then we could both pound Ross!"

"We have more serious problems to talk about," Mom said, sighing. "Let's drop the twin talk." She opened the refrigerator and pulled out a bottle of water. She raised it to her mouth and took a long drink.

"But I saw a kid who looks just like me," I said. "I mean, exactly like me. He could have been my twin!"

Mom took another drink, then shoved the bottle back into the fridge. "Were you looking in a mirror?"

I rolled my eyes again. "Ha ha. Another good one, Mom. Remind me to laugh later."

"I'm going to bed," Mom said. She clicked off the kitchen lights and started out of the room.

"No, wait." I hurried after her. "I really did see my twin."

As Mom turned back, she looked troubled and sad. "Ross, what am I going to do with you?" she whispered. "You really can't go two minutes without making up a story."

I felt my anger rise. I balled my hands into tight fists at my sides. "I'm not making this up," I screamed. "It's the truth!"

I pushed Jake out of the way and ran up to my room.

I couldn't get to sleep that night. I kept thinking about that boy swimming toward me in Max's pool. I kept picturing the angry expression on his face. I kept seeing him mouth the words *Go away*.

And then he vanished.

And I kept thinking about Cindy and Sharma. How angry they were over a simple mix-up.

Mom's words kept repeating in my mind: "I don't think you know the difference between the truth and a lie."

That was crazy. Totally wrong.

But how could I prove it to her?

Finally I drifted into a restless sleep. I dreamed that I was running through an endless field of tall grass, being chased by Cindy and Sharma. They were waving their arms furiously, calling to me, shouting their lungs out—but I couldn't hear them. And I couldn't stop running through the tall grass.

I was awakened by voices.

I sat straight up in bed, breathing hard. My pajama shirt clung wetly to my skin.

I glanced at my clock radio. Two o'clock in the morning.

Who was talking at this time of night? I held my breath and listened hard.

The voices came from downstairs. I heard a woman's voice. She was speaking loudly, sharply. But I couldn't make out her words.

Had Dad come home early from his shoot? Were he and Mom talking down there?

I slid out of bed and tiptoed to the hall. Nearly to the stairs, I stopped and listened again.

It was dark downstairs. No lights on in the living room. They must be in the kitchen, I realized.

The woman was talking. It was Mom. I recognized her voice.

I leaned into the stairwell to try to make out her words.

"Are you going crazy or something?"

That's what she said. She didn't sound angry. She sounded worried.

"You don't have a twin," she said. "No twin. Why would you say such a crazy thing?"

And then I heard a boy answer.

"But I saw him!" the boy said. "Really. I saw him."

I let out a low gasp. I gripped the banister to keep from falling.

The boy . . .

The boy . . . had MY voice!

CHAPTER 10

"I'm not making it up," the boy said—in my voice. "I saw him, and he saw me."

"It's late. We should be asleep," Mom said. "Come on. Turn off the lights."

"Why don't you believe me?" the boy demanded shrilly.

Gripping the banister, I realized my whole body was trembling.

How can he have my voice? Who is he? Why is Mom talking to him in the middle of the night?

I had to see what was going on. I took a step—and stumbled.

My bare foot slid over the wooden stair, and I started to fall, tumbling down step by step.

A painful thud with each step.

I landed hard on my elbows and knees. My heart pounding, I waited for the pain to stop. And listened for approaching footsteps, for cries of surprise from the kitchen.

Mom must have heard me thumping and

bumping down the stairs.

Why didn't she come running to see who had fallen?

Silence in the kitchen now.

I picked myself up and straightened my pajamas. One knee throbbed with pain. I rubbed it carefully as I limped toward the kitchen.

"Who's down here?" I called. "Mom? Is that you?"

No reply.

The kitchen was dark. No lights on. Silvery moonlight poured in from the windows. No color in the room, only shades of gray.

I suddenly felt as if I were in a black-and-white movie.

"Mom? I heard you talking!" I called.

I made my way across the kitchen, running my hand along the counter. "Anyone in here?"

No.

I peered out at the backyard. Under the bright moonlight, the swimming pool shimmered, and the grass glowed like silver.

Unreal.

I turned away—and the kitchen lights flashed on. Blinking from the shock of the light, I saw Mom in the doorway.

"Ross? What are you doing down here?" she asked, holding a hand over her mouth and yawning loudly.

"I—I heard you talking," I said.

She tightened the belt of her robe. "Me? It wasn't me. I was asleep."

"No," I said. "I heard voices. You were here in the kitchen, talking to a boy."

Mom rubbed her eyes with both hands. "No. Really, Ross. Why are you down here?"

"I told you," I said, clenching my fists. I banged one fist on the Formica counter. "Why don't you believe me?"

"Because I wasn't in here talking to anyone," Mom said. "I was in my bed, sound asleep. Until I heard you wandering around."

She yawned. "You must have been having a nightmare. Sometimes nightmares can seem very real."

"I didn't dream it," I insisted. "I know the difference between a nightmare and what's really happening."

I could see she wasn't going to believe me. So I shrugged and followed her out of the kitchen, clicking off the lights as I left.

I didn't get back to sleep that night.

I lay in bed, staring up at the ceiling. Listening for the voices downstairs. Waiting . . . listening for Mom and the boy with my voice.

I didn't know I would see the boy in a few hours.

I didn't know how dangerous he was.

I didn't know the terrifying trouble I was in.

Cindy stopped me after school Monday afternoon. I was kneeling down in front of my hall locker, lacing my new tennis sneakers. She stepped in front of me and stomped down hard on one of them.

"Hey!" I snapped angrily. "Why'd you do that?"

She shrugged. "Just felt like it."

I tied the laces quickly, then spit on my fingers and tried to rub off the scuff mark she'd made. "If you're still angry at me about Max's party . . ."

"I've decided to be nice to you again," she said.

"Nice? By stomping on my foot?"

She laughed. "That was just to be funny." She raked her fingers through her straight black bangs. "Why did you leave the party so early Friday night? Afraid Sharma and I would toss you in the pool again?"

"You almost drowned me!" I grumbled.

"You deserved it," Cindy replied. "So why did you leave in such a hurry, Ross?"

"Oh, I was worried about my little brother," I said.

"I don't like to leave him alone for long."

Cindy stared hard at me. "Is that the truth?"

I slammed my locker shut. "Of course," I said.

Cindy shifted her backpack on her shoulders. "Maybe you could come over to my house now. We could study for the government test together."

I waved to some guys down the hall. "I can't," I told Cindy. "I have tennis team practice."

I glanced at the clock above the principal's office. "I'm already late."

Cindy frowned at me. "Where's your tennis racket?"

I started jogging to the back doors. "Steve Franklin said he'd bring an extra one for me. I left mine at home this morning."

"Where are you really going?" Cindy called after me. "Why don't you tell me the truth?"

"It's true!" I shouted. I trotted out of the school building and hurried across the playground to the tennis courts.

I heard the *thock thock thock* of rackets hitting tennis balls. Guys on the team were already warming up.

I searched the long row of courts for Steve Franklin. He had a bucket of balls and was hitting one after another, practicing his serve.

I started jogging over to him to get the racket he'd promised to bring. But Coach Melvin blocked my way. "Ross, you're ten minutes late. We really need you here on time. You missed the whole warm-up."

"Sorry, Coach," I said. "I . . . uh . . . had a really bad nosebleed."

He squinted at my nose. "You okay now?"

I nodded.

"Well, go warm up. Practice your serves, okay? Take the court next to Steve."

I took a basket of tennis balls and trotted over to Steve. He stopped serving and tossed me an old racket of his. "What's up, Ross?" he asked.

I swung the racket hard a few times to get the feel of it.

"I'm thinking of quitting the team," I said. "I might go pro."

Steve laughed. "Yeah. Me, too."

"Not a bad racket," I said, twirling it in my palm. "Not a good racket. But not a bad racket."

"You want to come over and practice some time this weekend?" Steve asked. "My dad built a new court in our backyard. It's clay. Very sweet."

"Cool," I said. I dragged the bucket of balls over to the next court and started practicing my serve. The first three flew into the net.

I turned and saw Coach Melvin frowning at me from the next court.

"Just testing the racket," I called to him.

I served a few more. My arm felt stiff. I hadn't practiced in a while.

Down the long row of courts, guys were volleying back and forth. The afternoon sun suddenly appeared from behind a high cloud. The bright light swept over me.

I shielded my eyes with one hand—and saw him.

Squinting into the sunlight, I saw the boy—me!—my twin. He was six or seven courts down, at the far end.

He was volleying with Jared Harris. He was dressed in the same tennis whites I wore. His dark hair flew up as he ran to the net.

He looked just like me!

The racket fell out of my hand and bounced in front of me.

"Hey!" I shouted. I waved frantically.

He didn't hear me. He returned a serve from Jared, then ran to the corner to return Jared's shot.

"Hey—you!" I cried. "Wait!"

My heart pounded. I squinted hard, trying to block out the bright sunlight. Trying to make sure I wasn't seeing things.

No. It was me.

It was my exact double on that court.

And suddenly he turned—and saw me.

I saw his eyes go wide. I saw his expression change. He recognized me.

For a long moment we stared at each other down the long row of tennis courts.

And then his mouth formed the words . . . the same words they had formed underwater in Max's pool: *Go away.*

Even from so far away, I could see the angry scowl on his face. Cold . . . His glare was so cold.

"GO AWAY!" he repeated.

"No!" I screamed. "No!"

I started to run, shouting and waving my arms wildly.

I got about two steps and tripped over the racket I had dropped.

The racket slid under my feet. I fell onto my stomach and bounced hard over the asphalt.

"Owww!"

Ignoring the pain, I scrambled to my feet. Lurched a few steps toward the far court—and stopped.

The boy—my twin—was gone. Vanished again.

I stared into the light. Jared had his back turned. He was leaning over, pulling a white headband out of a canvas bag.

He had missed the whole thing!

Finally Jared turned around. "Hey, Ross," he called. "Are you going to play or not?"

I ran over to him. "Th-that wasn't me," I said.

He narrowed his eyes at me. "Excuse me? I thought we were playing a practice game."

"It wasn't me," I repeated shakily.

The guys in the next court had stopped playing. They were staring at me now.

I saw Coach Melvin jogging over from the other end of the courts.

"That boy—" I said to Jared. "Did he tell you his name or anything?"

Jared laughed. "I don't get the joke, Ross."

"It—it wasn't me!" I cried shrilly.

Jared shook his head. "Well, he looked like you, and he talked like you, and he sounded just like you. And he played like you. So . . ."

"What's the problem, Ross?" Coach Melvin hurried up to us, gazing at me sternly. "What's happening?"

"Uh . . . nothing," I said. "Really. Nothing."

I felt dazed. Kind of dizzy.

The bright sunlight turned white . . . white . . . whiter. It flashed in my eyes.

What's going on? I wondered.

Who *is* that kid?

CHAPTER 12

"Sharma—hey!" I saw her on the steps in front of school and ran over to her. "You stayed after?"

She nodded. "I had a makeup test in government. It wasn't too bad."

"That means you aced it," I said. Sharma is a total brain, but she doesn't like kids to say it. Her idea of a bad test score is anything below 110!

"Are you walking home?" I asked. "Can I walk with you?"

She nodded again. She pulled a bug or something off my tennis shirt. "How was tennis practice?"

"Totally weird," I said. As we started to walk, I decided to tell her the whole story. I had to tell someone!

"This kid is my exact twin," I told her. "But he keeps disappearing before I can talk to him. Today, he was at tennis practice, playing with Jared. But it wasn't the first time I saw him. I saw him in Max's pool Friday night. He was swimming right at me!"

Sharma laughed. "You make up the dumbest stories."

"No. I'm serious!" I said. "He is my exact twin. In every way. He even wears the same clothes as me."

"Give me a break," Sharma said. "You should be a writer, Ross. You have such an awesome imagination."

I groaned. "But I'm not making it up. Why won't anyone believe me?"

"Because it's crazy?" Sharma suggested.

We stopped at a corner. "I'm telling the truth," I insisted. "I saw this boy twice. And he was me. Really."

Sharma narrowed her eyes at me. "Do you believe in ghosts?"

"Ghosts? No," I said. "Why?"

"Well, I saw this movie on TV about a girl who kept seeing her twin. And her twin turned out to be her ghost. The ghost came back from the future because she wanted to possess herself and take over her own life."

"That doesn't make any sense at all," I muttered.

"I know," Sharma said. "But maybe the boy you keep seeing is your own ghost."

"But don't I have to die to have a ghost?" I asked.

Traffic drowned out Sharma's answer. Cars whirred through the intersection. The afternoon sun was lowering behind the hills. People were speeding home from work.

The light turned green. I started to walk.

"Hey—stop!" Sharma pulled me back. "Where are you going?"

"But the light—" I protested.

"You're so busy making up invisible twins, you don't know what you're doing!" Sharma said.

"He's not invisible," I told her.

The light turned red. Sharma tugged me into the street. "We can go now."

"Huh? You're going to get us killed!" I cried.

I pulled back and stumbled over the curb. Sharma laughed as I fell flat on my back on the grass. "What is your problem, Ross? Have you totally lost it?"

I pulled myself up and brushed off the back of my jeans. "Sorry," I said. "But you started to walk on red, and—"

I realized she was staring over my shoulder. Not listening to me. She was waving at Cindy who was coming our way.

I glanced down—and uttered a cry of surprise.

The grass where I had fallen—it had turned brown. You could see the outline of my shoulders and my back and one of my arms.

The grass along the curb was all green—except for where my body had touched it.

And as I stared, the patch of brown grass made a sizzling sound, as if it was on fire. Black smoke floated up.

The grass burned away until the outline of my back and shoulders was bare dirt.

"Wow," I murmured. "That is so weird! Sharma—look at this."

I glanced up to see Sharma walking away. "See you, Ross." She gave me a quick wave. "I have to talk to Cindy."

"Wait, Sharma! Come back!" I shouted.

"We'll walk home together tomorrow, Ross. Hey, why don't you invite your ghost? We can all walk home together!" She laughed as she headed down the street to Cindy.

"Sharma! Hey—Sharma!" I called after her. But she didn't slow down or turn back.

I stared down at the grass again. "What is that about?" I muttered. I waited for the traffic to stop. Then I ran across the street and kept running until I reached home.

The gardeners were just finishing for the day, packing up their truck. I ran through the front lawn sprinklers. The cold water felt great!

To my surprise, Mom was waiting for me at the front door. "What's wrong?" I cried.

"Nothing is wrong," she said. "Your karate teacher just called. He said—"

"My what?" I interrupted.

"Mr. Lawrence said he's coming early. Right after dinner. So, if you have homework to do . . ."

"But—but—but—" I sputtered. "I don't take karate lessons, Mom!"

Her mouth dropped open. She narrowed her eyes at me. "Only since you were seven," she said.

I felt a chill run down my back.

She wasn't joking.

But how could she say that?

The only karate I ever did was in Nintendo games!

"Don't just stand there, Ross. Come in," Mom said. "How was your tennis practice?"

"Weird," I said. I opened my mouth to tell her about seeing my twin again. But I stopped myself. She'd just think I was making it up.

"Why was it weird?" she asked.

"Well . . . I played so well for a change. No one could touch my serve. Coach Melvin thinks I'm going to be the star player on the team this year."

"Excellent," Mom said. She hugged me. "We'll have an early dinner since your karate lesson is early. You can thank me in advance. I made your favorite."

"My favorite?"

"Yes. Brussels sprouts. Jake won't eat them. But I know you love them."

Huh? Brussels sprouts? I HATE them! Just thinking about them makes me want to puke!

"Mom?" I cried weakly. "What is going on here?"

CHAPTER 13

She didn't hear my question. The phone rang, and she hurried to answer it.

I was going to ask where Jake was. But then I remembered that he has his guitar lesson on Mondays. Amelia, our housekeeper, always brings him home around dinnertime.

I made my way up to my room to change out of my tennis whites. I opened my closet door—and gasped.

A white karate robe hung on the door hook.

How did that get here? I wondered.

I backed out of the closet and glanced quickly around my room. Had anything else changed? Was I into other activities that I had no memory of?

My eyes swept over my Jimi Hendrix posters, my autographed baseballs, my snow globe collection, my stuffed leopard from when I was four.

Everything was there. Everything was the same.

Except for that white robe in my closet.

And the sour smell of brussels sprouts floating up

from the kitchen downstairs. How could Mom forget how much I hate brussels sprouts?

I started to change into a clean pair of baggy jeans and a black T-shirt. But as I pulled the shirt from my dresser drawer, a sharp pain shot through my forehead.

"Huh—?" I gasped. The shirt fell from my hands.

I grabbed my head as another pain rocked through it. I saw a white flash, like a lightning bolt. I pressed my hands tightly to my head.

"Ohhh . . . what is happening?"

Stab after stab of pain pierced my head. I felt as if someone kept jamming a knife into my eyes.

I dropped to my knees, weak from pain. Flash after flash of white light blinded me.

"Whoa . . ."

And then it stopped.

I blinked several times. Still holding my head, I waited for the pain to return.

But I felt normal again. I opened my eyes. I could see clearly.

Shaking my head, I climbed to my feet. What was that about? I'd never had a headache like that before.

I stared out the window, breathing slowly, trying to get my head straight—when Mom called me from downstairs. "Ross, I need you to do me a favor."

I pulled on the T-shirt, brushed back my hair. Then, still feeling shaky, I made my way down the stairs and met her at the bottom.

"I just had the worst headache," I groaned.

She rolled her eyes. "Ross, why do you always have a headache when I need you to do me a favor?"

"No. Really," I insisted. "But I'm okay now. What's the favor?"

"The milk went sour," she said, holding her nose. "I need you to go to the store and buy another carton."

My mouth dropped open. "Huh? Walk to the store? This is Beverly Hills, Mom. People don't walk to the store. That's too weird. Why don't you drive?"

"I can't," she said. "I'm waiting for a call from your dad. He's been so busy on the set, I haven't spoken to him in three days."

"But he can call you in the car," I said. "It's almost four blocks to the store, and—"

"Ross, just go," Mom said. She stuffed a twenty-dollar bill into my T-shirt pocket.

Normally, I'd come up with a great excuse: "I can't walk that far. I sprained my ankle at tennis practice. Coach Melvin said I should stay off my foot all week."

But I decided it would be good to get out of the house. It would give me time to think about all the weird stuff that was happening.

"Back in a few minutes," I said. I took off, walking fast.

I had walked about two blocks—halfway to the

store—when I saw my twin. He was half a block ahead of me, walking fast.

He was wearing baggy jeans and a black T-shirt, just like me. He had Walkman headphones over his ears and was snapping his fingers, jiving along.

I stopped in shock. My heart started to pound.

"This time you're not getting away!" I said out loud.

I took off, running full speed to catch up to him. He had the music blasting in his ears. So he didn't hear me.

You're not getting away. You're not getting away. I chanted those words in my mind as I ran.

I stretched out my arms as I caught up with him.

I grabbed him by the shoulders. He was real!

I grabbed him from behind. Spun him around.

And gasped in shock.

CHAPTER 14

Not him! It wasn't my twin!

It was another guy, a stranger.

His dark eyes bulged in surprise. His mouth dropped open.

I held my grip on his shoulder. I was too startled to move.

And then I felt the shoulder move under my hand. It started to wriggle . . . then shrink . . . to melt away.

I uttered a cry. My hand flew off his shoulder.

And I stared in horror as the boy's shoulder shrank under the sleeve of the black T-shirt. And his hand . . . his hand clenched in a tight fist . . . grew smaller . . . melted away . . . melted into the wrist.

And then the arm curled like a fat snake. Boneless . . . No longer a human arm, it twisted and curled, and reached out for me like the tendril of a plant.

"You . . . You . . . You . . ." the boy choked out in a hoarse gasp.

"Huh?" I gasped. I stepped back, trying to escape the curling tendril of an arm.

He uttered a gurgling sound, tore off the headphones, and staggered toward me.

I slapped my hand over my mouth to keep from screaming as his face began to change.

The skin peeled away. Peeled off like onion skin . . . flaked away in chunks . . . until he had no skin.

No skin on his face at all!

His hair fell off in thick clumps. And then the pale skin flaked off his scalp. And now his whole head glowed bright red. Red and wet.

Just like raw meat.

His face was raw meat, chunks of meat, crisscrossed with bulging purple veins.

His dark eyes stared out at me from wet sockets.

No nose. Just two deep holes, two gaping nostrils carved into the meaty slab.

"The pain. It hurts," he moaned.

His whole face jiggled and throbbed.

I staggered back. "What—what's happening to you?" I stammered, raising my hands to shield myself from the hideous sight of his raw face. From his arm, wriggling in front of him like a pale snake.

He tossed back his throbbing, glistening red face and uttered a shrill howl.

And then he spun away—and took off, howling as he ran. And screaming at the top of his lungs, "Help! Help!"

I grabbed my stomach. I felt sick.

What just happened? I wondered, hugging myself, trying to stop trembling.

I shook my head to try to clear it.

But I couldn't force the picture of the kid's face from my mind. The throbbing red meat, glistening and wet. The purple veins pulsing in his choppy face.

"I've got to get away from here!" I said out loud. I started to jog—but another sharp pain shot through my head.

On fire, I thought. My head is on fire!

I grabbed my head with both hands. Stab after stab of pain made me cry out. I shut my eyes. I pressed my hands tighter over my throbbing head.

Once again the pain stopped as abruptly as it had started.

I shook my head hard. I saw the little grocery store up ahead. It'll be cool inside, I decided.

And normal.

Please, I pleaded silently, let everything be normal again.

The store was nearly empty. A couple of teenagers were discussing candy bars at the front counter. A boy was trying to get his friend to buy a Zigfruit bar. His friend said only freaks buy Zigfruits. He was sticking with Four Musketeers.

Zigfruits? Four Musketeers?

Since when did they add another musketeer?

I picked a carton of milk off the shelf and carried it to the woman behind the counter. "Is that all?" she asked.

I nodded. "Yes. Just the milk."

I shoved the carton across the counter.

And felt the cardboard carton melt away in my hand.

The milk poured out, steaming . . . making a loud hissing sound.

"Oh!" I gasped as the hissing milk poured out in thick lumps. It spread over the counter. Bubbling . . . steaming . . . turning bright yellow.

A sick, sour smell rose up from the yellow clots.

The shocked woman gazed down at the steaming mess. Then raised her eyes to me—frightened eyes—and opened her mouth in a scream: "GET OUT! OUT! GET OUT OF HERE!"

"S-sorry!" I choked out. My stomach lurched from the sick smell. I gagged. Spun away from the counter—and staggered outside.

I stumbled to the curb, feeling dazed, sick. I glimpsed the two guys from the store, holding strange candy bars, staring at me from the doorway.

"Hey—!" I called to them. My legs shaking, my whole body trembling, I walked up to them. "What just happened?" I asked. "Did you see—?"

"Don't touch us!" one of them screamed.

They both raised their hands as if shielding

themselves from me.

"Keep back! Don't touch us!"

"But—but—" I sputtered. "What's wrong? What's happening?"

CHAPTER 15

The two boys scrambled away. One of them dropped his candy bar. He didn't stop to pick it up.

I ran all the way home. Gasping for breath, sweat pouring down my face, I burst into the house.

"Mom? Where are you? Mom?"

"In the dining room," she called. "Jake and I started without you."

I lurched into the dining room. Mom and Jake sat at one end of the long table. Jake opened his mouth wide and showed me a disgusting, chewed-up blob of spaghetti inside.

I ran up beside Mom's chair. "I—I have to talk to you," I said.

"Sit down," Mom said sharply. "What took you so long? Mr. Lawrence will be here any minute."

"Listen to me!" I cried. "Something strange is going on and—"

"Your face is strange!" Jake shouted. He burst out laughing at his own dumb joke.

"At least my nickname isn't Rat Face!" I shot

back. "Hi, Rat Face! What's up, Rat Face!"

"I'm not a Rat Face! You're a rat! You're a whole rat!" Jake screamed. "Go eat some cheese, Rat!"

"Stop it! Stop it right now!" Mom cried. She turned to me. "Where's the milk?"

"That's what I'm trying to tell you," I said breathlessly. "I couldn't—"

"You came home without milk?" Mom sighed. "Sit down, Ross." She pushed me toward my seat. "Don't talk. Try to eat something before your lesson."

"But—But—"

"Don't talk! Just eat!" She scooped a mound of spaghetti onto my plate. Then she piled on a ton of brussels sprouts.

Yuck.

The smell made my stomach lurch.

Mom leaned over the table, watching me. "Go ahead. Try the sprouts. I know you love them."

"We have to talk—" I started. "You see, I don't like brussels sprouts. I'm trying to tell you—"

She shook her head. "Stop it. Not a word. I've heard enough of your crazy stories to last a lifetime. Just eat."

I had no choice. I speared one of the disgusting, squishy balls on my fork. I raised it slowly to my mouth.

I felt sick. My stomach tightened.

I started to gag.

Mom stared across the table at me.

I held my breath. And slid the brussels sprout into my mouth. So squishy and slimy and sour . . .

I swallowed it whole.

Mom sat back in her seat. "Good?"

I couldn't reply. I was trying with all my strength to keep from puking.

The front doorbell rang. I saw Amelia, the housekeeper, hurry to answer it.

"That's Mr. Lawrence," Mom said. "Hurry, Ross. Get into your karate robe. You'll have to eat later. We'll keep dinner warm for you."

I gulped down a glass of apple juice, trying to get the brussels sprouts taste out of my mouth. "Uh . . . maybe I should skip the lesson tonight," I said. "I have a big homework project, and—"

"Mr. Lawrence drove all the way from Burbank," Mom said. "Get upstairs and get changed. What's wrong with you tonight?"

That's what I want to know! I said to myself as I hurried to my room.

What's wrong with me tonight?

I stared at the white robe hanging on my closet door. Which way does the belt go? I wondered. Does the collar stay up or down?

How am I going to fake my way through this lesson? I asked myself. I can't. I don't know anything about karate. And I've never seen this Mr. Lawrence before in my life.

Why did Mom say I've been taking lessons since I was seven?

How can she be so totally confused?

I pulled on the robe and tied the belt in front of me. My hands were trembling.

This guy could kill me, I realized.

I can't go through with this. I've got to stop it.

Downstairs, I heard voices coming from Dad's gym in the back of the house. Dad has a Stairmaster, a weight bench, and a treadmill in there.

As I stepped into the room, I was surprised to see a canvas floor mat spread out in the center of the gym. Jake was on the mat, kidding around with a huge, bald, red-faced man in a white robe. Mr. Lawrence.

The karate teacher was letting Jake throw him over his little shoulder. Jake laughed as Mr. Lawrence flipped over and landed with a hard thud on his back.

"You didn't know you were so strong, did you?" Mr. Lawrence asked Jake.

"I'm stronger than Ross!" Jake bragged. He crooked both arms to show off his pitiful, pea-sized muscles.

Mr. Lawrence sprang easily to his feet and turned to me. "Hi, Ross. You ready?" He bowed to me.

I bowed back. "Uh . . . I don't think I can do this tonight," I started. "You see, I've had these terrible headaches—"

"Tension," Mr. Lawrence said. "This lesson should help."

"No. Really," I insisted. "Maybe . . . uh . . . Jake would like a lesson tonight. I can't—"

He wasn't paying any attention to me. "Let's practice what we were doing last time, okay?"

He stood stiffly, facing me, hands placed firmly on his hips. He stared straight ahead, concentrating. His round, bald head glowed under the ceiling light.

What is he waiting for? I wondered. What is he going to do?

It didn't take long to find out.

With a grunt, he swung off the floor. Flew up off the mat. Both legs rose sideways—and landed a hard, pounding kick in my stomach.

"Unnnnh!" I groaned in pain.

I doubled over. It hurt . . . hurt so much . . . I couldn't breathe . . . couldn't breathe . . .

I felt my stomach tighten—then heave.

"Unnnnnh." The whole brussels sprout flew out of my mouth and plopped onto the mat.

Gasping, holding my aching stomach, I collapsed to the floor.

Mr. Lawrence huddled over me. "What happened?" He knelt beside me, his heavy arm on my shoulders. "Ross, you've defended against that a hundred times. Why didn't you move?"

"Uh . . ." I couldn't speak. My breaths were rasping in my throat.

Somehow I managed to stand. My stomach ached. I felt about to heave again.

"Ross, are you okay? Why didn't you defend yourself?" Mr. Lawrence asked.

I turned away. Bent over, I started to run. Out of the gym. Down the back hall.

"Ross, come back!" Mr. Lawrence shouted after me.

I was nearly to the stairs when a figure jumped out to stop me.

My twin.

I let out a startled cry. "You—?"

Scowling at me furiously, he grabbed my arm. "I'm late—and you try to take over my life! It's not going to work, Rosssss," he hissed. "Give me that robe—and get out of here!"

"But—" I groaned weakly.

"Get out! Go away!" he cried in a harsh whisper. "I've been warning you! You don't belong here!"

CHAPTER 16

Angrily I pushed his hand away. "Get off me!" I cried.

"Go away, Rossss!" he hissed. He shoved me. "You don't belong here. You have to leave."

"But—it's my house!" I cried. "Who are you? What are you doing here?"

He raised a finger to his lips and glanced nervously down the hall. "Keep it down. I can't explain. But I'm trying to tell you—you're in danger. Don't say anything. Don't touch anything. Just give me that robe and get lost! Fast!"

"I won't leave!" I insisted. "You have to leave! I'm going to tell Mom. I'm going to explain that you aren't me!"

"She's *my* Mom!" my twin declared. "Please! Leave! Just—go!"

"No way!" I said.

I heard voices from the gym. Footsteps in the hall.

"Get upstairs!" my twin whispered frantically. He grabbed the robe and struggled to tug it off me. I let him take it. Then he pushed me to the stairs.

"What's going on?" I demanded. "Who are you? Why do you look like me?"

"I can't explain now. Go up to my room—quick!"

"It's my room!" I protested.

"Get upstairs before they see you!" he ordered.

"But I have to talk to Mom!" I said.

"No way." He twisted my arm up hard behind my back.

"Ow."

He's real, I realized. He's a person. He's not a ghost. A ghost couldn't shove me or twist my arm like that.

Squeezing my arm behind my back, he forced me up the stairs and into my room. "You can't—" I started to say.

But he practically heaved me into the room. "I'll come back after the lesson. I'll explain," he said breathlessly. "Don't try to escape. And don't touch anything. I'm warning you."

Then he hurried back out to the hall and closed the bedroom door behind him.

"No! Wait!" I shouted.

I grabbed the doorknob and started to pull the door open. But I heard the lock click on the other side.

He'd locked me in.

"Hey—come back!" I shouted. I pounded on the door with my fists. "Give me a break! Let me out of here!"

I pounded till my fists hurt. Silence out there.

With a defeated sigh, I slumped away from the door. I'm a prisoner, I realized. A prisoner in my own room.

But was it my room?

I spun around. My eyes swept over all the familiar things. My Jimi Hendrix posters . . . my snow globe collection . . . my things.

Yes. I was in my own room. My room in my house.

But why does everything seem right and wrong at the same time?

I remembered falling. Then watching the grass burn.

I thought about the boy on the street. I had grabbed his shoulder, and his arm had changed until it slithered and curled. And his face . . .

I didn't want to think about that hamburger face.

The milk in the store. I held the carton . . . and it blew up or something! And then everyone started screaming at me.

What was going on?

Did I cause those things to happen?

Why? How could I?

I paced back and forth, my heart pounding. I clenched and unclenched my fists. I stopped at the window and peered out.

A warm, clear night. Stars in a purple sky. The olive tree below the window shimmered in a soft wind, as if inviting me. Inviting me to climb out and lower myself down its trunk.

Yes!

I'll escape, I decided. Then I'll run back inside the house and find Mom. I'll show her the other Ross. I'll tell her he's an impostor, a total fake. I'll make her believe me. And I'll tell her about all the other weird things that have happened. There's got to be a logical explanation for all of it. Once Mom sees the other Ross, she'll know I'm not lying. She'll help me figure out what's going on.

My hands trembled as I reached for the window. I slid it up as high as it would go. Warm, damp air floated into the room. It smelled so sweet and fresh.

I lowered myself onto the windowsill and slid one leg over the side.

This was the tricky part. The nearest branch was a foot or two below the window. I had to lower my feet onto it carefully, then swing my body out and grab onto the slender trunk.

If I slipped . . .

I didn't want to think about it.

I turned and started to swing my other leg out the window.

But I stopped when I saw the bedroom door open behind me. My twin burst in, still wearing his karate robe. His eyes searched the room, then stopped when he spotted me at the window.

"Good!" he said. "Go. You have to go. There isn't room for both of us!"

And then I gasped as he dived forward, arms out-stretched. Running to push me out the window.

CHAPTER 17

I spun to fight him off.

But my leg caught on the side of the house.

He grabbed my arm with both hands. And to my shock, pulled me back into the room.

I landed on the floor, breathing hard, my body bathed in a cold sweat.

He stared down at me, a crooked smile on his face. My crooked smile.

"Did you think I was going to push you out?" he asked, breathing hard.

"Well . . . maybe," I muttered.

I climbed slowly to my feet. I stood facing him, tensed and ready.

"I'd love to push you out," he said, squinting at me angrily. "But the fall wouldn't kill you. And I have to get you out of here—out of here for good."

"So why didn't you let me go out the window?" I demanded.

"You wouldn't get very far," he said menacingly.

"What do you mean?" I demanded.

"You don't understand. You don't know anything," my twin said, shaking his head. "I guess I have no choice. I have to explain it all before you go."

"But I'm not going," I said firmly, crossing my arms in front of me. "You are going. You are the one who doesn't belong."

He made a disgusted face and motioned for me to sit down.

I dropped down tensely on the edge of the bed. He tugged off the white robe and tossed it into the closet. Then he pulled out the desk chair and sat on it backward, resting his hands on its back.

"This is your own fault," he said bitterly. He glanced to the door. I guessed he was making sure it was closed.

"My own fault?" I cried. "What are you talking about?"

"You told a lot of lies—didn't you!" he accused. "You lied and lied and lied. You told so many lies, you broke the fabric of truth and reality!"

"I didn't lie that much!" I protested.

"Ross, you lied so much, you lost all track of what's real and what isn't real," he continued. "You slipped into a parallel world. Into a whole different reality. Out of your world—into my world."

I jumped to my feet. "Are you crazy?" I shouted. "What are you talking about?"

"Didn't you learn about parallel worlds?" my twin asked. "What kind of school do you go to? We study that in fourth grade."

"You're totally crazy," I muttered, dropping back onto the bed.

"Well, didn't you notice things are a little different here?" my twin demanded. "Didn't you notice that things are almost the same—but not quite?"

"Well . . . yeah," I replied.

My twin climbed to his feet. He shoved the chair back under the desk. "You lied and lied until you lost your reality," he said.

"No—" I said.

"Now you're in a world where you don't belong. And it's your fault. All your fault."

"How do you know?" I screamed. "What makes you the expert? How do you know anything about me?"

"Because I *am* you!" he shouted back. "I'm Ross Arthur in this reality, in this world. And you don't belong here! You're an Intruder. A dangerous Intruder. You can't stay!"

"No!" I cried again. "You're not Ross—I am!" I screamed.

But I knew I didn't belong here.

I couldn't belong here. Too many weird things had happened. Things I couldn't explain.

My twin said I broke the fabric of reality. But that sounded totally crazy.

Was I really in a parallel world?

My head began to throb. I didn't know what to believe.

"You have to go," my twin ordered. "Get out—now!"

"GO? Where am I supposed to go?" I shouted. "I'm staying. You leave!"

And then I lost it.

I jumped on him. In a wild fury, I grabbed him around the neck.

I dropped him to the floor.

I kicked him hard in the stomach.

With an angry groan, he rolled on top of me. Punched me in the chest.

And we wrestled, wrestled frantically, rolling over the floor, punching, clawing, pounding each other.

"Only one of us belongs here, Ross," he gasped. "Only one of us can stay. Me! You can't survive here! I'm telling the truth. You can't survive. You're going to die!"

CHAPTER 18

I wrapped my twin in a headlock. I tightened my grip until his face turned red.

"I'm not going to die!" I gasped.

He twisted free and slammed me to the floor. He jumped on top of me and started to twist my arm.

"Owwwwww." I let out a howl of pain.

A hard knock on the bedroom door made us both stop. We were wheezing, choking, gasping for breath. My side ached. My head throbbed. My neck was stiff.

He had a deep, red scratch down his left arm.

"Ross, what on earth are you and Jake doing in there?" Mom called in.

"Uh . . . nothing," my twin answered, wiping a gob of spit off his chin. "We're just . . . kidding around."

"No! Mom, help me!" I cried. "It's me! Please! Open the door! I—"

My twin clamped his hand over my mouth before I could say more. He furiously motioned for me to be quiet.

I struggled to get free.

My twin clamped his hand tighter over my mouth. I couldn't move. I couldn't make a sound.

Please, open the door! I silently begged. Please, Mom!

But the door remained closed. "Just don't wreck your room. It was cleaned this morning," Mom called in.

"No problem," my twin answered.

We listened to her footsteps padding down the stairs.

When she was gone, my twin finally lifted his hand from my mouth. "That was very stupid," he muttered. "She wouldn't help you. She would know instantly that you don't belong here."

"What are you saying?" I cried weakly.

I pulled myself to a sitting position on the floor and leaned my head against the bed.

"You just don't get it, do you," he said.

I wiped sweat off my forehead with the sleeve of my T-shirt. "Get what?"

"You don't understand what is happening here," he said, rubbing the red scratch on his arm. "You really never studied parallel worlds?"

I shook my head.

"Well, there are many, many parallel worlds," he said. "I live in one world, and you live in another."

"You live in the world of the cuckoos," I muttered.

He sighed and continued. "That night at Max's

party, the portal between our worlds opened up."

I frowned at him. "You mean in the swimming pool?"

He nodded. "I saw you there in the water. I couldn't believe what I was seeing. I was so scared. It took me a while to figure out what had happened."

"What happened?" I asked.

"You slipped into my world, Ross. You slipped through the portal. You swam into my world."

I rolled my eyes. Something weird was definitely going on. But portals? Parallel worlds? "I don't think so," I said.

He jumped to his feet. "I'm trying to explain," he snapped. "I'm sure it looked to you like your world. The people were all the same. The places were all the same. But it's different in a lot of ways. It's a parallel world. It's my world."

"Tell me another one," I muttered.

This guy was as good a liar as I was! He was so good, he almost had me believing him.

"Since that night at Max's party," he continued, "you've been slipping in and out of my world. You've been going back and forth between our worlds. And now you seem to be stuck here. But you can't stay in this reality. You don't belong."

"Then why don't *you* leave?" I shot back.

All this talk about parallel worlds was starting to give me the creeps.

"You don't belong," he repeated. "And you . . .

you can do a lot of damage."

I swallowed hard. "Huh? What do you mean?"

"You are from another world. You can't just barge in and interfere with our world. You are dangerous. You are an Intruder. That's what we call people like you."

An Intruder?

"Intruders are very dangerous," my twin continued. "Even if they don't mean to be. Sometimes when they touch things, they change them. Sometimes they destroy things completely."

"Okay. I get it," I said. "I'm an Intruder. If I touch something, I destroy it."

"You believe me?" he asked.

"Yes," I replied.

I crossed the room and grabbed him with both hands.

"Goodbye!" I shouted. "Goodbye!"

CHAPTER 19

He jumped up and shoved me away. "Nice try," he muttered. "But you can't control it. You can't just grab people and destroy them any time you want."

He glared at me angrily. He balled his hands into fists. "Don't ever try anything like that again," he said.

And then he lowered his voice. "But there isn't much point in worrying about you. You're going to die in a day or two."

"You're crazy," I muttered, breathing hard. I balled my hands into fists, too. I was ready to fight again if I had to.

"Haven't you already started to feel the pain?" he asked. "The pain of being in a world where you don't belong? Intruders always feel more and more pain."

I swallowed hard. The headaches? The powerful, stabbing headaches I'd had this afternoon? Is that what he was talking about?

No way. Everyone gets headaches from time to time.

"And when the pain becomes unbearable, Intruders start to fade away," my twin continued. "They get lighter and lighter . . . they fade until you can see right through them . . . lighter and lighter . . . until they blow away like a dead leaf."

"Nooooo!" A scream of protest burst from my throat. "You're crazy! You're a liar!"

A crooked smile spread slowly over my twin's face. "You'll see," he murmured.

"No!" I shouted again. "No—you'll see!"

I lowered my shoulder and rammed right into him, shoving him hard. He let out a startled cry and toppled onto the bed.

By the time he regained his feet, I had the bedroom door open and burst out into the hall.

"Mom! Mom—help me!" I shouted, running to the stairs.

I leaped down the stairs, two at a time. "Mom! Where are you?"

I ran through the house, calling for her. Back to the gym. Down to the family room. No sign of her.

I peered into the garage. Her car was gone. She must have gone out, I realized.

My heart pounding, I ran out onto the driveway. I've got to get away from here, I decided. I've got to get away and think.

I took off, running across front lawns. It was a hot, smoggy L.A. night. The air felt heavy and wet. I was already sweating. My shoes thudded over the perfectly trimmed lawns.

A Jeep rolled past, music blaring out the window. Its headlights rolled over me as it passed.

Normal. Everything normal.

Max's house came into view on the other side of the long, low hedges. Maybe Max is home, I thought. Maybe I'll stop in and see what's up with him. Try to talk to him. Maybe he can help me figure out what's really going on.

I ducked through the spot in the hedge that I always use. The backyard was dark. One terrace light on at the garage. The house was dark, too.

No one home, I decided. I wiped sweat off my forehead. Despite the heat of the night, I felt chilled. The back of my neck tingled. I'm just tense, I decided.

I started back toward the street but stopped when I heard a sharp yip. I turned and saw Flash, the O'Connors' Dalmatian, come trotting across the grass.

"Flash!" I called. I was glad to see him. I'd known Flash since he was a puppy.

The O'Connors live across the street. Sometimes when they go on vacation, we take Flash to our house. "Hey, Flash—how's it going?"

The dog stopped suddenly, a few feet from me. He began sniffing the air furiously. His ears perked straight up.

"Hey—Flash?" I called. I knelt down and motioned for him to come get some hugs. "Here, boy. Come on, boy."

To my surprise, the dog lowered his head—and started to snarl.

"Hey—" I jumped to my feet.

Flash pulled back his lips, revealing two rows of sharp teeth. He snarled menacingly, his entire body arched, tense.

"Flash—it's me!"

With a furious growl, the big dog leaped at me.

I dodged to the side. Lost my balance. Slid on the grass. Landed hard on my side.

The snarling dog turned. Eyes red. White drool making the sharp teeth glisten.

He uttered another angry growl. Leaped hard. Lowered his head—and sank his teeth into my arm.

CHAPTER 20

I let out a howl of pain and tried to roll away.

But the dog was too heavy, too strong.

Pain shot down my arm, my entire side.

With a groan I reached up both arms and grabbed the dog around the neck. I shot my hands forward, struggling to pull the furious Dalmatian off me.

He snapped his jaws angrily, snarling, clawing at me.

I held on to his neck. Held on tight, trying to push him away.

And then suddenly he uttered a high, soft cry. Like the mew of a cat.

Flash's red eyes appeared to dim. He backed off me, staggered back. He raised his head and opened his mouth wide in a high, shrill howl. A howl of pain.

I rolled away. Stumbled to my feet, gasping for breath, rubbing my throbbing arm.

And I saw the white fur on Flash's neck. Saw it blacken. Saw the red handprints on the dog's bare skin.

And then Flash uttered a choking sound. A gurgling from deep in his throat.

He gazed up at me—no longer angry, but surprised. Confused.

The fur fell off his body. And his skin peeled. Flaked away.

"Ohhhhhh." A moan of horror escaped my throat as the dog toppled onto its side.

It dropped heavily onto the grass and didn't move again.

And its skin—its skin and fur—melted away as I stared down at the lifeless form.

"No!" I cried. I knelt down and grabbed the dog in my hands. "Flash! Flash!"

His skin peeled off in my hands. Warm, wet chunks of skin.

I gagged. Jumped away, frantically wiping my hands on my jeans.

The dog's skin all melted away until I was staring at the gray skeleton. Shimmering in the light from the low half moon, gray rib bones curling up from the grass. And an eyeless, silvery dog skull, jaw open in a silent cry.

I did this!

The words rang in my ears.

I did this to Flash!

No. I didn't want to hear it. I didn't want to believe it.

Holding my hands over my ears, I turned and ran. Ran without seeing. Ran without thinking.

The dog's last pitiful howl repeated in my ears. I

kept running as if trying to escape from it, to escape from the sound in my own head.

I don't know how long I ran. I suddenly found myself on Rodeo Drive. The classy shops were all closed. The sidewalks were empty, except for a few window-shoppers, peering into the brightly lit store windows.

I stopped running. I was drenched in sweat, my hair matted to my head. My T-shirt stuck to my body. My chest ached from running for so long.

I leaned in a doorway and gazed down the street. It all looked normal to me. The shops, the restaurants. The same as always.

I stepped away from the building when I heard shouts. Angry, excited shouts. Across Wilshire Boulevard, a block away.

I crossed Wilshire, followed the voices—and found myself on a street lined with small stores. They were all closed. The sidewalk was deserted—except for the shouting men.

Three L.A. cops surrounded a young man. Two of the cops held the guy tightly by his arms. The third cop stood in front of the guy, blocking my view of him.

What's going on? I wondered.

I ducked behind the trunk of a huge palm tree and watched from my hiding place.

The cops were wearing uniforms I'd never seen before. Uniforms that looked like spacesuits, shiny silver and padded, and helmets just like the ones astronauts wear. Weird.

"Looks like we caught one," one of the cops said.

"Yep. He's an Intruder," another one said excitedly. "I've never seen one—have you?"

"No. But let's keep this quiet," he answered. "We don't want the neighborhood in a panic."

I moved in the shadows. Ducked behind another tree to get a closer look.

Finally I could see the young man. He had long, blond hair. Wild, blue eyes. A tattoo snaking along one arm.

He was struggling to free himself from the two cops who held him. Bending and twisting. He started screaming at the top of his lungs, his hair flying up, head tossed back.

"I'm not an Intruder!" he shrieked. "I'm not! You've got the wrong guy!"

The cops weren't buying it. "Calm down," one of them said. "Save your strength."

"Why fight?" the other cop shouted. "You don't have much time."

"Give up."

Instead, the man lurched forward with a furious cry, struggling to burst free.

The two cops lost their hold for a moment. Crying out, they made a wild grab for him. And ripped off the man's sport shirt.

One of the cops screamed. Another one shut his eyes and turned away.

I gaped in amazement at the man's bare chest. I could see his heart pumping inside him . . . see his stomach churning and bobbing . . . see blue blood pulsing through his veins, his guts twisting and curling.

I could see right through him!

Suddenly the man doubled over. He uttered gasp after gasp. The light faded from his eyes. He hugged himself tightly. "The pain . . ." he moaned. "Ohhhh, help me. I can't stand the pain."

His screams and cries rang in my ears. My head started to throb.

I shrank back. Pressed myself against the tree. I shut my eyes and covered my face with my hands.

It was all true, I realized.

My twin had told the truth about Intruders. He had told the truth about me.

I didn't belong here. I was an Intruder, too.

And in a day or two . . . in a day or two . . .

I'd be gone. Forever.

CHAPTER 21

The cops shoved the poor Intruder into the back of a van. The van sped off quietly. No flashing lights. No siren.

I was the only one on the sidewalk. I felt paralyzed, frozen with fear.

How could I save myself? How could I return to my own world before I faded away?

My head felt ready to burst. My panic made my heart leap around in my chest.

How did I get here in the first place? I asked myself.

The portal . . . The portal . . .

"Whoa!" I let out a cry. My twin had already told me the answer. It was so simple!

Max's swimming pool! That's where he and I had seen each other for the first time. That's the portal between our two worlds!

I had just been there a few minutes ago, in Max's backyard. I was so close . . . so close to returning home . . . and didn't even realize it.

Yes!

I pumped both fists in the air. I let out a happy shout.

I turned and made my way back across Wilshire Boulevard. Back down Rodeo Drive. I knew what I had to do. It was so clear, so easy.

I'll return to Max's backyard, I told myself. And I'll jump into the pool. Clothes and all. I'll dive down . . . swim underwater . . . through the portal . . . swim back to my world.

I'm so lucky, I decided.

I figured out how to return home before I got too weak. Before I started to fade away. Before the pain became unbearable.

So lucky . . .

I was just a block from Max's house, walking fast, swinging my arms, when the black-and-white police cruiser pulled up beside me.

"Stop right there," a gruff voice barked.

CHAPTER 22

I froze. A cold shudder shook my body.

Panic choked my throat. My knees felt about to collapse.

They know!

They know I'm an Intruder!

How did they find out?

A round-faced cop with a flat buzz cut and tiny, round black eyes leaned his head out of the patrol car. "Where you headed, son?" His tiny eyes studied me up and down.

"H-home," I choked out.

He frowned and kept his eyes locked on me. "You live around here? Or are you out sight-seeing?"

"No. I live down there." I pointed. I told him the address.

"What's your name, son?" The radio in the car squawked loudly. A low voice on the radio was calling out numbers. "Do you have any ID?"

"ID? N-no," I stammered. I reached for my back pocket. "I left my wallet at home. But I'm Ross

Arthur. My Dad is Garrison Arthur. He's with Mango Pictures."

"We don't need your family history," the cop's partner said from behind the wheel. "You shouldn't be walking around at night, kid."

He turned to the other cop. "Let's go. We've got a 308 on Sunset."

They sped away without saying good-bye.

I stood there trembling, watching the patrol car whirl around the corner. I hugged myself to stop the shaking. Cold sweat clung to my forehead, my cheeks.

A close call, I knew.

I have to get out of here, I told myself. I won't be safe for a second—until I get back to my own world.

I took off running. I didn't stop until I got to Max's house.

I was halfway up the front lawn when I saw the dog skeleton poking up from the grass near the hedge. The pile of bones gleamed dully under the moonlight. The ugly sight made my stomach lurch.

Poor Flash.

I've got to get home before I harm anything else, I told myself.

Max's house was dark except for a porch light. Still no one home.

I made my way along the side of the house to the back. A dim yellow light spilled out from one of the bedrooms. Otherwise, I moved through total darkness.

I stepped onto the terrace in back. My heart started to pound with excitement.

I was so hot and drenched with sweat. I could use a cold swim.

Especially a swim that would bring me home.

I'll jump into the shallow end and swim toward the deep water, I told myself. Just as I did that night at Max's party.

I'll swim to the deep end . . . slip through the portal . . . and be out of this frightening world forever.

My shoes scraped the stone terrace as I jogged to the pool.

I stepped eagerly to the edge. Peered down.

And stared at bare concrete.

"No! No! No!" I pounded my fists against my sides.

The pool had been drained.

CHAPTER 23

I had no choice. There was no water in the pool, and I was out of ideas. I had to go back to my twin's house. I had to talk to him. He was the only one who might be able to help me.

I sneaked in through the back door and crept upstairs to his room. He looked up from his computer as I walked in, and flashed me a disgusted scowl. "You're back?" he sneered.

He stood up, walked to the window, and gazed out into the blackening night.

From far in the distance I heard the shrill call of a bird, a strange, trilling sound I'd never heard before.

A sound from a different world.

A different reality.

"You've got to help me," I pleaded. "Tell me, how . . . how do I get back to my world? What do I have to do?"

He turned slowly and stared at me for a long while. Finally he snickered coldly. "I don't know. It's your problem."

"No!" I cried. I jumped up and crossed the room

to him. I grabbed him by the front of his T-shirt. "You have to know!" I screamed. "You have to know!"

He pulled free and stumbled away from me. "I—I don't want to fight again," he said.

"Then tell me!" I demanded. "You know all about this—right? You studied it in the fourth grade. You know about portals and parallel worlds. You know it all—don't you?"

I backed him into a corner.

He tensed his body. Raised his hands, as if expecting another fight.

"Tell me!" I screamed.

"Okay, okay," he replied, motioning with both hands for me to back off. "Just sit down, okay? I think I know how you can do it. But stop screaming."

Breathing hard, I took a few steps back. "Tell me," I demanded again.

"Okay. Sit down," he said. "You've been a liar your whole life, right?"

I glared at him. "Excuse me?"

"Just go with me on this," he said. "You've been a liar your whole life."

"Whatever," I muttered. And then I snapped, "How do you know?"

"I already told you. Because I'm you," he replied. "You slipped into my world because your whole world became a lie, okay? If you want to get back to your world, you have to reverse it."

I scratched my head. "Huh? Reverse it?"

He nodded. "Yeah. You have to tell the truth. You have to tell the truth to someone about what has happened to you."

I swallowed. "You mean I have to explain to someone from your world that I'm an Intruder? That I came here from another world?"

"Yes. And you have to make them believe you." he said.

"But—everyone knows I'm a liar!" I cried. "Everyone knows I make up stories all the time. Who would believe me? Who?"

He shrugged. "Beats me."

And suddenly, I had an idea.

CHAPTER 24

"Where can I sleep tonight?" I asked.

My twin yawned. "I don't care. Go sleep in a tree."

"Can I sleep on the floor?" I asked.

He shrugged. "Do what you want. Just leave me alone."

A short while later my twin clicked off the lights and climbed into bed. I struggled to get comfortable on the rug.

We live in different worlds, I thought. But our lives are a lot alike.

If his Mom was like mine, she would get up early. And she would go into the kitchen to make coffee and call her friend Stella, who also gets up early.

And if I came downstairs while my twin was still asleep, I could talk to her. And I could quietly, calmly explain the whole thing.

Then I would bring her upstairs—and she'd see the proof. Two Rosses!

This is going to work. I'm practically home, I

thought as I drifted off to sleep.

When I woke up, gray morning light filled the window. I raised my head and squinted at the clock-radio beside the bed. Six-ten.

I had overslept a little. But it was okay.

My twin was sound asleep on his stomach, covers pulled up to his head.

If he was like me, his alarm wouldn't go off for another hour.

Yawning silently, I dragged myself to my feet. My back ached from lying on the hard floor. I'd slept in my underwear. I pulled on my jeans and T-shirt from yesterday.

I bent to tie my sneakers. Then I crept out of the room on tiptoes, and down the stairs to the kitchen.

The aroma of fresh coffee floated out to greet me. The kitchen was dark, except for the pale gray light from the windows.

Mom sat with her back to me on a tall stool at the counter. She had a white mug of coffee steaming beside her. The telephone was pressed to her ear.

The same Mom, I thought. The same blue bathrobe. Her hair unbrushed. One blue slipper on her foot, the other on the floor.

"I know, I know," she was saying into the phone. "Stella, tell me something I don't already know. Nothing changes. Really."

I tapped her on the shoulder.

A mistake.

She let out a startled squeal and dropped the phone. "Ross—what on earth!"

"Sorry, Mom," I said softly.

"What are you doing up so early? You scared me to death!" Mom exclaimed.

She picked up the phone and returned it to her ear. "Sorry, Stella. It was Ross. What were you saying?"

"I want to tell you something," I said. "Something kind of crazy."

She shrugged and pointed to the telephone. I could hear Stella's voice at the other end. She sounded like a quacking duck.

"Go make yourself some cereal," Mom whispered, waving me away.

"Okay," I said. "But I need to tell you something."

"I know, I know," she said into the phone. "You're not the only one, Stella. It happens. It happens a lot."

I went to the cabinet. I pulled down a bowl and a box of cornflakes. "I really have to talk to you," I told Mom.

She lowered the phone from her ear. "Stella got another call. She put me on hold. What do you want to tell me?"

"Well . . ." I shoved the cereal box away. I didn't really know where to begin. I knew I had to tell it right. I had to make her believe me.

"Are you in trouble, Ross?" Mom asked, her face wrinkling in concern.

"Well . . . yes and no," I said. "You see, Mom—a strange thing happened to me."

"How strange?" She had the phone pressed to her ear, but she was studying me, her eyes locked on mine.

"Pretty strange," I said. "You see, you're not really my mom. I—"

"Oh, Ross! Not another one of your crazy stories!" she cried. "It's too early! Go back to sleep, okay? You've got another hour to sleep."

"Just listen to me," I said. "I know I've made up a lot of things in the past. But not today. Today I'm really serious, and I really need your help, okay?"

I took a deep breath. I stared at the cereal box. For some reason, I couldn't look at her. I didn't want to see her face in case she didn't believe me.

"Just let me tell the whole thing, Mom. And please believe me," I begged. "Please. I'm not making this up."

I stared at the cereal box. "The portal was open, and I slipped into a parallel world," I continued. "You probably know all about parallel worlds. Ross—I mean, the other Ross, your Ross—said he studied them in school. Well, that's what happened to me."

I took a deep breath. "I'm Ross, but I'm not the same Ross you know. I belong in a different world. I'm what you call an Intruder. And I need to get back there fast. I need you to believe me, Mom, so I can get back there. If you come upstairs, I can prove it to you. The other Ross—your Ross—is still in bed. Sleeping."

Whew. I got it all out.

I took a deep breath and hesitantly raised my eyes from the cereal box to Mom. "Do you believe me?" I asked in a whisper. "Do you? Will you come upstairs?"

CHAPTER 25

I held my breath. "Mom?"

She hung up the phone. "What is it, Ross?" she snapped.

"Do you believe me?" I repeated.

"Believe what? I have to run over to Stella's house. She's very upset."

She waved me away. She hadn't heard a word I said.

"Just stop in my room before you get dressed," I begged. "I have something to show you. It's an emergency!"

"I'm not getting dressed, Ross. I'm only going next door." Mom grabbed her raincoat from the coat closet and threw it over her bathrobe. "Stella has an emergency. A real emergency. She doesn't make up stories."

Mom stepped out the back door. I watched her hurry across the lawn to Stella's house.

I sighed and slumped out of the room. Strike one.

I trudged back upstairs to my room. My twin was

still sound asleep. He had kicked all the covers onto the floor. I do that sometimes, too.

I suddenly felt so homesick. I wanted to be back safe and sound in my real room. I wondered what my real mom was doing. I wondered if the real Jake was awake yet.

I stood over the bed and stared at my twin for a long moment. It felt so weird to see myself, how I looked, how I slept. He was me in every way.

And this was his room. I didn't belong here. And if I didn't find someone to believe my story, I wouldn't be here much longer.

"Wake up," I whispered. I bent down and shook him by the shoulders. "Come on. Wake up."

He blinked one eyelid open. "Huh? What's your problem?" he asked, hoarse from sleep. "What time is it?"

"It's early," I said. "But I don't have much time. I want to go to school with you."

He opened his other eye. "Excuse me?"

"I have to find someone to believe my story. So I have to go to school with you. As soon as my friends—your friends—see the two of us, they'll believe me. I know they will."

He sat up sharply. "No way," he said.

"Huh? You won't let me go to school?" I cried.

"Of course I'll let you go to school." A slow smile spread across my twin's face. "But I'm not going with you. You're going to have to make someone believe you all by yourself. No way I'm helping." He let out a loud yawn.

"Fine. I'm going to school now," I said. "I'm going to school—and I'm going to make someone believe me."

I stepped out into a warm, smoggy day. The air already heavy and damp. Along the block, gardeners were unloading their trucks. A woman in a gray maid's uniform was walking two white standard poodles along the curb.

It seems so much like home, I thought sadly. But I guess I'm as far away from home as a person can be.

I didn't have much time to feel sorry for myself. I saw Cindy on the next block, and I ran to catch up with her.

"Hey, wait up! Cindy—wait up!"

She was riding her bike, pedaling hard, her black hair bobbing behind her.

"Hey, wait!"

She finally stopped and turned around. "Ross? What's up?"

I ran over to her. "I have to tell you something," I said breathlessly.

She started pedaling again. "We're late. What is it, Ross?"

"I'm not really Ross," I said, struggling to keep up. "I'm Ross in a different world. And I have to get back there."

"You have to get back to the insane asylum!" She laughed. "You and your crazy stories."

"Cindy—please," I begged. "I'm not kidding about this. I'm really, really, really serious."

Her smile faded. "I don't get it. What's the joke?"

"It's not a joke," I said. "I don't belong here. I can't stay in this world. I have to get back to where I belong. If I don't . . ." My voice cracked.

"All I need is for you to believe me," I pleaded. "To believe what I'm telling you."

She rolled her eyes. "You want me to believe that you're an alien from another planet?"

"No!" I cried. "I want you to believe that I'm Ross in a parallel universe. I—I'm an Intruder!"

As she stared at me, her eyes darted back and forth. I could see she was thinking hard, trying to decide.

I crossed my fingers behind my back. "Do you believe me, Cindy?" I asked. "Do you?"

"Okay," she said finally. "Okay. I believe you."

CHAPTER 26

"Great!" I cried. "Thank you! Thank you!"

"I also believe that the moon is made of Limburger cheese," Cindy said. "And I believe that I can flap my arms and fly to Mars anytime I want." She burst out laughing.

"Wait! I can prove it to you!" I said.

I don't know why I didn't think of this before. But I could show Cindy that I was an Intruder!

"Watch this!" I said. I fell onto the grass, landing on my back. "Intruders destroy things. Right?"

Cindy just rolled her eyes.

"When I get up, the grass will burn and sizzle. You'll see."

I pressed my back hard into the grass. I wanted to make sure the grass turned totally brown.

I stood up. "Okay. Look."

We both stared down at the ground.

"Whoa." Cindy's eyes opened wide. "That's unbelievable. Flat grass."

Flat grass. That was it. The grass lay flat where I

had fallen. Still green. Not burned at all.

Why didn't it work this time? I wondered, staring at the grass. My twin could probably tell me, but it really didn't matter now.

The only thing that mattered was making Cindy believe me.

"Cindy—" I glanced up, but she was gone. I watched her pedal away, bumping over the curb, onto the next block. "I'm not giving up," I said out loud. "No way."

But a sharp stab of pain made me grab my head. I shut my eyes, trying to force the pain away.

"Ohhh," I groaned as my stomach started to ache. I bent over as the pain increased, as if thousands of razors pierced my stomach. The pain was so intense, I couldn't walk.

I hunched at the curb, doubled over in agony. My head. My stomach. It's happening, I realized. Just as my twin predicted. The horrible pain . . .

I forced myself to walk to school. I knew I didn't have much time. I had to find someone to believe my story.

I tried Max next. I found him at his locker across from Miss Douglas's class. "Max, listen to me," I said. "I'm an Intruder. I'm not really Ross."

He laughed. "Whatever," he said, and started toward class.

"Max—wait!" I called. "Please! If I told you a totally wild, totally insane story about me slipping between parallel worlds . . . if I told you that I'm not really the Ross you know, and that I don't belong here in your world . . . if I swore it was all true . . . would you believe me? Is there any chance at all you would believe me?"

He opened his mouth to answer. "No way—" he started.

"Think about it," I said. "Don't answer right away. Think about it, okay?"

He nodded. "I've thought about it."

"And?" I asked.

"And I think you're trying to get out of helping me wash my father's car," he said. "Nice try. But it won't work. You promised. See you after school. And don't forget to bring the car wax."

"Max—why won't you believe me?" I shouted.

"Everyone knows your crazy stories, Ross," he said grinning. "Everyone."

The bell rang.

Max shouted goodbye and hurried down the hall to class. I watched him for a moment, his words repeating in my mind.

Words of doom.

I could feel panic tighten my throat. My legs shook again as I slumped into Miss Douglas's classroom. I saw her standing at the side of her desk, straightening a pile of papers.

And suddenly I realized: She has to believe me.

She's a teacher. She has to believe her students.

If I beg her to believe me, she'll see how desperate I am. She won't be like my friends and think it's all a big joke.

Because why would I joke with a teacher? And I bet she knows all about parallel worlds.

I began to feel hopeful again. Just a little hope. But enough to make me think I might be able to return home after all.

"Miss Douglas!" I called.

Eyes turned as I tossed my backpack to the floor and took off running to the front of the room.

"Miss Douglas! Can I tell you something?"

CHAPTER 27

Miss Douglas didn't believe me, either.

She thought I was trying to get out of taking a test. "But I have to admit this is one of your better stories, Ross," she snickered, shaking her head.

"Go take your seat," she said, waving me away. "I'm sure you'll have an even better story for me tomorrow."

I trudged across the room to my desk.

There won't be a tomorrow, I thought bitterly.

There won't be a tomorrow for me because no one will believe me.

So what if I'm a liar? So what if I make up stories all the time?

Why can't someone believe me when I do tell the truth?

After class I tried to stand up. But I felt weak. I could feel my strength draining away.

My backpack suddenly weighed a ton. It took real effort to raise my shoes from the floor and make my way to my next class.

No one is going to believe me, I realized. Even my teacher thinks it's a big joke.

But I knew I had to keep trying.

In line at the lunchroom I asked one of the lunch servers if she believed in parallel worlds. She stared at me and asked if I wanted pizza or macaroni.

I looked for Sharma. But some kids told me she and her family went away for a few days.

After school I told my story to the tennis team coach. Coach Melvin listened silently, squeezing a tennis ball in one hand.

When I finished, he thought for a moment. Then he said, "I once had a dream like that. You can skip practice today, Ross, if you're upset about your dream."

He hurried off to start practice.

With a sigh I tried to sling my tennis racket onto my shoulder. But I didn't have the strength. I couldn't raise it that high.

My backpack felt too heavy to carry. My legs felt so weak, I kept stumbling on the sidewalk. The wind blew me off the grass onto the curb.

Feeling lost and defeated, I headed for home. It's as good a place to disappear as any, I thought sadly.

My twin greeted me at the front door. "You're back?"

I nodded weakly, struggling to catch my breath. Stomach cramps made it hard to breathe. My head throbbed with pain.

My twin followed me outside. I slumped wearily against a tree.

"You failed, huh?" he said. He had a crooked smile on his face, as if he was enjoying my suffering. "Sorry," he said. "The sun is heading down. I don't think you have much time."

"I . . . know . . ." I whispered.

I stared hard at him. The sinking sun made his face glow. His gray eyes gleamed in the soft light.

I gazed at him, so healthy, so strong, so . . . alive.

And suddenly I had an idea.

Suddenly I knew how I could save myself.

CHAPTER 28

I pointed at the other Ross. "You!" I said.

He took a step back. And narrowed his eyes at me. "Me? What about me?"

"YOU believe me!" I cried. "YOU believe the story. So—I'm safe! You said I need only one person to believe my story—and it's YOU!"

To my surprise, he burst out laughing.

"I've won!" I insisted. "I can go back to my world now."

He shook his head and laughed again.

"What's so funny?" I demanded. "This is serious. I did exactly what you told me to do. I found someone to believe me. You! You! You! So now I'm safe."

"No, you're not," he replied, still grinning. "I lied."

"You what?" I cried.

"I'm you—remember?" he said. "I'm your exact double, Ross. You're Ross—and I'm Ross. We're the same, right? So . . . sometimes I make up stories."

"You mean . . . you mean . . ." I swallowed hard.

I suddenly felt weaker. I staggered back onto the front lawn. Smacked hard into the tree trunk.

A gust of wind pushed me away. I pressed my back into the trunk.

"You mean . . . that's not the way to return to my world?" I whispered.

He raised a hand to his mouth. "Oops! Guess I made up a little story."

"But—but—that's so cold!" I gasped.

He shrugged. "Whatever. I'm you, remember? I'm you in every way. Except that I belong here, and you don't."

The wind lifted me off my feet. I grabbed the trunk to pull myself back to the ground.

"You're fading away," my twin said. "You're practically gone."

I glanced at my hands. I could see right through them. I could see through my arms.

The wind picked me up again. I dived for the tree trunk and flung my filmy arms around it.

I'm going to blow away, I realized. Like a dead leaf.

I felt so weak . . . weak and drained.

Holding tightly to the tree trunk, I turned to my twin. "Aren't you going to help me?" I pleaded. "Are you just going to let me disappear?"

"I can't help you," he said. "It's too late."

CHAPTER 29

I clung to the tree, but my grip was slipping. In a few seconds I knew I would flutter away. "You've . . . got to . . . help me," I whispered.

My twin crossed his arms over his chest. "I just want you gone, Ross. If I tell you how to get back to your world, you'll only tell more lies. And you'll end up in my world again."

"No!" I whispered. "No. Tell me how to get back. Tell me! Please! I promise—no more lies. I swear! Only the truth!"

"You're lying!" he shouted. "I know you are!"

"No—please!" I begged. "Please—tell me what I can do."

My twin shook his head. "No way."

I lost my grip on the tree. A blast of wind lifted me off my feet.

"I'll never tell another lie!" I swore. My voice came out so weak, I didn't know if he heard me.

"Okay, okay," he muttered. His expression softened. "Okay. I'll give you a break. I can't stand to see another Ross suffer."

"Thank you," I whispered. "Thank you."

He pointed. "See my garage? There's a room above the garage."

"Yes," I said. "An empty room. I know it. I have the same garage."

"Well, that room is a portal," he continued. "It's a passageway between our two worlds."

"Wow," I murmured.

"Climb up to the room and wait for a door to open," my twin instructed. "Go through that door—and you will be home. You will be home and strong again."

"Thank you," I whispered. "Thank you and good-bye. I promise you'll never see me again."

"Better hurry," he replied. "You've only got a few minutes." He turned and started to jog back into the house.

I gazed at the garage. It stood at the edge of the lawn, only twenty or thirty steps away. But to me, it was a mile in the distance.

Could I walk that far?

Was I strong enough to make it to the garage and up to the top room?

If I let go of the tree, will I just blow away like a leaf? I wondered.

My whole body trembled. I knew I had no choice. I had to try for it. It was my only hope.

My last hope.

Slowly, slowly I let my hands slide off the smooth

tree bark. I sank to my knees in the grass.

Should I crawl?

No.

I took a deep, shuddering breath and pulled myself to my feet.

A gust of wind blew against me. I gritted my teeth and leaned into it.

I took a step forward. Then another.

It felt as if the wind was trying to keep me from the garage. But I had to get there.

I lowered my head and pushed forward. I tried to think heavy thoughts.

I'm a ship's anchor, I told myself. I'm an elephant.

Forward. Step by step. Pushing my light body against the steady, stiff breeze.

I'm nearly there, I realized. Just a few more steps.

I uttered a cry as a sharp gust lifted me off the grass. It sent me flying back. A few seconds later I dropped heavily onto the grass.

I'm not going to quit, I told myself. I'm going to get there. I'm going to get to the portal.

I leaned forward again, lowering my head and shoulders—and trudged ahead. One step. Another. Another.

Breathing hard, my chest heaving from the effort, I stepped into the cool darkness of the garage.

I hugged myself, trying to stop my trembling. And peered at the stairs, half-hidden in darkness at the back wall.

The stairs to the portal between our worlds.

The portal . . . the portal . . .

"NO!" I let out a hoarse, angry scream. "NO! NO!"

I shouted in fury—in terror—because I suddenly knew this was wrong.

My twin had lied to me again.

CHAPTER 30

He lied. He lied.

The garage room can't be the portal.

Because I've never been up in the garage room!

I couldn't move from one world to the other from there—since I'd never been there!

"Get up there, Ross!" a voice barked, right behind me.

I turned and saw my twin. His expression was cold, angry. He gave me a hard shove. "Get up there," he repeated. "I don't want anyone to hear your last screams."

"N-no, please—" I begged weakly.

But he gave me another shove. "It will all be over in a few minutes."

I stumbled forward. He moved to block my escape.

I felt so weak. Pain shot up and down my body. I wanted to curl up . . . curl up into a tiny ball and disappear.

But I couldn't give up. I couldn't let him do this to me. I wouldn't!

It wasn't fair. It wasn't right.

"AAAAAAAGH!" With a cry of fury I spun around—and threw myself onto him.

Startled, he stumbled back.

I clung to him, my arms wrapped around his shoulders. I clung to him with all the strength I had left.

"Get off! Get off me!" he shrieked. He backed out of the garage, twisting, turning, trying to pry me off.

But I held on tight, wrestling with him. Struggling against the pain that pulsed over me. Feeling so light . . . so light . . .

He backed across the lawn. He grasped my arms and squeezed them. "Get off me!"

"No!" I whispered. "I won't give up! I want to go home!"

We wrestled over the grass. I gasped for breath. I knew I couldn't hold on much longer.

And suddenly we were at the edge of our swimming pool. Wrestling. Thrashing. Bending and twisting.

I gazed into the water, sparkling so blue under the afternoon sunlight.

And in the gently rippling water, I saw our reflections. Both of our faces, side by side in the shimmering water.

Just like the first time I saw him.

Exactly like the first time we met.

"Go!" my twin screamed, wrestling hard. "Go forever, Ross!"

I couldn't hold on to him any longer. He flung me

off him. I fell into the pool like a sagging inner tube.

But I reached out—and grabbed his arm.

And pulled him in with me.

We both sank into the cold water. Down . . . down . . .

So cold and clear . . . shimmering with a million dots of sunlight . . . so unreal . . .

We stared at each other underwater . . . stared face to face as we had that night . . . gazed with the same eyes at our identical faces . . .

Lower . . . lower into the cold, clear water.

And this time it was me who mouthed the words: *Go away*.

And as I said it, the water began to darken. As if someone had dimmed the lights.

My chest felt about to explode.

My twin faded away. Vanished in the blackening water.

All dark. All dark now.

I swam in blackness. My chest burning. My whole body throbbing.

The horror rose up . . . rose up around me.

For I knew that I had failed . . . failed.

I was fading into the blackness.

Fading away forever.

CHAPTER 31

Choking . . .

I'm choking, I realized. Can't breathe.

I blinked my eyes open. Felt water slide down my cheeks. Stared through a film of water over my eyes.

Am I still underwater?

So dark. Dark as night.

I coughed up water. Choked and gagged.

Tried to blink the water from my eyes.

And stared up at Cindy and Sharma. Their faces tight with worry. Tears staining Sharma's pale face.

"Hey—he opened his eyes!"

My ears rang. The cry sounded so far away. But I recognized Max's voice.

Cindy leaned over me. "You're okay, Ross," she said in a trembling whisper.

"You're going to be okay," Sharma added.

I opened my eyes wide. I could see clearly now.

I was lying on my back. Staring up at a lot of faces. Beyond the two girls I saw Max and his father. And other kids I knew, all in swimsuits, all huddled together, worried and tense.

Above them the moon floated above a layer of clouds. Night. It was night.

And I was lying on my back on the terrace beside Max's swimming pool.

"I'm so sorry," Cindy said, leaning over me.

"We were just kidding around," Sharma said, holding my arm. "It was supposed to be a joke. We didn't mean to hold you under so long."

"But then you started to choke," Cindy whispered. "It—it was so horrible! You weren't breathing, and—" Her words caught in her throat. She turned away.

"My dad saved your life," Max said.

"It's a good thing I took that CPR class," Max's father said. He leaned over me. "Do you feel okay, Ross?"

"Yeah . . . I guess," I said weakly. I sat up. I was lying in a puddle of cold water.

"We're so sorry," Cindy repeated. "Really, Ross. We didn't mean to hold you under so long. We were so stupid. Please—please forgive us."

The two girls went on apologizing, but I wasn't listening.

I was thinking about my parallel world adventure. Was it all a crazy dream?

It had to be.

It all never happened. I was drowning and my mind hallucinated the whole thing.

I breathed a long sigh of relief and jumped to my feet.

I felt so happy—so happy to be alive, to be back with my friends. I ran around and hugged everyone—even Max!

I'm in my world, I thought gleefully. I'm in the real world. And I'm going to stay here!

Everyone started talking and laughing at the same time. The music rang out again. The party was back underway.

I thanked Max's father, said goodbye to Max, and started running through the backyards to my house. I suddenly remembered about Jake.

I had left him all alone. I wasn't supposed to go out.

Was I going to be in major trouble?

I didn't care. I was so happy, so happy to be back!

I burst into the house and ran up to Jake's room. "Hey—" I called. "What's up?"

Jake was sitting on the bed with his back to me. He turned slowly.

And I opened my mouth in a scream of horror.

His face—his face was gone.

I gaped at his skull . . . his gray, rutted, worm-infested skull . . . empty eye sockets staring blankly back at me . . . his jaw open in an evil toothless grin.

CHAPTER 32

My scream choked off in my throat. I staggered back as Jake's laugh rang out from under the ugly skull.

He raised both hands and tugged the skull off. "Gotcha!" he grinned at me.

A mask.

"You're a wimp," Jake said. "You scare like a little baby!"

I didn't care about his dumb joke. I was so happy to see my brother, I hugged him, too.

"Get off me!" he cried. "What's your problem, Ross? Yuck!"

I backed off, laughing.

I'm here! I thought. Here in my normal world.

Normal. Everything normal!

I tossed back my head and let out a joyful shout.

My cry was cut short when I heard voices in the hall.

I turned—and gasped—as two more Jakes stepped into the room!

"N-no—!" I stammered. "It—it isn't possible!"

The three identical boys stared at me as if I was crazy.

Mom burst into the room. "Ross, you didn't go out, did you?" she asked angrily. "I need you to stay home and take care of the triplets."

My mouth dropped open. I couldn't speak.

My eyes went from face to face to face.

I messed up, I told myself. I really messed up.

Somehow, I ended up in another parallel world.

How do I get out of here?

I can't live with three Jakes. I can't! I can't!

"Well?" Mom demanded, hands on her waist. "Are you going to stay home and watch your brothers?"

"Well . . ." I said.

Think fast. Think fast, Ross.

Think of a good story to get yourself out of this!

THE NIGHTMARE ROOM
DEAR DIARY, I'M DEAD

CHAPTER 1

DEAR DIARY,

My hands are shaking so badly, I don't know if I can write in you today. I was so scared last night. I'm still trembling.

Maybe I should start at the beginning. You know my friends Chip and Shawn and I have been talking about camping out in Full Moon Woods for nearly a year. Well, last night we finally did it.

What a mistake!

We thought it was going to be cool. We loaded all our gear into my dad's van, and he dropped us off at the dirt path that leads into the woods.

"Stick to the path, Alex," Dad called. "It will lead you to the creek. I'll pick you up right here tomorrow morning." The tires spun in the dirt as he drove away.

It was a cloudy afternoon. As soon as we stepped into the woods, it grew even darker. Our backpacks were bulging. And the canvas tent weighed a ton.

But we didn't mind. We were finally on our own in the woods. We walked quickly, following the path, making our way toward the creek.

Shawn started to sing an old Beatles song. Chip and I joined in. I loved the way our voices echoed off the trees.

"We should have brought our guitars," I said. All three of us play guitar, and we're starting a band.

Chip laughed. "Great idea, Alex. Where would we plug them in?"

"We'd need a very long extension cord!" I replied.

We were laughing and singing, enjoying the fresh cool air and the crunch of our shoes over the carpet of fat brown leaves.

The path ended, but we kept walking. I was pretty sure the creek was straight ahead. It grew even darker, and a cold wind swirled around us.

We walked for at least an hour before we realized we were totally lost.

"We should be able to hear the creek," Shawn said. He set down his backpack and stretched. "Where is it? Did we go in the right direction?"

"We'll never find it now," Chip sighed. "It's too dark."

A gust of wind sent dead leaves flying all around us. "Are there bears in these woods?" Shawn asked. He sounded a little frightened.

"No. But there are bunny rabbits that can chew you to bits!" I joked.

Chip laughed but Shawn didn't. I shivered and wrapped my yellow windbreaker tighter around me.

"Which way is the path?" Shawn asked, turning back. He pointed. "Is that the way we came? Maybe we should go back that way."

A hooting sound made me jump. A bird on a low tree branch. It hooted again, peering down at us.

"I don't want to go back," I said. "Let's keep going. The creek is this way. I know it."

But Shawn and Chip wanted to stay right there and pitch the tent. It wasn't a bad place. A circle of tall grass surrounded by tall trees. So I agreed.

We tossed our backpacks in a pile and started to unroll the tent.

That's when I had the feeling for the first time— the feeling that we were being watched.

I felt a prickling on the back of my neck. I heard a snapping sound behind us, like someone stepping on dry twigs.

I spun around. But I didn't see anyone. The trees tilted toward each other, as if closing in on us.

"What's your problem?" Shawn asked. "Did you see an animal?"

I laughed. "Yeah. A herd of buffalo."

We struggled with the tent. The gusting wind kept blowing it out of our hands. We finally got it to stand. But then the wind kept blowing out our campfire.

By the time we finished dinner, it was late. All three of us were yawning. My shoulders ached from

135

carrying the heavy backpack.

We decided to climb into the tent and go to sleep. Shawn and Chip crawled inside. I started to follow them—then stopped.

I had the strange feeling again. The prickling on the back of my neck. Who was watching us?

I squinted through the misty darkness. I sucked in my breath when I saw dull gray circles—several pairs of them—floating low between the trees.

Eyes?

I dove into the tent. We slept in our clothes under wool blankets. The wool felt scratchy. The tent was damp from dew.

We couldn't sleep. We started to tell each other jokes. We were kidding around and laughing a lot.

But we stopped laughing when the howls started.

They were low at first, like ambulance sirens far in the distance. But then they sounded closer, louder. And we knew they were animal howls.

"I . . . hope it's dogs!" Shawn exclaimed. "Maybe it's just some wild dogs."

We huddled close together. We all knew we weren't hearing dogs. We were hearing wolf howls.

So close. . . . So close we could hear the harsh, shallow breaths between the howls.

And then the soft crunch of footsteps outside the tent.

They were here! The howling creatures! The tent flap blew open.

My friends and I let out screams.

Two men in black leather jackets leaned down to peer into our tent. One of them raised a flashlight. He moved the light slowly from face to face. "Are you kids okay?" he asked.

"Wh-who are you?" I asked.

"Forest Patrol," the other man said.

"Yeah. Right. Forest Patrol," his partner repeated.

They both stared at us so hard. Their eyes were cold, not friendly at all.

"The woods really aren't safe," the man with the flashlight said. "Not safe at all."

His partner nodded. "First thing in the morning, you should get yourselves to the road. It's right up there." He pointed.

We promised we would. We thanked them for checking on us.

But I didn't like the way they stared. They didn't look like forest rangers. And as soon as they left, the frightening howls started up again. Howls all around us.

We didn't sleep at all that night. We lay awake, staring up at the tent walls, listening to the animal howls.

The next morning, as soon as sunlight began trickling down through the trees, we jumped up. We hurried out of the tent and began to pack.

I started to fold up the tent—but stopped when I saw something strange on the ground. "Hey—!" I called out to Chip and Shawn. "Look!"

I pointed to the footprints in the soft dirt. Two pairs that led from the woods to the front of our tent.

The Forest Rangers' prints.

All three of us stared, stared in shock and horror.

Their prints weren't human. They were animal paws.

Animal paws in the dirt.

Wolf prints!

CHAPTER 2

"Alex, is any of that true?" Miss Gold asked.

I rolled the pages of my story between my hands. "No," I told her. "I made it all up."

"You and Chip and Shawn never went camping?" she asked, peering at me over the rims of her glasses.

"No. Never," I said.

"He's afraid of poison ivy!" Chip called out.

The whole class laughed.

"He's afraid of *trees*!" another kid chimed in.

The whole class laughed even harder.

"He's afraid of bugs!" Shawn added.

No one laughed at that. No one ever laughs at Shawn's jokes. He's a good guy, but he just isn't funny.

"Well, that is an excellent short story," Miss Gold said. "One of the best we've heard this week. Thank you for sharing it with the class, Alex. Very good work."

She waved me back to my seat. But I didn't move

from the front of the classroom. "Aren't you going to tell me my grade?" I crossed my fingers behind my back.

"Oh. Right." Miss Gold pushed the glasses up on her nose. "I'll give you a B-plus."

"Huh?" I let out a groan. "Not an A?"

"B-plus," she repeated.

"But—why?" I demanded.

She brushed her blond hair off her forehead. "Well . . . you did very well with the plot. But I think you need to work on describing your characters better. We don't really know what Chip and Shawn look like—do we?"

"But they're sitting right there!" I protested, pointing at my two friends. "You *know* what they look like!"

"Real ugly!" a kid shouted from the back of the room.

Big laughter.

But I wasn't laughing. I needed an A.

"You need to describe them in the story," Miss Gold continued. "And we don't know what's different about them. You didn't give them real personalities."

"But—" I started.

"And I think you need more description of the woods," she said. "More detail. You know, Alex, the more little details you add to a story, the more *real* it becomes."

Tessa Wayne was waving her hand frantically in

the air. "There's something I don't understand," she said. "If the two men were wolves, where did they get the leather jackets? I mean, they were completely dressed, right? But they're wolves? And how did they get the flashlight?"

"Good questions, Tessa," Miss Gold said.

I rolled my eyes. Tessa always asks the good questions. That's why I hate her guts.

"The men were werewolves," I explained, sighing. "Not regular wolves."

"Well, the bell is about to ring," Miss Gold said, gazing up at the wall clock. She turned back to me. "I just had an idea. You did such a good job with the diary format. I mean, writing your story as a diary entry was very clever."

"Thanks," I said weakly. So why didn't she give me an A?

"You should keep a *real* diary, Alex," she continued. "Write in it every day. You can hand it in at the end of the year for extra credit."

"Really?" I said. "Okay. Thanks."

I saw Tessa's hand fly up. I knew what she was going to say.

"Miss Gold, I want to start a diary too. Can I do a diary for extra credit?"

"Yes," Miss Gold replied. "Anyone in class can keep a diary. Very good idea."

The bell rang.

I hurried to my seat and started to shove my story

into my backpack. I felt a sharp tap on my back. I knew who it was.

"Pay up, Alex," Tessa said. She stuck her hand in front of my face.

"Excuse me?" I tried to play innocent.

"Pay up," she insisted. "You bet me five dollars you'd get an A on that story. You lost."

"A B-plus is almost an A," I said.

She waved the hand in my face. "Pay up."

I reached into my jeans pocket. "But . . . I only have *three* dollars," I said.

"Then why did you bet me?" Tessa demanded. "You know you never win a bet against me. You always lose."

"Wait a sec," I said. I caught up with Chip and Shawn at the door. "Pay up," I said, blocking their way.

They both groaned. Then they reached into their pockets, and each of them handed me a dollar bill.

I hurried back to Tessa. "Okay, I've got the five," I said. I handed it to her.

"What was *that* about?" she asked, motioning toward Chip and Shawn.

"I bet them each a dollar that after you heard my story, you'd want to write in a diary too."

Tessa blushed. Her cheeks turned an angry red. "Big deal," she muttered. "So you won two bucks from your friends. But you're such a loser, Alex. Now you're totally broke—right?"

I pulled out my pockets. Empty. "Yeah. I'm broke."

Tessa grinned. "I love making bets with you," she said. She held the money up in front of my face and counted the five dollars one by one. "It's like taking candy from a baby."

"Wait a minute—" I told her.

An idea had flashed into my mind. An awesome idea. An idea that would turn me from a loser into a winner.

"I want to make one more bet with you," I told Tessa. "A really big bet."

CHAPTER 3

"You did *what*?" Shawn screamed. "Alex, are you totally whacked?"

"I'm going to win this one," I said.

"But you *never* win a bet with Tessa," Chip said. "How could you bet a hundred dollars?"

We were in Chip's garage after school, tuning up our guitars. The garage had only one electrical outlet, so we could plug in only two amps. That meant that one of us had to play acoustic, even though we all had electric guitars.

"I won't need a hundred dollars," I said, "because I'm going to win."

Sproinnnng.

I broke a string. I let out a groan. "I'll just play without it," I muttered.

Shawn shook his head. "You're crazy, Alex. After what happened with McArthur and the flag . . ."

"That was a sure thing!" I cried. "I should have won that bet!"

Just thinking about it made me angry.

A few weeks ago, I made a deal with Mr. McArthur. He's one of the janitors at school. Except he's not called a janitor. He's called a maintenance engineer.

McArthur is a nice guy. He and I kid around sometimes. So I made a deal with him.

He raises the flag every morning on the flagpole in front of our school. So I paid him five dollars to raise it upside down on Wednesday morning.

Then I dragged Tessa to school early and bet her ten dollars that he would raise the flag upside down.

"You're crazy, Alex," Tessa said, rolling her eyes. "McArthur has never slipped up like that."

He will *this* morning, I thought happily. I started planning how I'd spend Tessa's ten bucks.

How was I to know that Mrs. Juarez, the principal, would arrive at school just when McArthur was raising the flag?

She came walking up the steps and saw McArthur. So she stopped in front of the pole, raised her hand to her heart, and waited to watch the flag go up.

Of course McArthur chickened out. He raised the flag right side up.

I didn't blame him. What could he do with her standing right there?

But I had to pay Tessa the ten bucks. And then McArthur said he'd pay me back my five dollars in a week or so. Not a good day.

"It's my turn," I told my two friends. "Tessa has won about three hundred bets in a row. So it's definitely my turn!"

"But why did you bet her that your diary would be more exciting than hers?" Shawn asked.

"Because it will be," I said. "Tessa is real smart and gets perfect grades. That's because all she does is study. She spends all her time on homework and projects for extra credit. She's so totally boring! So her diary can't be exciting. No way!"

"Who's going to decide whose diary is the best?" Chip asked.

"We're going to let Miss Gold decide," I said. "But it won't be a hard choice for her. This is one bet I'm not going to lose."

"Want to bet?" Chip asked.

I squinted across the garage at him. "Excuse me?"

"Bet you five dollars Tessa wins this bet too."

"You're on!" I said. I slapped him a high-five.

"Count me in," Shawn said. "Five bucks on Tessa."

"You guys are real losers," I groaned. "Let's play. What's the first song?"

"How about 'Purple Haze'?" Chip suggested. "It's our best song."

"It's our *only* song," I muttered.

We counted off, tapping our feet, and started to play "Purple Haze." We played for about ten seconds, when we heard a loud, crackling *pop*.

The music stopped and the lights went out.

We'd blown the fuses again.

A short while later, I dragged my guitar case into the house. Mom greeted me at the door. "I've been waiting for you," she said. "I have a surprise."

I tossed my backpack onto the floor. Then I tossed my jacket on top of it.

"Don't tell me. Let me guess," I said. "I'll bet you five dollars it's a puppy. You finally bought me that puppy I asked for when I was six?"

Mom shook her head. "No puppy. You know your dad is allergic."

"He can breathe at work," I said. "Why does he have to breathe at home?"

Mom laughed. She thinks I'm a riot. She laughs at just about everything I say.

"I'll bet five dollars it's . . . a DVD player!" I exclaimed.

Mom shook her head. "No way, Alex. And stop betting every second. That's such a bad habit. Is that why you're broke all the time?"

I didn't answer that question. "What's the surprise?" I asked.

"Come on. I'll show you." Mom pulled me upstairs to my bedroom. I could see she was excited.

She moved behind me and pushed me into the room. "Check it out, Alex!"

I stared at the big desk against the wall. It was made of dark wood and it had two rows of drawers on the sides.

I stepped up to it. The desktop had a million little scratches and cracks in it.

"It's . . . it's old!" I said.

"Yes, it's an antique," Mom replied. "Your dad and I found it at that little antiques store on Montrose near the library."

I ran my hand over the old wood. Then I sniffed a couple of times. "It's kind of smelly," I murmured.

"It won't be smelly after we polish it up," Mom said. "It will be like new. It's a beautiful old desk. So big and roomy. You'll have space for your computer and your PlayStation, and all your homework supplies."

"I guess," I said.

Mom gave me a playful shove. "Just say 'Thank you, Mom. It's a nice surprise. I really needed a desk like this.'"

"Thank you, Mom," I repeated. "It's a nice surprise. I really needed a desk like this."

She laughed. "Go ahead. Sit down. Try it out." She wheeled a new desk chair over to the desk. It was chrome with red leather.

"What an awesome chair!" I said. "Does it tilt back? Does it go up and down?"

"Yes, it does everything," Mom said. "It's a thrill ride!"

"Cool!" I dropped into the chair and wheeled it up to the old desk.

The phone rang downstairs. Mom hurried to answer it.

I tilted the chair back. Then I leaned forward, smoothing my hands over the desk's dark wood. I wonder who owned it before me, I thought.

I pulled open the top desk drawer. It jammed at first. I had to tug hard to slide it open. The drawer was empty.

I slid open the next drawer. The next. Both empty. The air inside the drawers was kind of sour smelling.

I leaned down and pulled open the bottom drawer.

"Hey—what's that?"

Something hidden at the back of the drawer. A small, square black book.

I reached in and lifted it from the drawer.

Then I blew the thick layer of dust off the cover and raised it close to see what it was.

A diary!

CHAPTER 4

I stared at the dusty book, turning it over in my hands. What a strange coincidence!

I rubbed my hand over the black leather cover. Then I opened the book and flipped quickly through the pages.

They were completely blank.

I'll use this to write my diary for Miss Gold, I decided. I'll write my first entry tonight. And I'll write it in ink. Miss Gold will like that.

I set the diary down on the desk and thought about what I would write.

First, I'll describe my friends, I decided. Miss Gold said I needed more description, more details. I stared at the old diary and planned what I would say.

I'll start with me. How would I describe myself?

Well, I'm tall and kind of wiry. I have wild brown hair that I hate because it won't stay down. My mom says I'm always fidgeting. I can't sit still. My dad says I talk too fast and too much.

What else? Hmmm . . . I'm kind of smart. I like to hang out with my friends and make them laugh. I'm a pretty good guitar player. I'd like to make a lot of money and get really rich because I'm always broke, and I hate it.

That's enough about me. What about Chip? How would I describe Chip?

Well . . . he's short. He's chubby. He has really short brown hair and a round baby face. He looks about six, even though he's twelve like me.

Chip wears baggy clothes. He likes to wrestle around and pretend to fight. He's always in a good mood, always ready to laugh. He's a terrible guitar player, but he thinks he's Jimi Hendrix.

Shawn is very different from Chip. He's very intense, very serious. He worries a lot. He's not a wimp or anything. He just worries.

Shawn has brown eyes, orangy hair that's almost carrot colored, and lots of freckles. He gets better grades in school than Chip and me because he works a lot harder.

Who else should I describe? Do I have to describe Tessa? Yes, I guess I should. She'll probably pop up in the diary from time to time.

I guess Tessa is kind of cute. But she's so stuck-up, who cares?

She has straight blond hair, green eyes, a turned-up nose like an elf nose, and a little red heart-shaped mouth. She's very preppy and perfect-looking.

Yes. That's good. Tessa wants to be perfect all the time. And she hangs out only with girls who are just like her.

I flipped through the empty diary one more time. I'm pretty good at description, I decided. I couldn't wait to write this stuff down.

And what else should I write about? I'll write about how my parents bought me a new desk, and how I found a blank diary in the bottom drawer just when I needed a diary. Very cool!

I leaned back in the new desk chair, very pleased with myself. I tilted the chair back a few times. Then I raised and lowered the seat, just to see how it worked.

I heard Dad come home. Then I heard Mom calling me to dinner. I tucked the diary into the top desk drawer and hurried down to the dining room.

"How's the new desk?" Dad asked.

"Excellent," I told him. "Thanks, Dad."

He passed the bowl of spaghetti. "Did you have band practice this afternoon?"

"Yes, kind of," I replied. "We blew the fuses again. We really need a better place to rehearse."

Mom chuckled. "Your band needs a lot of things. Like a singer, for example. None of you guys can sing a note. And how about someone who *doesn't* play guitar?"

I rolled my eyes. "Thanks for the encouragement, Mom."

Dad laughed too. "What do you call your band? Strings and More Strings?"

"Ha-ha," I said. Dad has such a lame sense of humor. He's not even as funny as Shawn, who is never funny!

"Bet you ten dollars that we get good enough to win the junior high talent contest," I said.

"Alex, no betting," Mom said sternly.

They started talking to each other, and I concentrated on my spaghetti and turkey meatballs. We used to have real meatballs. But Mom became a health freak. And now all of our meat is made out of turkey.

After dinner, I practically flew upstairs to get started on my diary. I found a black marker pen to write with. Then I sat down in the new desk chair and pulled the diary out of the drawer.

I'll start with an introduction about how I found the diary, I decided. Then I'll describe my friends and me.

I opened the diary to the first page. And let out a gasp.

The page had been completely blank when I found the book this afternoon. But now it was covered with writing. There was already a diary entry there!

At the top of the page, a date was written: *Tuesday, January 16.*

"Huh?" I squinted hard at it. Today's date was

Monday the fifteenth.

"This is too weird!" I said out loud.

A diary entry for tomorrow?

My eyes ran over the handwritten words. I couldn't focus. I was too surprised and confused.

And then I uttered another gasp when I made another impossible discovery.

The diary entry was written in *my handwriting*!

A diary entry for tomorrow in my handwriting? How can that be? I wondered.

My hands were shaking. So I set the open book down on the desktop. Then I leaned over it and eagerly started to read.

CHAPTER 5

DEAR DIARY,

The diary war has started, and I know I'm going to win. I can't wait to see the look on Tessa's face when she has to hand over one hundred big ones to me.

I ran into Tessa in the hall at school, and I started teasing her about our diaries. I said that she and I should share what we're writing—just for fun. I'll read hers, and she could read mine.

Tessa said no way. She said she doesn't want me stealing her ideas. I said, "Whatever." I was just trying to give her a break and let her see how much better my diary is going to be than hers.

Then I went into geography class, and Mrs. Hoff horrified everyone by giving a surprise test on chapter eight. No one had studied chapter eight. And the test was really hard—two essay questions and twenty multiple choice.

Why does Mrs. Hoff think it's so much fun to surprise us like that?

The diary entry ended there. I stared at the words until they became a blur.

My hands were still shaking. My forehead was chilled by a cold sweat.

My handwriting. And it sounded like the way I wrote.

But how could that be? How did an entry for tomorrow get in there?

I read it again. Then I flipped through the book, turning the pages carefully, scanning each one.

Blank. All blank. The rest of the pages were blank.

I turned back to tomorrow's entry and read it for a third time.

Was it true? It couldn't be—could it?

What if it is? I asked myself. What if Mrs. Hoff *does* spring a surprise test on us? Then, I'd be the only one who knew about it.

I'd be the only one to pass the test.

I closed the diary and shoved it into the desk drawer. Then I found my geography textbook, opened it to chapter eight, and studied it for the next two hours.

The next morning, I ran into Tessa in the hall outside Mrs. Hoff's room. "Nice shirt, Alex," she sneered, turning up her already-turned-up nose. "Did you puke on it this morning, or is that just the color?"

"I borrowed it from *you*—remember?" I shot back. Pretty good reply, huh?

"How is your diary coming?" Tessa asked. "Or do you want to give up and just pay me the hundred dollars now?" She waved to two of her friends across the hall, two girls who look just like her.

"My diary is going to be awesome," I said. "I wrote twelve pages in it last night."

I know, I know. That was a lie. I just wanted to see Tessa react.

She sneered at me. "Twelve pages? You don't know that many words!" She laughed at her own joke.

"I have an idea," I said. "Why don't we share each other's diaries?"

She frowned at me. "Excuse me?"

"I'll read your diary, and you can read mine," I said. "You know. Just for fun."

"Fun?" She made a disgusted face at me, puckering up that tiny heart-shaped mouth. "No way, Alex. I'm not showing you my diary. I don't want you stealing my ideas!"

Oh wow.

Oh wow!

That's just what Tessa said in the diary entry.

Was the diary entry coming true? Was it all really going to happen?

I suddenly felt dizzy, weak. How could a book predict the future?

I shook my head hard, trying to shake the dizziness away.

"Alex? Are you okay?" Tessa asked. "You look so weird all of a sudden. What's wrong with you?"

"Uh . . . nothing," I said. "I'm fine."

The bell was about to ring. I gazed into Mrs. Hoff's classroom. It was filling up with kids.

I turned back to Tessa. "Uh . . . you haven't read chapter eight yet, have you?" I asked.

"No. Not yet," Tessa replied. "Why?"

"No reason," I said, trying to hide my grin.

I followed her into the room. I waved to Chip and Shawn. Then I dropped my backpack to the floor and slid into my seat at the back of the room.

Mrs. Hoff was leaning over her desk, shuffling through a pile of folders. She has straight black hair and flour-white skin, and she always wears black.

Some kids call her Hoff the Goth. But that doesn't make sense, and it doesn't even rhyme.

I sat stiffly in my seat, watching her, tapping my fingers tensely on the desktop. My heart started to race.

Is she going to give the test? I wondered.

Is the rest of the diary entry going to come true?

CHAPTER 6

My heart thudded in my chest. I leaned forward so far, I nearly fell off my seat.

Is she going to announce the test? Is she?

Gripping the desktop with both hands, I held my breath and watched her.

"Let's all settle down now," Mrs. Hoff said, straightening one sleeve of her black sweater. "We are going to have a busy morning."

A busy morning? What did that mean?

A test?

I couldn't hold my breath any longer. I let it out in a long *whoosh*.

"Please clear your desks," Mrs. Hoff said. "Take out paper and pencils, everyone. We're having a surprise test on chapter eight."

"YESSSS!" I cried.

My shout rose up over the groans and moans of all the other kids.

Everyone turned to gape at me.

I could feel my face growing hot. I knew that I was blushing.

Mrs. Hoff tossed back her black hair and snickered. "Since when do you like tests, Alex?"

"I . . . uh . . . didn't hear you right," I answered, thinking fast. "I thought you said we were going to have a *rest*!"

The whole class burst out laughing.

I like making people laugh—but I hate being laughed at. At least it got me off the hook.

Mrs. Hoff handed around the test papers. I checked mine out carefully. Two essay questions and twenty multiple choice.

Yes! Just like in the diary entry.

It was all true. All of it!

The diary predicted the future.

Several times I had to stop myself from humming as I took the test. This was sweet, so sweet! I knew everything! It was going to be my best geography score ever.

I could hear the other kids moaning unhappily. Across the room, Shawn was slapping his forehead, frowning down at his test paper.

I finished ten minutes before the bell rang. The other kids were still writing like crazy, groaning in misery, scratching their heads.

When the bell rang, the room was silent. Kids slowly handed in their test papers. Their faces were green, sick looking.

"I flunked it," Chip sighed out in the hall. "I totally flunked it."

Shawn slumped behind him. "I didn't know enough to flunk it!" he declared.

A pretty good joke for Shawn. Only I don't think he was joking.

"How did you do, Alex?" he asked.

"Not bad," I said. "I might have aced it."

I turned away from their shocked stares to greet Tessa.

She slunk into the hall, defeated, wrung out. Even her hair looked wilted.

"That was rough," she groaned. "Why didn't she tell us to study that chapter?"

I couldn't keep a grin from spreading across my face. "Tessa, bet you five dollars I aced it," I said.

Her mouth dropped open.

"Alex, save your money!" Shawn warned. "That's crazy. You know you never win a bet against Tessa."

"You can't win that bet!" Chip chimed in.

"Five bucks," I repeated, ignoring them. "Want to bet, Tessa?"

She narrowed her eyes at me. She studied me hard. "You want to bet me that you aced that surprise test?"

My grin grew wider. I tried to keep a straight face. But I just couldn't.

"I don't like that grin," Tessa said. "No bet."

"But, Tessa—" I started.

She spun away and trotted around the corner, her blond hair sagging limply behind her.

"Alex, you can't win against her," Shawn said. "Why do you keep trying?"

"Maybe I can win," I told him. "Maybe I'm going to start winning big-time."

"Are we going to practice after school?" Chip asked. "I found a better extension cord for the garage. Maybe it won't blow the fuses."

"We need to learn some new songs," Shawn said. "I downloaded the chords for 'Stairway to Heaven.'"

"Cool," Chip said. He began strumming his stomach, humming the melody, doing a loud air-guitar version of the old Led Zeppelin song.

"Uh . . . I can't do it after school," I said. "I have to get home."

They both groaned with disappointment. But I didn't care.

I had to get home to check the diary. I had to see if another entry had appeared.

Would it be there, waiting for me? Waiting to tell me about tomorrow?

CHAPTER 7

I saw Tessa watching me as I left school that afternoon. She was talking to another girl, but she had her eyes on me.

I didn't stop to talk to her.

I ran out the front doors and leaped down the front steps. It was a blustery, wintry day. Heavy, dark clouds covered the sky.

I was so eager to get home, I hadn't zipped my parka. As I ran, it billowed up behind me like a cape.

I'm a superhero! I thought. And what is my superpower? The ability to know the future!

The gusting wind helped to carry me the four blocks to my house. I felt as if I were flying.

I was half a block from home when I saw the little orange kitten dart into the street.

"Help! Get him! Get him!" a little red-faced boy came running frantically to the curb. I recognized him. Billy Miller, a kid I baby-sat for sometimes.

Billy's kitten was always running away.

Alex to the rescue! I thought. I was feeling like a superhero. I flew into the street, scooped up the kitten easily, spun around, and ran it back to Billy.

Billy was so happy to have the kitten back in his hands, he nearly squeezed it to death! He thanked me a hundred times and went running back to his house.

A few seconds later, I trotted up our gravel driveway. I stopped at the kitchen door. I swallowed hard, trying to catch my breath.

I had been feeling like a superhero. But now unpleasant thoughts forced their way into my mind.

The wind died, and my coat drooped around me. I suddenly felt as heavy as a rock.

Will the diary have an entry about tomorrow? I wondered.

Will it tell me the future every day?

Or was that some kind of accident or coincidence?

Why was that entry in the diary in the first place? And why was it written in my handwriting?

I didn't want to think about those two questions. They were kind of scary.

I crossed my fingers on both hands. "Please, please—show me another entry," I muttered.

Knowing the future was so totally cool. It meant that my grades were going to be better than ever. It meant that I could win a thousand bets with everyone! I could be *rich* by the end of the school year!

Rich! How sweet!

How totally sweet!

It meant that I'd never be broke again. It meant that I'd be a winner. A winner—and everyone would know it.

And . . . it meant that I'd always be *one day ahead of Tessa*.

I'd had the diary for only one day. One single day. But already I knew that I needed it.

Needed it!

My heart was racing as I tore open the back door and burst into the house. Clara, our housekeeper, was at the sink. I called "hi" to her and ran to the front stairs.

Then I pulled myself up the stairs two at a time.

I stumbled on the top step and nearly fell on my face. My backpack slid off my shoulders and bumped to the floor.

I didn't bother to pick it up.

I ran to my room.

And dove for the desk.

I pulled out the black leather diary.

"Please . . . please . . ." I muttered, gasping for breath.

I flipped open the cover. Gazed at the first page— the entry for today. So true. All of it, so true.

And what about tomorrow?

Breathing hard, I carefully turned to the next page.

I stared wide-eyed at the page. And let out a cry.

Nothing.

Nothing there.

CHAPTER 8

I shuffled through the pages. All blank.

I closed the book and opened it again. But still the only entry was the first one.

I tossed the diary down and pounded my fists on the wooden desktop.

I felt so disappointed. As if someone had given me a really awesome Christmas present and then taken it away the next day.

I sat there for a few minutes, staring at the diary, trying to get over my disappointment. Then I dragged my backpack into my room and tried to do some math homework.

But it was hard to think about algebra.

Every five or ten minutes, I reached for the diary. And I opened it, hoping to find an entry about tomorrow.

At dinner, Mom and Dad were talking about going on a winter vacation to some island. They expected me to be excited about it.

But I barely heard a word they said. I kept thinking about the diary.

"Alex, are you feeling okay?" Mom asked, clearing my half-eaten dinner away. "You're very quiet tonight. That's not like you."

"I'm just thinking," I replied.

Dad laughed. "That's not like you either!" he joked.

Ha-ha.

I slid my chair back. "May I be excused?"

I didn't wait for an answer. I took off, running up the stairs to my room. I dove to the desk and grabbed the diary.

"Yes!" I cried happily. "Yes!" I did a wild dance around my room.

A new entry had appeared about tomorrow. Again, it was in my handwriting.

How is this happening? I asked myself. Is it some kind of strange magic? Do the new pages always arrive after dinner?

My hands were shaking from excitement. What is going to happen tomorrow?

I held the book steady in both hands and eagerly read:

DEAR DIARY,

Wow! What a great day! Chip, Shawn, and I went to the basketball game after school. And it was amazing! The Ravens won in overtime!

Everyone in the gym went crazy. I thought they
were going to tear the building down!

"Whoa!" I murmured. My heart was pounding. I
read that first part again.

Our team will win in overtime tomorrow. And
then the diary gave me the final score of the game.

Wow!

I can win a few bets with *that* information!

If the diary tells me the score of every game
before it happens, I'll *never* lose another bet! I'll be
the richest kid in school!

And everyone will think I'm some kind of genius!

I turned back to the diary:

Tessa is suspicious about the geography test. I
saw her watching me. She is very curious about how I
did so well on the test when everyone else flunked.

I'm going to have to be a lot more careful around
Tessa. I don't want her to know about this diary.

She would ruin everything for me if she found out.
I know she would.

I heard a cough.

From behind me.

"Huh?" I turned quickly—and gasped.

Tessa stood in the doorway, scowling at me. Her
eyes were on the diary.

CHAPTER 9

I slammed the book shut and shoved it into the top desk drawer. Then I jumped to my feet, ready to protect the diary from Tessa.

She stepped into the room, shaking her head. "I'm not interested in your stupid diary," she said. "You don't have to hide it, Alex. I wouldn't read it if you *paid* me!"

I let out a sigh of relief. But I didn't move away from the desk. I didn't trust her.

"I—I haven't started my diary entry for today yet," I said. That was *kind of* true. "I'm going to write it tonight."

"Don't bother," Tessa replied. "It won't be as good as mine."

"Why did you come over?" I asked. And then I flashed her an evil grin. "Need help with your geography homework?"

She groaned and narrowed her eyes at me. "How did you know about that test this morning, Alex?"

she asked. Her green eyes burned into mine.

"Uh . . . what makes you think I knew about it?" I said.

"You knew about it," she replied, still studying me. "You had to know about it. Or else you never would have passed it."

Wow! Tomorrow's diary entry is already coming true, I thought.

I crossed my arms over my chest. "That's stupid," I said. "How would I know about a surprise test?"

"That's what I'm asking you," she replied, tossing back her blond hair with a snap of her head. "Are you going to tell me?"

"I . . . just had a hunch," I replied. "Just a weird hunch. So I read over chapter eight last night. You know. Just in case my hunch was right."

She twisted up her heart-shaped lips and squinted hard at me. "A hunch?" She snickered. "You cheated somehow. I know you cheated. Did Mrs. Hoff tell you about the test in advance?"

"Huh?" I made a face at Tessa. "Why would Mrs. Hoff tell me anything? It was a wild hunch. Really."

I uncrossed my arms, feeling a little more relaxed. "Is that what you came over to ask me?"

Tessa seemed to relax too. "No. Not really . . ." She dropped down on the arm of a chair. "I was talking to Shawn. . . ."

"About what?"

"About your band," she said. "You see, I'm a really

good singer, and I've always wanted to sing with a band. And I know you guys don't have a singer. So—"

"You like to sing?" I interrupted. I couldn't picture it. Tessa was so stiff, so serious.

My stomach suddenly knotted in dread. Tessa wants to join our band. No! Please—no!

"I sing along to CDs all the time," she said. "And everyone says I'm very good. I'm really into pop, and I can sing oldies too. I've never tried rap, but—"

"Please!" I cried out. I couldn't help myself. The idea of Tessa singing rap made my stomach churn.

She jumped to her feet. "So do you think I could be in your band?"

"Well . . ." I swallowed hard. "Maybe," I said.

"Maybe?"

"I'll talk to Chip and Shawn. We'll take a vote or something. Then I'll let you know—okay?"

She seemed a little disappointed. She started to the door. "Okay," she said softly. "Thanks."

I couldn't wait for her to leave. As soon as I heard the door slam behind her, I pulled out the diary. And I read the entry about tomorrow five or six more times.

I memorized the score of tomorrow's Ravens game. And I made a plan for betting my friends on the game.

I was so excited, it took me a long time to fall asleep. When I finally drifted off, I dreamed about the diary.

I dreamed I was sitting at my desk. Thunder

roared outside, and lightning flashed in my bedroom window. The white light flickered in my room.

I lifted the diary from my desk drawer and began to read it by the flashing lightning.

In the dream, I turned the pages slowly. They were all filled in, but I didn't stop to read them.

Until I got to the last page.

Thunder boomed all around me. I raised the last page close to my face to read it.

And I saw one word on the page. Only one word, in bold black ink.

In the dream, I stared at the word as the lightning made it flicker on the page:

DEAD.

One word on the last page of the diary:

DEAD.

In my handwriting:

DEAD.

The dream ended in a blinding white flash of lightning.

I opened my eyes and sat straight up in bed.

Drenched with sweat, my pajamas stuck wetly to my skin.

Morning sunlight poured into the room. Mom stood at my bedroom doorway. She smiled at me. "Alex, you're already up? I came to wake you for school."

"Mom?" I asked, my voice hoarse from sleep. "Do dreams ever come true?"

CHAPTER 10

"Move over," Chip boomed. He bumped me hard, forcing me to slide along the bleacher seat. Then he bumped me again, even harder, making me bounce into the guy next to me.

Chip laughed. He just likes bumping people. It's kind of his hobby.

The bleachers in the gym were filling up with kids and parents and a few teachers. Everyone cheered as the Ravens came running onto the floor in their black and gold uniforms, each player dribbling across the court.

The other team came running out of the visitor locker room. Their uniforms were yellow, and they were called the Hummingbirds.

Chip bumped me hard in the ribs with his elbow. "What a geeky name for a basketball team," he said. "The Hummingbirds."

"Yeah. Tweet-tweet," I said.

Shawn turned around from the bench below us.

"It's not so bad," he insisted. "Hummingbirds are very fast. And some people think they bring good luck."

Good old Shawn. He always has all the info.

Chip reached down and messed up Shawn's hair. Then he cupped his hands around his mouth and shouted at the Hummingbirds as they warmed up. "Tweet-tweet! Tweet-tweet!"

Some other kids laughed and joined in, until the chant spread across the gym.

The Hummingbirds were making most of their warm-up shots. One of their players was a giant. He had to be seven feet tall!

"Who is that guy?" I asked.

"His name is Hooper," Shawn said, turning around again.

Chip laughed. "He plays basketball and his name is Hooper? Cool!"

"He's only in seventh grade, and he's already six foot three," Shawn reported.

"Wow. He's a big Hummingbird!" I said.

A lot of kids laughed at that.

The game was about to start. I knew it was time to get serious.

"We're going to beat these birds," I said. "Anyone want to bet on it?"

Shawn turned around again. "Alex, you want to bet on the Ravens? Look at this guy Hooper. They're going to stuff us!"

"Yeah. This guy Hooper can block every shot," Chip said. "Look at him. He's a *tree!*"

A guy behind me tapped me on the shoulder. "You want to take the Ravens? I'll take the Hummingbirds. How much do you want to bet?"

"Yeah. I'll take the Hummingbirds too," Chip said. "Bet you five bucks."

This is too easy, I thought. Way too easy.

I had a plan. It was time to put it into gear.

"I don't want that bet," I said. "I want to do another kind of bet."

About a dozen kids were leaning in, listening to me now.

The referee's whistle echoed off the gym walls. Kids were cheering and shouting. The teams were gathering at center court.

"I'll bet anyone five dollars that this game goes into overtime," I announced.

"Huh?"

"Get serious!"

"Overtime? No way!"

I heard cries of disbelief all around.

"Alex, that's stupid," Shawn whispered. "Don't throw away your money."

"Who's got five dollars?" I called out. "Five dollars says the game goes into overtime. If it doesn't, I pay you five bucks."

More cries of disbelief. Guys were muttering that I'd totally lost it.

But ten kids took the bet. Ten times five. That's fifty bucks I was about to win.

If the diary's prediction came true . . .

I sat on the edge of the bench the entire game. My muscles were all tensed and I kept my hands clenched together in my lap.

The Hummingbirds got out to an early lead. The Ravens had a lot of trouble scoring because of Hooper. He stood under the basket and batted away just about every shot the Ravens took.

At halftime, the 'Birds were ahead by eight points. It looked pretty bad.

Chip, Shawn, and the other eight guys who bet against me all had big grins on their faces. "No way this game goes into overtime," Chip said, and he bumped me so hard, I fell into the aisle.

"We'll see," I said. But my stomach was doing flip-flops. I knew I didn't have fifty dollars to pay off the bet if I lost. In fact, I had only six dollars to my name.

The diary had to be right. Or else I was dead!

Dead.

The frightening dream suddenly flashed back into my mind. Once again I saw the single word written in big, bold script on the back page:

DEAD.

I blinked the picture away. Then I leaned forward and concentrated on the game, which had started up again.

The 'Birds scored first. Hooper hardly had to jump to slam-dunk the ball through the net.

I let out a groan. The Ravens were down by ten points now. If the game was going into overtime, they had to get to work.

I crossed my fingers on both hands and watched the game intently. I barely breathed. I kept seeing those ten guys with their hands stuck in my face, demanding their five dollars.

With a few minutes to go in the game, the Ravens had pulled to within two points. The seconds ticked by. The teams moved up and down the court.

A shot—and a miss.

A bad pass out of bounds.

Only a few seconds left. The Ravens had the ball. The kid with the ball drove right at Hooper. Hooper tripped. The Raven sent up a short layup.

Yes!

The Ravens tied the score at twenty-six just as the final buzzer went off. The game was going into overtime.

The gym practically exploded with cheers and startled cries. Kids stamped their feet so hard, the bleachers creaked and shook.

I leaped up and began jumping up and down on the bleacher floor. I pumped my fists in the air.

"Overtime! Overtime! I win! I win BIG-time!"

I went around and made everyone pay up. Ten times five. My biggest win ever.

How did it feel? Try *great!*

Chip was grumbling to Shawn. "This didn't happen," he muttered. "How could Alex know it would go into overtime?"

"So he got lucky once," Shawn replied.

Time for part two of my plan.

I stood up and turned to the guys who had bet me. "I'll give you a chance to win your money back," I announced. "I'll bet five dollars that the final score is 34 to 30, Ravens."

They were even more surprised at this bet. Some of them laughed really hard. The others just shook their heads.

"Come on, guys," I urged, "I'm giving you a chance. If the score isn't 34 to 30, I'll pay you back your money."

Only eight guys took this bet. The other two said they didn't have any more money to lose.

"You're crazy," Shawn told me. "You're totally whacked." But he took the bet anyway.

I sat back and concentrated on the game.

Would the diary come through again? So far, it had been totally right each time.

The overtime period was only five minutes. I didn't have long to wait.

Kids were screaming and cheering and stomping their feet. The game was tied at thirty. Then the Ravens scored two straight baskets right over Hooper's head.

Now the screams were so loud, I had to cover my ears with my hands.

I gazed at the scoreboard: 34 to 30, Ravens. Only five seconds left to play.

"Pay up, guys!" I shouted. "Check out the score! Alex the Great wins again!"

Out of the corner of my eye, I saw Hooper move to the basket. He sent up a long jump shot just as the buzzer rang out.

Swish! It dropped through!

Final score: Ravens, 34 to 32!

I lost the bet.

CHAPTER 11

I paid the guys their money. They were laughing and goofing, slapping me on the back.

Chip kept chanting, "Alex the Great! Alex the Great!" He wrapped me in a headlock and rubbed his knuckles against the top of my head until my skull throbbed.

I finally pulled free and hurried down the bleacher steps. I saw Tessa watching me from the other bleacher. I waved to her, but I didn't stop.

I pushed through the crowd and made my way out of the school building. I had to get home to check the diary.

I ran all the way. I was totally out of breath, my right side aching, by the time I got to my room.

I pulled the diary from its drawer and turned to the second entry, the page for today.

I ran my finger down the page until I came to the final score of the basketball game. Yes. The final score in the diary was 34 to 32.

The diary had it right.

You see, I had deliberately lost the bet. I'd bet on the wrong score on purpose. I'd let them win.

The idea was to sucker them all.

I wanted them to think that I was crazy, that I didn't have a clue. So, the next time, they wouldn't be suspicious at all.

Next time, they'd take any bet I offered.

And I'd clean them out.

I closed the diary and gave the cover a big kiss.

I was feeling great.

Sure, I'd just lost big-time. I'd won fifty dollars, then lost forty.

But I was still ten dollars ahead. And there was plenty more where that came from. As long as the diary told the truth.

I'll be a millionaire by the end of the year, I thought.

A millionaire!

I didn't check the diary again until after dinner. That's when the new entries seemed to appear.

"Why do you keep grinning like that?" Dad asked. We were having ice cream sundaes for dessert. I didn't realize I was grinning.

I shrugged. "Just grinning."

"Who won the basketball game today?" he asked.

I wiped chocolate sauce from my chin. "We did. In overtime. It was awesome."

"I heard a rumor," Mom said, frowning at me. "I heard that kids in your school have been betting on the basketball games. Is that true?"

I swallowed a lump of ice cream. "That's dumb," I said.

Mom squinted at me. "The rumor is dumb? Or betting on the games is dumb?"

"Both," I said.

I don't like to lie to my parents. I always try to be as honest as I can.

"The school should clamp down on kids who bet," Dad said, squirting more Reddi-wip on his ice cream. "You're too young for that."

Mom kept staring at me. Did she suspect something? Did someone tell her that I was the one making the bets?

I grinned at her. "Bet you ten dollars the school catches those kids!" I said.

Mom and Dad both burst out laughing. When things start to get tense, I can always make them laugh.

I finished my sundae and hurried up to my room to read the diary.

Would it tell me about tomorrow?

As I opened the diary, my hands shook with excitement.

This was so totally cool! Knowing things that no one else knew was just about the most awesome thing that could happen!

Little did I realize as I began to scan the words in the entry for tomorrow . . . little did I realize that sometimes knowing things can be really bad news.

CHAPTER 12

I was so excited, the words kept blurring on the page.

I took a deep breath and held it to calm myself down. Then I started to read the entry—in my handwriting—moving my finger over the page, word by word.

DEAR DIARY,

Here is a big surprise. Tessa is in the band! I told her she could join. Chip and Shawn were really upset about it. They didn't want Tessa anywhere near our band. They didn't even want her to listen to the band! But then I explained to them why I let her in.

You see, Tessa told me about her uncle Jon. Uncle Jon has a big garage that's mostly empty. He told Tessa the band could rehearse there.

He's Tessa's favorite uncle, and I can understand why.

You see, Uncle Jon owns a restaurant downtown.

And he told Tessa that if we rehearse a lot, and if he thinks our band is good enough, he'll let us play at his restaurant! And he says he'll pay us!

I had no choice. I couldn't turn that down. I had to let Tessa into the band.

Such awesome news! I wanted to call Chip and Shawn and tell them about it.

But I couldn't tell them until Tessa told me. I had to keep things in the right order. Or else I'd get totally messed up and confused.

I returned to the diary to see what else was going to happen tomorrow . . .

Mrs. Culter was out sick. Everyone in her algebra class was really happy at first. They all thought that meant they wouldn't have the algebra test.

But then the substitute teacher came in with the algebra test. And we had to take it anyway.

I'd better study the algebra problems really hard tonight, I decided. Algebra is my worst subject. Having this info about the test tomorrow was really helpful.

There was one more entry in the diary. I leaned over the little book to read it—when the phone rang.

I let out a groan. I didn't want to talk to anyone. I wanted to finish learning about tomorrow.

I jerked the telephone off the desktop and raised

it to my ear. "Hello?"

"Hi, Alex." I recognized Tessa's voice instantly. "What are you doing?" she asked.

"Uh . . . working on my diary," I said. "I really don't have time to talk. This is the best diary entry I've ever written. Miss Gold is going to go nuts when she reads it!"

Tessa laughed. "At least you're modest."

"I've got to go," I said.

"Well, I just want to ask one question," Tessa replied. "Can I be in the band or not? Did you talk to Chip and Shawn?"

"Yes," I told her. "You can be in the band, Tessa. If you really can sing."

"Yay!" she cheered. "You won't be sorry, Alex. Really. I'm good. And guess what?"

I'll bet I can guess, I thought.

"I talked to my uncle Jon. And he may have a place for us to rehearse."

"That's great!" I exclaimed, trying to sound surprised.

"Uncle Jon wants to hear us," Tessa said. "He says if we're good enough, we can play at his restaurant."

"Cool," I said.

"Maybe I could come over tonight, and we could work on some songs together," Tessa said.

I made a disgusted face at the phone. "No. Not tonight," I told her. "I can't. I have to study for the algebra test."

"Don't bother," Tessa replied.

"Huh? Don't bother? What do you mean?" I asked.

"Mrs. Culter is sick," Tessa replied. "She came to see my mom at her office this afternoon."

Tessa's mom is a doctor.

"Mom says that Mrs. Culter is really sick," Tessa continued. "She won't be back in school for at least the rest of the week. So . . . no way we'll have the algebra test tomorrow."

I almost burst out laughing. I had to smack a hand over my mouth to keep silent.

"That's great news," I managed to choke out.

"I've been calling everyone and telling them the test is off," Tessa said.

"Cool!" I exclaimed.

I held my hand over the phone and let out a wild giggle. I couldn't hold it back.

That's one more test that I'll ace, I told myself. And one more test that Tessa will flunk!

I felt so happy, I *kissed* the diary!

It took me a few more minutes to get Tessa off the phone. When I finally hung up, I jumped to my feet. And I did another crazy dance around my room.

"Tessa flunks!" I chanted, pumping my fists in the air. "Tessa flunks! Tessa flunks!"

Poor Tessa, I thought. She just doesn't have the right diary. She doesn't have a diary that can tell her the future.

I suddenly remembered I hadn't finished tomorrow's entry. There was still one last sentence to read.

I felt so happy, almost giddy, as I picked up the diary from my desk.

But my mood changed as my eyes swept over the last sentence in tomorrow's entry.

I gasped—and squinted at the words in disbelief . . .

Bad news, diary. On my way home from school, I was hit by a car.

CHAPTER 13

"No!"

I let out a cry. "No way!"

I stared at the words. I blinked a few times, then read them again:

On my way home from school, I was hit by a car.

"That is *so* not going to happen," I said out loud.

The diary must have made a mistake. I'm a really careful guy. I never run out in the street without looking.

Why did it say that?

How could it be wrong when it had been right about everything else?

I slammed the book shut and slid it into the desk drawer.

My heart was pounding. I'll just have to be careful tomorrow, I told myself. I'll just have to be super careful—and make sure the diary prediction doesn't come true.

Last night's frightening dream suddenly flashed

into my mind.

DEAD. . . . The one word glowing in bold black ink in the diary. DEAD. . . .

Is it going to come true?

The diary only says I get hit by a car, I told myself, tapping my fingers nervously on the desktop.

It doesn't say how badly I get hurt. Or if . . . if I die.

Why doesn't it say? Why does it stop there?

Why doesn't it tell me what happens?

I swallowed hard.

Is it because *there's nothing more to tell?*

CHAPTER 14

I jerked open the desk drawer and pulled out the diary.

Maybe it will tell me more, I thought. Maybe it will tell me if I'm going to be okay.

My hands were so sweaty, the pages stuck to my fingers. I finally turned to tomorrow's entry and read it again.

Bad news, diary. On my way home from school, I was hit by a car.

Nothing more. Nothing.

Mom came to wake me for school at seven the next morning. I groaned and rolled over.

"I have an upset stomach," I moaned. "It hurts. I really feel sick."

Mom bit her bottom lip. She leaned over my bed and pressed her hand over my forehead. "You don't feel hot. Should I call Dr. Owens?" she asked.

"No. I just need to sleep," I whispered, doing my

best sick act. "I think I'd better stay home today."

I'd thought about this plan all night. If I stayed home, there was no way I could be hit by a car.

"Well, okay," Mom said, frowning at me, studying my eyes. "I'll make you some hot tea. It might settle your stomach."

I nodded weakly. I listened to her make her way back downstairs.

I settled my head into the pillow. You're pretty smart, Alex, I told myself. Stay home all day, and the diary will have to be wrong.

The phone rang. I picked it up and clicked it on. "Hello?" I asked weakly.

"Don't forget your guitar. Are you *psyched*? I'm totally psyched!"

It was Chip. What was he so excited about?

"My guitar?" I croaked. "What—?"

"You didn't forget!" he exclaimed. "You couldn't forget that the three of us are playing in the lunchroom today."

Oh, wow.

I did forget. I was so busy worrying about the diary.

Mrs. Jarvis, the lunchroom supervisor, said we could play for everyone at lunchtime. Our first time in public!

"Can you bring your amp?" Chip asked. "We can set up during study hall."

"Uh . . . yeah. Sure," I replied.

I couldn't let my friends down. I had no choice. I had to go to school.

And, of course, there was the algebra test first period. A test I was ready to ace.

Okay, okay. I'm going, I decided, climbing to my feet.

I'll just be careful after school, I decided. Real careful . . .

When I arrived at school carrying my guitar and amp, I had a surprise in store. Chip and Shawn were not glad to see me. In fact, they were totally steamed.

They came stomping toward me, swinging their fists tensely at their sides. I set the equipment down and turned to face them.

Chip bumped me hard with his chest, so hard I went sprawling against the wall of lockers.

"Hey—good morning to you too!" I said, trying to click my shoulder back into place.

"Why did you tell Tessa she can be in the band?" Shawn demanded.

"Yeah. Why?" Chip repeated. He bumped me again, a little harder. "Are you crazy?"

"Guys, give me a break," I pleaded. I raised both hands in front of me as a shield.

"We don't want Tessa in the band," Shawn said.

"We don't like Tessa," Chip added.

"I know, I know," I said. I dodged away from another bump from Chip. The guy was a *mountain*!

"But it's going to work out," I told them. "You'll see. We'll be glad about it."

"Have you lost it?" Chip demanded. "She says she's going to sing with us at lunch. And we haven't even rehearsed with her."

"No problem," I said. "Did Tessa tell you about her uncle Jon?"

"We don't care about her uncle," Chip said angrily. "We don't want her messing up our band."

"Did she *pay* you?" Shawn asked. "How much did she pay you, Alex?"

"She didn't," I said. "I promise. It'll work out, guys. Her uncle is going to give us our first big break."

"We have to talk about this," Shawn said, shaking his head. "I know we need a singer. But—Tessa?"

"I can't talk now," I said, trying to push past them. "I've got my algebra test first thing." I grabbed my stuff and took off, running down the hall.

"Didn't you hear?" Shawn called after me. "Culter is out sick. No test today!"

But of course he was wrong and the diary was right.

You should have heard the other kids groan and moan when the substitute passed out the test papers.

I watched Tessa turn bright red. Tears filled her eyes.

She lowered her head and wouldn't look at anyone. She was so embarrassed!

She had called everyone and told them not to study.

Ha-ha. I couldn't keep the grin off my face as I breezed through the test.

Score another victory for Alex the Great!

I finished early and took my test paper up to the substitute. I flashed Tessa a big thumbs-up as I walked back to my seat.

She scowled and turned away. I could see that her test paper was a mess.

I dropped back into my seat, feeling really good about myself.

Our band was excited at lunchtime.

Chip, Shawn, and I set up our amps at a side of the lunchroom. Tessa brought a list of songs she knew, and there were a few on the list the three of us could play.

We started to tune up. Tessa kept clearing her throat. "I'm a little nervous," she confessed, "since we've never rehearsed or anything."

"Don't worry," I told her. "You'll be fine."

But she wasn't fine.

In fact, she was *horrible*!

Chip, Shawn, and I played "Purple Haze" to get things started. It's our best song, and the kids in the lunchroom seemed to like it. A few kids even clapped.

Then Tessa stepped up to sing. But she didn't sing—she screeched! Her singing sounded like fingernails being scraped down a chalkboard! Only more painful.

She sounded like a wounded animal howling in pain. She couldn't hit a single note. I couldn't even tell what song she was singing.

Kids stopped eating and started to beg for her to stop. That made Tessa sing even louder. I saw some kids running out of the lunchroom. One boy stuck his finger down his throat and pretended to puke.

We were supposed to play for half an hour. But Mrs. Jarvis stopped us after Tessa's first song. "Good work," she said. "Pack up quickly—okay?"

As we packed up, Chip and Shawn scowled angrily at me.

But Tessa seemed really cheerful. "That wasn't bad. But I'll get even better," she said, smiling at me. "I just need to rehearse a little."

"She embarrassed us for life," Chip muttered sadly as we carried our guitars down the hall. "How could you let her in our band?"

I didn't answer. I had other things to think about.

Mainly, the diary.

Why didn't the diary say that Tessa was the worst singer in history? Why did it leave out that part?

When her uncle Jon hears her sing, he won't let us anywhere near his restaurant! I thought bitterly. Why didn't the diary tell me that?

What else did the diary leave out about today? I wondered. What else?

I felt a shiver of fear. I kept picturing myself hit by a car . . . flying into the air . . . flattened, crushed, mangled, wrecked.

Was it going to come true? Was I a few hours away from my DOOM?

CHAPTER 15

"Let's get our bikes and go up to the dirt-bike track," Chip suggested after school. He slapped a heavy arm around my shoulders. "How about it, Alex?"

"I—I don't think so," I said quietly.

It was a cool, sunny afternoon. A tag football game had already started on the playground. Kids were running with their open jackets flapping behind them.

Everyone was laughing and shouting, happy to be out of school.

I didn't feel like laughing. My throat felt tight, and my stomach was doing flip-flops. I wanted to walk home slowly and carefully, and hide there till the day was over.

"Yeah, let's go!" Shawn said. "The track is empty during the week. We'll have it all to ourselves."

Chip laughed at him. "You'll have to take your training wheels off first!"

"Give me a break," Shawn muttered. He tried to shove Chip, but Chip danced away.

"I can't do it today," I said.

I turned and gazed down the street.

Was there a car out there with my name on it? Was there a car on its way right now, roaring down the street, coming to nail me?

With a shudder, I turned back to my friends. "Here's another idea. Why don't you guys bring your guitars to my house, and we'll practice some new songs."

Chip grinned at me. "We can't practice without Tessa, your *girlfriend*—can we?" he asked in a high, teasing voice.

Shawn laughed. "Alex and Tessa. What a gruesome twosome!"

I rolled my eyes. "You two are *so* not funny. Come on. Maybe Tessa was just nervous. Maybe we can teach her to be a better singer."

"Yeah. Maybe if we tape her mouth shut," Chip muttered.

They finally agreed to come over. But they said they had to stop at their houses first.

I turned and started walking toward home. I kept on the grass beside the sidewalk, as far from the street as I could get.

My legs trembled as I walked. My heart was racing in my chest.

"Don't be dumb. There's nothing to be scared

about," I told myself. "Two more blocks and you're home."

I walked slowly, carefully, keeping my eyes straight ahead.

I was half a block from home when I saw the little orange kitten run into the street.

"Not again!" I cried.

I heard Billy Miller's screams before I saw him come darting out from behind a hedge. "My kitten! My kitten!"

I glimpsed Billy's frightened face. I saw the little cat freeze in the center of the intersection.

I had no choice.

I had to rescue it.

I leaped into the street and started to run.

CHAPTER 16

"My kitten! Alex—help! Get my kitten!"

Running hard, I heard the blast of a car horn. Then the shrill squeal of tires on the pavement.

"Uhh."

I felt a hard bump. From behind.

My hands flew up.

And I was flying, flying through the air.

I flew into a bright white light. The street, the lawns, the sky—they all disappeared.

All colors vanished. I seemed to fly forever.

I landed in a shock of pain. The world rushed back. Colors and sounds.

I heard Billy crying. A car door slammed. A woman shouted, "Hey! Hey! Hey!" The same word over and over.

The sky spun above me, whirled so fast, as if I were on some kind of amusement park ride.

"Hey! Hey!"

The woman bent over me, her face red and twisted in fear. "Hey—are you all right?"

My skin prickled. Something scratched my arms. Blinking, I realized I had landed on a thick evergreen bush.

I struggled to catch my breath. I gazed up at the frightened woman.

"Are you all right? I—I almost stopped in time. I didn't hit you hard, but—"

"I . . . think I'm okay," I said. The sky stopped spinning above me. I saw Billy holding the kitten in his arms.

With a groan, I sat up. I pulled bristles off my arms and the front of my shirt. The bush had cradled my fall.

"Does anything hurt?" the woman asked. "Is anything broken? Should I call the police? An ambulance? Can you stand up?"

"I . . . think so," I said. She helped pull me up.

I felt shaky but okay. I tested my arms, my legs. I twisted my head around. Everything checked out okay. Nothing broken, nothing hurting.

"I'm so sorry," the woman said, her voice trembling. "I almost stopped in time. I . . . I just feel so awful."

I pulled more pine needles off my jacket. "It's okay," I told her. "I knew I was going to be hit by a car today."

Her frightened expression faded. She narrowed her eyes at me.

I knew instantly that I'd said the wrong thing. The words had just spilled out.

She studied me intently. "We'd better get you to a doctor," she said.

Mom and Dad took me to see Dr. Owens. She checked me out and said everything was all right. "You might feel a little stiff and sore tomorrow," she said. "But I think you can go to school."

Wow. Hit by a car, and I don't even get a day off from school!

On the way home, I slumped in the back of the car, feeling really glum. What a lost opportunity, I thought bitterly. I really blew it this time.

What if I had made a bet with Chip and Shawn? What if I'd bet them that I'd be hit by a car on the way home?

I could have won big-time!

"You were really lucky," Mom said, turning from the passenger seat to face me. "Really lucky."

No, I wasn't, I thought. What's lucky about being hit by a car and not winning a dime from it?

"Next time, Alex, look both ways before running out to save a kitten," Dad said.

Ha-ha. Very funny.

Chip, Shawn, and Tessa were waiting in the driveway when I got home. They cheered when I told them I was perfectly okay.

But Tessa tilted her head and stared hard at me.

"Alex, I know why you ran out into the street and got hit by a car today," she said.

"I do too," I replied. "To rescue a kitten."

She shook her head. "No. To make sure your diary is more interesting than mine. You'll do *anything* to win our bet!"

Chip and Shawn laughed. But I didn't think it was funny.

"I don't have to do a lot of crazy things to make my diary interesting," I told Tessa. "Because I'm a really good writer."

So far, of course, I hadn't written a single word in the diary. The diary had written it all for me.

Thinking about the diary gave me a chill.

What would it say about tomorrow? Would it have more bad news for me?

I suddenly realized I was afraid of the diary. I was so excited at first. But knowing the future was really creepy.

Maybe I shouldn't open it again, I thought. Maybe I should tuck the thing away in a drawer and never look at it again.

But would that change things?

Wouldn't the same things happen in my life even if I didn't read about them first in the diary?

"I talked to my uncle Jon." Tessa's words broke into my thoughts. "He says his garage is ready. We can use it anytime to rehearse in."

"Yaay! That is totally awesome news!" Chip

exclaimed. "Let's go right now!"

"I can't," I said. "I was just in an accident—remember?"

Chip nodded. "Oh, yeah. Right."

We made a plan to try to rehearse that weekend. Then, feeling sore and achy, I made my way into the house for dinner.

A noisy thunderstorm struck while we were eating. Lightning crackled over the backyard, and a boom of thunder made the house shake. Rain poured down. The lights flickered but didn't go out.

Mom and Dad kept glancing at me as I ate. I knew they were thinking about the car hitting me. But none of us talked about it.

After dinner, I hurried upstairs to my room. I slid the diary out from its hiding place in my desk drawer. Then, holding it between my hands, I stared at the cover.

I didn't open it. I wondered if I could keep myself from opening it.

My hands trembled as I held it. I was afraid of it now—and I had good reason to be.

I knew I was holding some kind of magic. But was it *evil* magic?

Diary, what is your secret? I wondered for the hundredth time. How do you know what's going to happen tomorrow?

And why are you written in my handwriting?

My hands moved as if on their own. As if I were

no longer in control.

My hands pried open the diary.

I shuffled through the pages.

Yes. There it was—an entry for tomorrow.

I didn't want to read it. I didn't want to know.

But I couldn't help myself.

I raised the book close to my face and started to read.

CHAPTER 17

DEAR DIARY,

The eighth-graders had their Junior Olympics at the running track in back of school today. The track was still wet from all the rain last night. Runners kept slipping and falling, and a couple of kids really cut up their knees.

The wind was blowing like a hurricane. Some of the javelin throwers had their javelins come flying back at them! It was a mess, but we seventh-graders got out of school all day to watch them. So we thought it was terrific.

The blue team won every single event. Except for the broad jump, which was a tie.

"Excellent!" I cried out loud. I set the diary down and pumped my fist above my head.

I hope Chip and Shawn and the other guys bring lots of money to school tomorrow! I'm going to win it all! All!

They won't believe that Blue can win every event. And then, when I bet them the broad jump is a tie, I'll clean them out!

Thinking about all the bets I would win really cheered me up. I could forgive the diary for the car accident. I suddenly didn't feel as scared of it. The little book was going to make me rich!

I raised it close and began to read the rest of tomorrow's entry. . . .

Tessa keeps giving me a hard time. I can't tell if she is teasing me or not.

She keeps saying that I'm doing things just to make my diary more interesting than hers. She says I'll do anything to win our bet.

It isn't true at all. But what is Tessa going to think when she hears the crazy thing I did after school?

Huh? After school?

My heart started to pound. As I gripped the diary, my hands were suddenly cold and wet.

What did I do after school?

I bent over the diary and read. . . .

You should have heard the screams. Everyone was in a total panic.

Maybe a hundred kids were watching me, and more were running over from the playground.

208

I heard kids shouting all down the block and out to the street.

What an adventure!

I don't even remember climbing up onto the roof of the school building. But there I was, teetering on the roof edge at the gutter.

And then, it's hard to believe—but I did it. I flapped my arms like a bird and jumped off the roof.

CHAPTER 18

"Ten . . . fifteen . . . twenty . . ."

After the Junior Olympics, I stayed in the bleachers to count the money I had won. The total came to thirty-five dollars.

Not a bad day's work.

I jammed the wad of fives into my jeans pocket and zipped my denim jacket up to my chin. I shivered.

What a cold, dreary day. The sky had been dull and gray all afternoon. The ground was still drenched from the heavy rains last night.

A cold wind kept gusting, swirling, blowing so hard, the bleachers behind the school trembled.

Leaning into the wind, I made my way into the school building. I had spent all afternoon watching the Junior Olympics. Cashing in big-time.

Now I had to pick up my backpack from my locker and walk home.

Walk home *without* climbing up onto the roof of the school.

This is one diary prediction that will not come true, I decided.

I waved to Tessa, who stood talking to a group of girls.

Tessa made a face and turned away from me. She was steamed because she lost ten dollars to me betting that the broad jump *wouldn't* be a tie.

Ha-ha. My diary is better than yours! I thought.

I had been thinking about the diary all day.

Of course, I didn't understand it. I didn't understand how it worked, how it knew the future.

It was kind of magical. It was totally scary.

But, so far, finding it was the best thing that had ever happened to me.

The next Ravens basketball game is tomorrow, I suddenly remembered. I know the score of the game will be waiting for me in tomorrow's diary entry.

I could feel the wad of five-dollar bills in my jeans. Maybe I'll let the guys win a few dollars at first, I thought. Just so they don't get suspicious when I totally clean them out again.

Yes, the diary was definitely great. Awesome. Fantastic.

If only it didn't bring any more bad news.

I felt a cold tingle of fear. Was the diary also evil?

I stopped in front of my locker. I shivered again. A frightening thought rolled through my mind.

What if the diary was *causing* these bad things to happen?

What if it wasn't just reporting what happened the next day? What if it was *causing* me to be hit by a car? What if the diary *forced* me to jump off the roof?

No. No way.

I shook my head hard, as if trying to shake that thought from my mind.

What a crazy idea.

That little book can't force me to do anything, I decided.

I am a free person. I have a mind of my own. I can decide what to do and what not to do.

No book can tell *me* what to do!

I swung my backpack over my shoulders and jogged out the back door of the school. The sky was even darker. Another storm was on its way. The air felt cold and wet.

I saw a couple of guys tossing a football back and forth at the edge of the playground. Their shoes sloshed in the wet grass. The gusting wind kept carrying the football out of their hands.

I turned away from the school. A blast of wind sent my hair flying straight up. I brushed it down with both hands. Then, leaning into the wind, I started toward home.

I had gone only two or three steps, when I heard the screams.

Frantic screams.

"Alex—help me! Help!"

CHAPTER 19

I froze at the sound of my name.

"Alex! Alex! Help me!"

I uttered a startled gasp and spun around.

A little boy stood in the grass near the back of the building, waving frantically.

I took a few steps toward him and his face came into focus. Billy Miller.

Not again!

"Alex—help!"

I took off running. "Where's your cat?" I cried.

Some other kids were also hurrying over to Billy. The two boys dropped their football and came running. I saw two of Tessa's friends trotting to help the boy.

I got to him first. "Where's your cat?" I repeated breathlessly. My eyes searched the playground.

"At home," Billy said. The wind blew his blond hair over his face.

I gaped at him. "Huh? At home?"

"It's not my kitten!" he wailed. "It's my Raiders cap! My new Raiders cap! Look!"

He stuck his arm up, pointing wildly. "Up there. The wind blew it!"

"Oh, noooo," I moaned. I raised my eyes to the slanted, black roof of the school. Squinting into the gray sky, I could see the black-and-silver Raiders cap. It rested on the rain gutter at the edge of the roof.

I'm not going up there to get it, I told myself.

I'm not going to make that diary entry come true.

I turned back to Billy. He had tears in his eyes. His face was bright red. His bottom lip kept quivering. "Please?" he whispered. "It's my brand-new cap."

What is up with this kid? I wondered. It's like he is *haunting* me! He already caused me to get hit by a car.

And now . . .

"Maybe the wind will blow it back down," I told Billy. "Maybe if you wait long enough . . ."

"NOOOO!" he wailed. "I WANT IT! I WANT MY CAP!"

"Get it for him, Alex," Nella, one of Tessa's friends, shouted. "Just climb up the drainpipe. It's not hard."

"Uh . . . I'm not a good climber," I said. "I . . . don't have the right shoes."

"Help the poor kid," another girl said. "Look at

him—he's crying!"

Tears were streaming down Billy's cheeks. He still had his hand raised, pointing to the cap.

"Maybe someone else could help," I said. I turned to the crowd of kids who had gathered around us. I counted at least twenty kids. "Does anyone else like to climb?"

"Help him, Alex," Nella repeated. "Just shinny up the drainpipe. It's not that high."

"Any volunteers?" I pleaded. "Anyone?"

No one.

"I WANT MY RAIDERS CAP!" Billy shrieked.

I swallowed hard. I gazed at the metal drainpipe running up the side of the building to the rain gutter along the edge of the roof. "Okay, okay," I muttered.

I had no choice. Everyone was staring at me. If I just left Billy standing there crying, no one would ever let me forget it.

So . . . I was doing it. I was heading up to the roof.

Kids clapped and cheered. I stepped up to the wall and grabbed the metal drainpipe with both hands.

It felt wet and slippery from all the rain. The wind blew, making the gutter above me rattle.

I gazed straight up. The building was only two stories high at this end. But the roof appeared a mile above me!

I could see the cap. It was hanging halfway over the gutter edge.

If only a gust of wind would blow it down and save me from having to do this!

But . . . no.

I took a deep breath and grasped the cold, wet drainpipe. I moved my hands high and wrapped my legs around the pipe.

Kids were still cheering, urging me on. I glimpsed Billy standing in front of the crowd. He had finally stopped crying. He had his eyes raised to the cap.

With a groan, I pulled myself up. My hands slipped on the wet metal. But I kept a tight grip on the pipe with my legs.

Slowly, slowly, I pulled myself up.

I was gasping for breath when I reached the roof. I leaned forward carefully and spread my hands onto the dark shingles. Then I pulled myself onto the roof.

The roof seemed to slant straight up. One slip, I realized, and I could roll right off.

I was on my hands and knees on the edge of the roof. A strong wind fluttered my jacket.

My whole body was trembling. My legs felt like rubber. I started to crawl forward. So carefully. Planting one hand. Then the other. Sliding one knee forward. Then the other knee.

The Raiders cap was only a few yards away. But I kept slipping on the wet shingles, sliding toward the edge of the roof.

Each time I slipped, a scream went up from the kids below. I turned and glimpsed other kids running from the playground.

I could hear their excited shouts. I knew they were cheering me on. But I couldn't make out their words.

I crawled forward, inch by inch. And then I stretched out one hand . . . stretched . . .

. . . and grabbed the cap.

Below, kids were cheering and shouting, slapping high-fives. Billy leaped into the air, laughing and clapping.

"Yes!" I cried, gripping the cap tightly in my fist. "Yes!" I jumped to my feet.

Why?

Why did I jump to my feet?

It was as if I had lost control. Some kind of powerful force had pulled me up.

There I was, standing on the edge of the roof, laughing, waving the cap in the air. A victory celebration?

No! I didn't want to be there. What had pulled me to the roof edge?

I lowered the cap to my side. And stared down, gripped with cold, sudden horror.

So far down to the ground.

What next? What next? I asked myself.

My whole body shuddered.

Am I going to flap my arms and jump off? Just as the diary said?

Is there nothing I can do to save myself?

The diary—it's always right, I realized to my horror. It always tells the truth.

And if it says I jump off the roof . . .

I'm going to break my neck. Or worse. Because the diary is . . . in control.

Trembling in the strong wind, I glanced down at the crowd again. The kids had grown silent. They all stared up at me tensely. No one moved.

I stared down at them, my mind swirling like the wind.

"Get down!" someone shouted.

"Alex—be careful!" I heard Nella cry.

"Alex—back up! Get back!"

Maybe I can make big bucks from this jump, I suddenly thought. If I'm going to break all my bones, at least maybe I can win a few bets.

I cupped my hands around my mouth and shouted down to them. "Does anyone dare me to jump?"

The wind blew the words back at me. And before anyone down below could reply, my shoes started to slide on the wet shingles.

"No—!" I gasped.

My arms flew up in the air as I lost my balance.

My legs slid out from under me.

My hands flapped wildly in the air.

One shoe caught in the gutter. The other slid over the edge.

I heard shrill screams. A rush of cold wind.

And flailing, kicking, and thrashing, I fell.

CHAPTER 20

The ground shot up to meet me.

It looked like a video game. All bright colors and screaming sound, and everything happening in jagged slow motion.

And then I saw a figure shooting forward. An alarmed face.

Arms straight out.

A hard *thud*.

I bounced. Bounced in someone's arms.

Colors swirled around me. And the screams—the screams all around, so shrill, I thought my ears would burst.

"Huh?" I uttered a choked cry as I realized someone had caught me.

A teacher. Mrs. Walker, the art teacher. I landed hard on top of her. We both tumbled to the grass. She let out a groan, then struggled to untangle herself from me.

How embarrassing, I thought, still dizzy, still falling

in my mind. Still feeling the ground rushing up to me.

How embarrassing. Caught by a teacher.

"Alex, are you okay?" she asked breathlessly, climbing shakily to her feet.

I jumped up quickly. "Fine," I said, trying to shake off the dizziness. "Fine . . . I guess."

Mrs. Walker let out a sigh. She brushed off her jacket. Then tested her arms. "You should go on a diet if you're going to jump off buildings."

Lots of kids laughed. I forced a smile.

Mrs. Walker's expression changed. "What on earth were you doing up there?"

"Billy's cap," I murmured. "I had to bring down his cap. . . ."

Where was it? What happened to the cap?

I glanced around. And saw a black-and-silver Raiders cap pulled down low over Billy's head. A big grin beneath the cap.

Billy was happy.

For the second time in one week, he had almost gotten me killed! And there he was, grinning his head off.

"That was really dangerous," Mrs. Walker said.

I nodded. "Yes, I know."

My whole life has become dangerous, I thought. My whole life is one frightening moment after another.

All because of the diary.

I picked up my backpack and started for home. Kids slapped me high-fives and congratulated me.

"Way to go, Alex!"

"That was totally cool!"

But I didn't feel totally cool. And I didn't feel like celebrating.

I wanted to hurry home and think. I had to think hard about this. Should I keep the diary? Or should I throw it in the trash?

Could I throw it in the trash?

No. No . . . it had a powerful hold on me, I realized.

I needed it. I needed to know what would happen next.

I couldn't fight it. I had tried to fight what it said. I had tried to make the diary wrong.

But it was always right. Always.

I burst into the house and tossed down my backpack. Then I leaped up the stairs two at a time.

I dove into my room. My heart pounding, I crossed to my desk.

Jerked open the drawer.

Reached for the diary. Reached for it.

"Huh?" I uttered a sharp cry.

Panic choked my throat.

My hand fumbled through the drawer. I pulled the drawer out all the way.

And stared down.

Stared wide-eyed.

Gone.

The diary was gone!

CHAPTER 21

I heard someone laugh.

Startled, I spun around.

Chip and Shawn sat on my bed, grinning. Chip waved the diary at me.

"Hey—!" I cried. "Where'd you get that?"

Chip's grin grew wider. He pointed. "On your desk. Shawn and I are going to read your deep, dark secrets."

"No!" I screamed. "Give it back!" I dove across the room and made a grab for it.

Chip giggled and dodged away from me. He tossed the diary to Shawn.

Shawn jumped to his feet and ran to the door.

"Come on—!" I shouted. "Give it!" I leaped at Shawn. Tackled him around the waist.

As I pulled him to the floor, he heaved the diary back to Chip. Chip reached for it—but it flew over his hand and bounced off the wall, onto the bed.

Chip and I dove for it, scrambling. I shoved him

hard. "Give it back to me!" I shrieked. "I mean it! Give it back!"

Then I totally lost it. I jumped on top of him and began pounding him with my fists. "Give it back! Give it back!"

Stunned, Chip rolled away. He dropped onto the floor and stared up at me in surprise. "Okay, okay," he muttered. "It's just a stupid diary."

I grabbed the little book and squeezed it tightly in my hand. I struggled to catch my breath. My heart was pounding.

"What is your problem, Alex?" Shawn asked, shaking his head. "We weren't going to hurt your diary."

"You didn't have to go totally berserk," Chip added.

"What's in that diary anyway?" Shawn asked. "Did you write stuff about *us* in there?"

"No," I said. "No way." I tucked the diary into the desk drawer and pushed the drawer shut. "I just . . . don't like people messing with my stuff."

"We're not people," Shawn replied, eyeing me intently. "We're your friends!"

"I know, but—"

"Forget about the diary," Chip said. He grabbed my arm and used me to pull himself to his feet. "Let's hang out or something. We could try those new video games you got."

"Uh . . . I can't," I said. "I've got to . . . uh . . . go

somewhere with my parents tonight. So I have to do my homework now."

They both stared at me. Could they tell I was lying?

I didn't want to hang out with them. I wanted to see the new diary entry. I wanted to sit and think about the diary.

They had given me a bad scare. When the diary wasn't in its right place, I totally freaked. Now I knew—I needed the diary. *Needed* it!

But I couldn't explain it to them. I couldn't really explain it to myself.

As soon as they left, I pulled the diary from the desk and eagerly shuffled through the pages. No new entry yet. I read over the old ones.

True. Everything in it was true. Every prediction had been exactly right.

I didn't know how it was happening. Or why. But as I stared at the blank pages, waiting for them to fill up with the next entry, I knew that I couldn't *live* without this book. I hated it—and I needed it at the same time.

After dinner, the next entry was waiting for me in the diary. But it was an entry I wished I hadn't read. An entry I didn't want to believe.

First, it gave me the score of tomorrow's Ravens game. Very handy.

But the rest of the entry filled me with dread:

After the basketball game, Shawn was riding his bike home. It was a cloudy, foggy evening, and Shawn was going really fast to get home before the rain started.

He wasn't looking where he was going. And I saw him crash. I saw the whole thing.

He smashed head-on into a parked truck. Poor Shawn. He flipped up into the air. He landed hard. Knocked unconscious. And he broke his leg in two places.

"No way!" I cried out loud, staring until the words blurred on the page. "No way. I won't let this happen. I *can't* let this happen."

The diary entries were becoming more and more frightening. Each prediction was more terrifying than the last.

But I can stop this one, I decided. I can stop it from happening.

Can't I?

CHAPTER 22

"Hey, Shawn, want to walk home with me after the basketball game?"

A cheer rang out as the Ravens scored. They were winning 35 to 25. Once again, the diary was right on target. I was about to win forty dollars from my friends.

"I can't. I rode my bike," he replied. He scratched his red hair, frowning. "I've got to stop making bets with you, Alex. You win every bet. I don't know how you do it. I'm totally broke."

"Just a lucky streak," I said, forcing myself not to grin. "Listen, leave your bike. You can get it tomorrow. Come to my house for dinner."

He shook his head. "I can't. It's going to rain. I want to get home fast."

"But—but—"

The final buzzer drowned out my protests.

I can't stop him from riding his bike, I realized. But I *can* stop him from having an accident.

I'll run along beside him. I'll make sure he pays attention and watches where he's going.

I can stop this accident from happening. I *will* stop it!

"Here's your five bucks," a kid grumbled. He shoved a five-dollar bill into my hand. "You're too lucky, Alex."

Two other guys each counted out five singles and handed them over to me. "Hey—double or nothing next time!" I shouted happily.

I collected all my winnings. Then I carefully counted the money to make sure I had it all. "Thirty-eight . . . thirty-nine . . . forty. Yes!"

If I kept winning like this, I'd soon have enough money to buy a new guitar!

I turned to Shawn. "Hey—"

He was gone. I thought he was standing right beside me.

The gym was emptying out slowly. I pushed my way desperately through the crowd and squeezed out the door. Some girls down the hall called to me, but I didn't turn around. I had to find Shawn.

I pushed open the back doors of the school building and burst onto the parking lot. It was a dark, damp evening. Black storm clouds spread over the sky. I felt a few cold drops of rain on my forehead.

"Shawn—?"

I spotted him on his bike, pedaling hard, speeding away from the bike rack.

"Shawn—stop!" I shouted, waving both arms. I took off, running after him.

I saw Tessa at the bike rack with two other girls. She looked up as I ran past. "Alex—what's up?"

I didn't slow down. I chased after Shawn, waving my arms frantically, shouting his name. "Stop! Hey—stop!"

He didn't hear me. He rolled down Park Street, picking up speed.

Rain began to patter down. I tried to run faster, ignoring the ache in my side.

"Shawn! Stop! Hey—Shawn!" I screamed.

Finally, he heard me.

He turned around.

"Stop!" I shouted, cupping my hands around my mouth. "Stop!"

He stared at me. He didn't see the large yellow moving van parked at the curb.

"Noooooo!"

My scream was too late.

His bike smashed into the broad back of the truck. I heard a sick crunch of metal. Then I heard Shawn's shrill cry.

The crash threw him into the air. His hands flew straight up. He smacked the back of the truck. Bounced off. Hit the pavement, landing on his side.

And didn't move.

I stood frozen in the middle of the street, staring in horror, my hands still cupped around my mouth.

My fault, I thought.

Then I heard a voice shouting. A familiar voice.

And I saw Tessa running along the curb, her blond hair flying behind her. She dropped down on the pavement beside Shawn.

"Alex—" she called. "Don't just stand there! Go get help! Get to a phone! Call for help! Hurry!"

Her cries broke through my thoughts. I shook myself alert and started to run up the driveway of the nearest house. They'll let me use the phone, I told myself. I'll call 911.

But as I ran up the drive, the same thought kept repeating in my mind.

My fault.

The accident was my fault. If I hadn't been there, Shawn wouldn't have turned around. If I hadn't been there, he'd be okay right now.

My fault . . .

The diary's fault . . .

I have to get rid of that diary, I decided. I have to get rid of it and never read another entry.

But will that help?

Will the horrible things stop happening to my friends and me?

CHAPTER 23

After dinner, I sat at my desk, staring at the diary. I held it between my hands, rubbing my fingers over the smooth black leather cover. I felt a chill of fear.

I'm not going to read another entry, I vowed.

How many frightening things had happened since I'd found the diary? I ran through them again in my mind. I was hit by a car . . . jumped off the school roof . . . and now Shawn was lying in the hospital with a badly broken leg.

I squeezed the little book tightly. My hands were sweating. They left wet fingerprints on the leather.

Can I really just toss this amazing book away? I asked myself. What about all the bets I've been winning?

The Ravens have four more basketball games to play. If I keep winning, I'll have more than enough for a new guitar. I'll be able to buy that Fender Strat I've been wanting for years!

No. Forget about that, Alex, I told myself. Give up

betting. Give it up before it's too late.

Be smart. Get rid of the diary. Throw it away.

But what if that doesn't help? I asked myself. The question sent a chill down my back.

What makes you think that all these frightening things will end just because you don't read the diary's predictions?

I stared hard at the book. It appeared to glow like a black jewel in my hands.

My hands trembled. I couldn't help myself. I couldn't stop myself. I started to open the cover.

I heard a cough.

I dropped the book and glanced up. "Tessa—?"

She stepped into my room. Her blond hair was brushed straight back, tied with a bright blue Scrunchie. Her green eyes locked on mine.

"What's going on, Alex?" she demanded. She walked up to my desk and crossed her arms in front of her.

"Excuse me? What do you mean?" I slid open the desk drawer and shoved the diary inside.

"I watched you this afternoon," Tessa said. "And I know there's something weird going on."

I crossed my arms too. "The only weird thing going on is you bursting into my room all the time," I said.

"Why did you run after Shawn like that?" she demanded. "Why did you shout like that?"

"Uh ... well ..." I couldn't think of a good answer.

"You knew he was going to crash," Tessa said. "That's why you were trying to stop him."

"No way—!" I cried.

"Yes, I watched you," she insisted. "How did you know he was going to crash?"

"I—I didn't," I told her.

Tessa wouldn't stop asking questions. "Why have you been acting so weird, Alex? I heard about you jumping off the roof at school. Why did you do that?"

"It was no big deal," I said.

She stared at me for a long time. "I have an idea," she said finally. "Remember, you wanted to share diaries. You read mine, and I read yours. Well, okay. Let's try it. Let me see your diary and—"

"NO!" I shouted. I jumped up from my desk and turned to block her way to the desk drawer. "Forget it, Tessa. I'm not sharing. I don't know why you came over here to spy on me. But I'm—"

Her expression changed. She looked really hurt. "I'm not *spying* on you, Alex," she whispered. "I'm just . . . worried about you. I mean, now that I'm in your band, I thought . . . I thought maybe we'd be friends."

"Friends?" My voice cracked on the word. "Well . . . I don't know . . ."

Now she looked even more hurt. Her red, heart-shaped lips were pushed forward in a sad pout. She sighed. "When is the band going to rehearse? Uncle Jon says the garage is all ready for us."

I was glad she had decided to change the subject. "Let's see if everyone can get together Friday night," I said.

A few minutes later, she was gone.

I made sure I heard the front door close behind her. Then I pulled the diary from its hiding place in the desk drawer.

"I'm not sharing you with anyone!" I told it.

I knew I shouldn't. But I couldn't help myself. I flipped quickly through the pages. Yes. A new entry, an entry for tomorrow:

DEAR DIARY,

What a wild day! Unbelievable!

When the driver got off the school bus for a few minutes, I took over the wheel. Do you believe it? I drove the bus! I raced it halfway across town.

Kids were crying and screaming. But what a thrill!

That is totally insane! I told myself.

I read the entry again. Then I burst out laughing.

Why would I do such a crazy thing?

Take over the school bus and drive it across town?

I would never do anything like that. This time, the diary is completely off. Completely wrong.

Besides, Mom picks me up on Thursdays. I don't even *ride* the school bus tomorrow. So it can't happen. It can't.

"Alex, are you up there?"

I heard Mom's shout from the stairs. "Yes? What is it?" I called.

"I can't pick you up after school tomorrow. I have an appointment. You'll have to take the school bus."

CHAPTER 24

After school the next day, I walked to the back of the school bus and plopped down in the very last seat. I fastened the seat belt as tight as I could. And I gripped the arms of the seat.

I'm not going to get up from this seat, I told myself. No matter what happens.

I'm going to show the diary that *I'm* the boss.

I decide what happens and what doesn't.

But I knew I didn't have much of a chance. I'd said the very same words before—and the diary's prediction always came true.

The diary was always right.

Why should I even try to fight it? I wondered.

I'm going to take over the bus, just as the diary said.

Before the ride is over, I'm going to be sitting behind the wheel, taking this thing through town.

I slumped sadly in the seat. The kid next to me said something, but I didn't even answer him. I stared glumly out the window.

Some kids were batting a balloon back and forth down the bus. I didn't even move when the balloon bounced off my head.

Some kids laughed at me. I didn't care.

You won't be laughing soon, I thought bitterly.

Soon you'll be screaming.

How is it going to happen this time? I wondered. What is going to cause me to run up to the front, drop behind the wheel, and drive this bus away?

I saw Billy Miller climb onto the bus, carrying a stack of comic books. He took a seat near the front and started shuffling through them. Was it going to be Billy's fault again?

What is going to make me do such a crazy thing?

I was so tense, I accidentally bit my tongue. I cried out in pain.

I can't take this suspense! I thought.

Finally, Mr. Fenner, the bus driver, climbed into the bus. He shouted for everyone to sit down. Then he slid into the driver's seat and started the engine.

The bus rumbled and shook. Mr. Fenner gunned the engine, making the bus roar and sending a white cloud of exhaust rising up to the back window.

He started to close the door, then changed his mind. The kids all groaned as he climbed up from his seat and stepped down off the bus.

I watched him cross the street to talk to two men at the corner. The two men laughed about something.

Mr. Fenner took off his cap and scratched his gray hair.

"We want to go! We want to go!" some kids started to chant.

Mr. Fenner kept on chatting with the two men. I think he was pretending he couldn't hear the chant.

Without even realizing it, I had unfastened my seat belt and stepped into the aisle.

Why am I doing this? I asked myself.

But the bus, the kids, the long aisle to the driver's seat, were all a blur. I was moving as if in a dream.

In a daze, I walked up the narrow aisle. Kids were chanting. "We want to go! We want to go!"

Billy Miller called out to me. A girl shouted, "Hey, Alex—sit down!"

But I paid no attention to any of them.

I have no choice, I told myself. Some strange force is pulling me forward . . . pulling me . . .

I slid behind the wheel. I gripped it with both hands.

"Alex—what are you doing?" a girl screamed.

"Go! Go! Go!" some kids were chanting.

I saw Mr. Fenner through the bus windshield. He had his back turned. He was shaking his head and laughing with the two men.

I closed the bus door. The engine hummed loudly. I leaned over the wheel. I pressed my foot down on the brake a couple of times, testing it. Then my foot found the gas pedal.

"Go! Go! Go!"

"Stop him!" someone shouted.

"Alex—get back to your seat!" a boy cried.

"Alex—don't!"

They didn't understand. I *had* to take over the bus. I had no control . . . no control at all.

Some kids were screaming for Mr. Fenner. A little girl right behind me started to cry.

I took a deep breath. Then I spun the wheel away from the curb, pulled back the gearshift, and stepped on the gas.

The bus squealed and lurched forward. "Whoa!" I cried out as the side of the bus scraped the car parked in front of us. I saw the car's mirror rip away.

Kids screamed and shrieked.

"Stop!"

"Somebody stop him!"

I spun the wheel harder and pressed the gas pedal down. "Hey—!" The bus rocked over the other curb onto the grass.

Kids shrieked louder.

Steering this thing was a lot harder than I thought.

Of course, I'd never driven a bus before. I'd never driven *anything* before—except in video games!

I jerked the wheel and aimed the bus back into the street. A car horn blared at my side. "LOOK OUT!" I screamed. The bus swerved sharply—and a kid went flying off his bike.

Close call!

"Stop! Alex—stop!" kids were shrieking and crying.

In the mirror, I saw Mr. Fenner running frantically after the bus. His cap blew off his head, but he kept chasing after me.

I leaned over the wheel and struggled to keep the bus on the street. My foot pressed harder on the gas.

How fast was I going?

I didn't dare take my eyes away from the windshield to check the speedometer.

I roared through a stop sign. My foot missed the brake pedal.

Driving was a *lot* harder than I'd imagined.

Behind me, my passengers had grown very silent. I heard a few kids snuffling, a few sobbing. But the screams had stopped. No one was talking.

The bus bounced hard along the street. On both sides, the lawns were a blur of green. I checked the mirror. I had left Mr. Fenner far behind.

When I heard the siren, my breath caught in my throat. I started to choke.

The high wailing sound grew louder. In the mirror, I saw a black police car, red lights flashing.

The diary didn't say anything about police! I thought.

And then my hands slid off the wheel as the bus lurched onto the grass.

The tree rose up in front of me. So dark and wide.

My scream rang out over the sound of the siren.

And then a thundering crash shook the bus.

The tree appeared to fly into the windshield. And all the sounds meshed together—my scream . . . the siren wail . . . the shattering glass . . . and the crunch of bending metal.

Then silence.

A terrifying, ugly silence.

CHAPTER 25

"Why did you do it, Alex?"

Dad held me by the shoulders. His eyes studied my face.

"I . . . can't explain," I whispered. "I'm . . . really sorry."

Mom and Dad came to the police station to take me home. They were too shocked and confused to be angry at me.

Why *had* I done it?

I really couldn't explain it. And if I told my parents about the diary, they wouldn't believe it anyway.

Luckily, none of the kids on the bus had been hurt. The front of the bus was pretty smashed in. And the tree I hit didn't exactly look great.

"You have no explanation?" Mom asked, biting her bottom lip. "No explanation at all for doing such a stupid, dangerous thing?"

"It won't happen again," I muttered.

And I meant it.

The diary had to go. I wasn't going to keep it for one more night.

Once again, Tessa appeared in my room after dinner. "I know why you're doing these things, Alex," she said, sneering at me. "I know your secret."

Had she really figured it out? I stared at her. "Secret?"

"It's the diary," she said.

I swallowed hard. How did she know? "What about the diary?" I demanded.

She narrowed her green eyes at me. "You're doing all these crazy, dangerous things *just so you'll have something exciting to write in your diary!*" she declared.

I laughed. She didn't have a clue.

"You've pulled all these crazy stunts so that your diary will be more exciting than mine," Tessa continued. "And then you'll win our bet."

She shook her head. "Alex, how could you risk all those kids' lives just to win a bet?"

I tried to explain to her that she was way off. That she didn't know what she was talking about. "I'm finished betting on things," I said. "I'm never going to make another bet as long as I live." But I couldn't convince her.

When she finally left, I grabbed the diary. I held it in my hands, staring at the cover.

I really wanted to read it. I really wanted to see

what it said about tomorrow.

Maybe just a peek . . .

No!

It was too dangerous. I could have killed those kids on the bus this afternoon. I could have killed myself! What if tomorrow's entry was even more dangerous and terrifying?

No. No way. This time I meant it.

Gripping the diary tightly in my hand, I crept out to the backyard. It was a dark night, but the three metal trash cans lined up at the side of the garage were easy to find. I lifted the lid off the first can.

A cold breeze made the trees shiver. A low tree branch cracked—and fell, thudding to the ground behind me.

Startled, I dropped the lid. My heart pounding, I tossed the diary into the can.

When I bent to pick up the lid, I heard a sound. A crackling. A scraping.

Another tree branch shifting in the wind?

Or was someone out there in the darkness, watching me?

"Who's there?" I called. "Is someone there?"

CHAPTER 26

Silence.

Shivering, I made my way back into the house. I was glad to be rid of the diary. I felt a hundred pounds lighter.

That night, I fell asleep quickly. I dreamed I was floating, floating on a puffy white cloud. The cloud suddenly popped and vanished—and I woke up.

I sat straight up, wide awake. Panic choked my throat. I glanced at the clock. Three in the morning.

I don't know what's going to happen tomorrow, I thought. I pictured the diary out back in the trash can.

I need it, I told myself. I need to know what's going to happen. I *have* to know!

I climbed out of bed. I straightened my pajama bottoms and crept barefoot down the stairs.

Once again, I was moving as if in a daze. As if under a spell. I knew I shouldn't be doing this. I knew I should leave the diary in the trash.

But I couldn't help myself. I had to read what it said about tomorrow.

I clicked on the light to the backyard. I silently prayed it wouldn't wake Mom and Dad. Carefully, I unlocked the kitchen door, pulled it open, and slipped out into the cold, moonless night.

Trees creaked and groaned. The wet grass felt icy cold against my bare feet. I saw an animal slither under a bush. I think it was a mole or a raccoon.

I tiptoed to the trash cans. The wind made my pajama shirt ripple. Shivering hard, I lifted the lid off the first can. I bent over it. Reached inside.

"Huh?"

No diary.

I leaned closer. Dipped my head into the can. No diary.

With a low cry, I began pawing frantically through the trash. It *has* to be here! I told myself. It has to!

Bending over the can, searching furiously, I dug deeper, deeper into the trash.

Where is it? Where?

In a panic, I lifted the can in both hands. Turned it upside down. And poured everything out.

Then I dropped to my knees on the wet grass and began tearing through the trash. Grabbing at it. Heaving it aside.

"Where is it?" I cried out loud, my heart thudding in my chest. "It's got to be here!"

I grabbed the next can and tilted it over. Nothing. No sign of the diary.

I turned the third can over too. Gagged on the smell of sour milk. Tore through the trash bags. Tore through spoiled eggs and wilted, decayed lettuce.

Tossed it all away. Tossed it over the lawn. Searching . . . searching in a choking panic.

But no. No diary.

The diary was gone.

CHAPTER 27

I stayed awake the rest of the night. I paced back and forth in my room, thinking about the diary.

It didn't just disappear, I knew. Someone had taken it.

Was it Tessa?

It didn't take me long to find out.

In school the next morning, I felt tense, shaky. One reason was that I'd been awake all night. But mainly, I was tense because I didn't know what was going to happen.

In algebra class, we had a pop quiz. I totally flunked it. I hadn't even opened my algebra book the night before.

As I slunk out of the room, I glimpsed the broad grin on Tessa's face. "That was so easy," she declared.

Later, I saw Tessa in the hall surrounded by a group of her friends. "Is it a bet?" she was saying.

"Let me get this straight," her friend Nella said. "You want to bet us five dollars there will be a gym locker inspection this afternoon?"

Tessa nodded, grinning. "Who wants to bet five bucks?"

"But we *never* have gym locker inspections!" Nella protested.

"If we don't, you win the bet," Tessa said.

I watched as the girls reached into their bags, pulling out five-dollar bills. Why was Tessa so sure about the locker inspection?

There was only one answer to that question. The diary. She knew the future. She must have the diary.

I balled my hands into tight fists. I gritted my teeth, trying not to explode in anger.

At lunchtime, I ran to catch up to her. "Hey, Tessa—wait up! I know what you did—"

"Better hurry, Alex!" she shouted, running ahead of me toward the lunchroom. "Pizza today!"

"How do you know?" I called.

Her green eyes lit up gleefully. "A little birdie told me!" She laughed and trotted into the lunchroom.

Again, I balled my hands into fists. Tessa has it, I knew. She waited till I went inside last night. Then she took the diary.

But she isn't keeping it for long, I decided. I'm going to get it back—tonight.

After dinner, Dad drove Chip and me to Tessa's uncle's house. We carried our guitars into the garage and set them down against the wall. Dad carried the large amp over to the electrical outlet near the door.

"I've got to go, guys," he said. "I'll pick you up in a few hours. Have a good practice."

"Thanks for helping us carry our stuff," Chip called as my dad climbed back into the car.

A few seconds after he backed away, Tessa appeared. She carried a tall stack of papers. "I brought some songs we can try," she said.

"Your uncle's garage is awesome," Chip said. He bent to plug his guitar into the amp. "We've got enough electrical power in here to rehearse an orchestra!"

Tessa nodded. "Uncle Jon is a good guy." She turned to the driveway. "Hey—look who's here!"

We all turned to watch Shawn struggle up the drive on his crutches. He had a heavy white cast on his broken leg that reached all the way to his waist.

Chip hurried to carry Shawn's guitar for him. "Hey, Shawn—how are you going to play guitar with those crutches?" he asked.

Shawn snickered. "I guess maybe I'll put the crutches down when I play," he said.

We all laughed. Chip blushed bright red.

The night was overcast, and a sudden flash of lightning made the garage as bright as day. A soft rain started to fall, tapping against the garage windows and the roof.

Chip attached a cable to Shawn's guitar. "I'll help you set up."

A boom of thunder shook the walls. "Great sound effects!" Chip cried.

I suddenly realized that Tessa was staring at me. "What's your problem, Alex?" she asked. "Why are you just standing around?"

"Oh. Uh . . . I brought the wrong guitar," I said. "I really wanted to play the other one."

I started toward the open garage door. Lightning flickered over the trees across the street. "I'm going to run home and get it," I said, shouting over another burst of thunder.

"In the rain?" Shawn called.

"It's only a couple of blocks," I said. "I'll be back by the time you're set up." I pulled my jacket over my head, grabbed my backpack, and ran out of the garage.

Of course, I wasn't going to my house. I was going to Tessa's house.

I had planned this all afternoon. I was going to Tessa's house to get back my diary.

The rain came down a little harder. My shoes splashed through shallow puddles as I jogged along the sidewalk. Lightning streaked the sky, making the trees and lawns flash like silver.

A few minutes later, I stepped onto Tessa's front stoop. Tessa's mom answered the door. "Alex? What's wrong?" she asked, very shocked to see me. "You're soaked!"

"Tessa forgot some song sheets," I said. "She asked me to get them from her room."

Thunder boomed. Dr. Wayne shook her head. "I hope you kids are all right in this storm. Practicing in a garage . . ."

"It's a very well-built garage," I said. "No leaks or anything."

I wiped my wet shoes carefully on the welcome mat, then made my way to Tessa's room. I clicked on the light—and saw it instantly.

The diary. *My* diary. Lying on top of a stack of papers on Tessa's desk.

"Yessss!" I cried happily.

I dove across the room and grabbed it.

She stole it. Tessa stole my diary! How could she do a thing like that?

Well, it doesn't matter, I decided. The diary is back with its proper owner.

I held it in my hands. Rainwater dripped from my hair onto the leather cover. I brushed the water away with my finger.

I've got to open it, I decided. I've got to see what the diary says about tonight.

I've felt so lost without it . . . so totally lost.

My hands shook as I flipped the book open.

I shuffled past the old entries till I came to the last page.

The new entry. The entry for tonight.

My eyes bulged as I read it. One word.

Only one word on the page:

DEAD.

CHAPTER 28

DEAD.

I stared at the word, the book trembling between my hands.

My frightening dream flashed into my mind. The dream had come true. The diary entry read: DEAD.

And the diary never lied.

"Alex—did you find what you need?" Dr. Wayne's voice broke into my thoughts.

"Yes. No problem!" I called. I slammed the book shut. I stuffed it into my backpack. Then I headed back to the front of the house.

DEAD.

Whoa. Wait a minute.

Tessa stole the diary yesterday. And now the entry for today was that one frightening word.

It means that Tessa is in danger, I realized. Not me.

I called good night to her mother and ran back into the rain. It was coming down harder now. Sheets of rain lit up by bright flashes of crackling lightning.

I pulled my jacket over my head and ran.

Tessa is in danger. The diary says that Tessa will be dead.

I can't let that happen, I decided. I have to warn her.

Thunder boomed. A jagged bolt of lightning snapped over the grass, so close, I jumped back.

My shoes splashed up waves of water.

DEAD. DEAD.

I'm going to save Tessa, I vowed. I'm going to save her.

But—how?

CHAPTER 29

A car rolled past, windshield wipers snapping. I leaped back as the tires sent up a tidal wave of water.

Through sheets of rain, the garage came into view. I could see my friends beyond the garage window.

My shoes pounded up the driveway. I was only a few feet from the garage when I heard a loud *crack*.

I glanced up in time to see a white bolt of lightning hit the tree beside the garage.

I heard a *snap*—and then a sizzling rip.

A large tree branch shuddered, then fell. It crashed with a wet *thud* to the soaked lawn.

Shaking, I struggled to pull open the garage door. As the door slid up, I saw Tessa. She was bending over to plug in a microphone cord.

Thunder boomed.

Tessa held the microphone in one hand while she struggled to plug in the cord.

She's going to be hit by lightning, I realized.

DEAD.

DEAD.

Tessa is going to be hit by lightning.

That's how the diary prediction will come true—unless I get to her in time.

Lightning streaked low over the garage roof. I heard the loud *crack* as it hit the wooden fence at the back of the yard.

Shaking off water, I lurched into the garage.

"Tessa—drop the cord!" I shrieked.

At the sound of my cry, all three of them turned.

"Drop it!" I shouted. "Tessa—drop it *now*!"

Tessa squinted at me. "Alex? What's your problem?"

She finished plugging in the cord. She held the microphone at her waist.

"Drop it!" I screamed.

And then I dove across the garage, my wet shoes slipping on the concrete floor.

Thunder roared.

I leaped across the garage—and grabbed the microphone from Tessa's hand.

As I grabbed it away, I saw the flash. A blinding white flash. So bright, so white, it forced my eyes shut.

And then I felt the jolt. A bone-crushing jolt of pain.

Like being hit by a locomotive.

The current crackled around me. My teeth chattered. My eyeballs burned.

And then the sizzling . . . the sizzling . . .

The sound of my own skin sizzling, burning away beneath the crackling electricity.

Hit by lightning . . .

Hit by lightning . . .

A roar of thunder was the last sound I heard.

CHAPTER 30

When the thunder faded, I slowly opened my eyes.

I gazed around my room. My own bedroom. I stood in my room.

"Surprise, Alex!" Mom cried.

Two men in blue uniforms were carrying an old desk into my room.

Mom smiled. "Do you like it? This is the desk you've needed for so long."

I gaped at it. "Huh? A desk? Hey—thanks!" I cried.

The phone rang. Mom hurried downstairs to answer it.

After the two men left, I began to examine the desk. It was very cool. Big. Dark wood. Very old-fashioned-looking.

I began opening the drawers. Some of them stuck a little. I had to struggle to pull them open.

"Hey!" I cried out when I found the little book in the bottom drawer. I lifted it out, blew the dust off it, and examined it.

A diary.

How strange, I thought. This morning, Miss Gold suggested that I keep a diary for extra credit. And then Tessa Wayne had wanted to keep a diary too.

And here it is—a diary. A blank diary.

Or *is* it blank?

To my surprise, I saw an entry already written in the book. In *my handwriting*!

But how could that be?

Very confused, I raised the diary close and began to read the entry:

DEAR DIARY,

The diary war has started, and I know I'm going to win. I can't wait to see the look on Tessa's face when she has to hand over one hundred big ones to me.

I ran into Tessa in the hall at school, and I started teasing her about our diaries. I said that she and I should share what we're writing—just for fun. I'll read hers, and she could read mine.

Tessa said no way. She said she doesn't want me stealing her ideas. I said, "Whatever." I was just trying to give her a break and let her see how much better my diary is going to be than hers.

Then I went into geography class, and Mrs. Hoff horrified everyone by giving a surprise test on chapter eight. No one had studied chapter eight. And the test was really hard. . . .

My hands were shaking. My heart was pounding. I stared at the diary in amazement.

That entry is for tomorrow, I realized.

But how does the diary know what will happen tomorrow?

IT'S AS IF IT ALREADY HAPPENED!

I glanced over the entry again.

"It can't be true—*can* it?" I asked myself.

Well . . . Just in case, I decided . . . maybe I'll study chapter eight right now!

THE NIGHTMARE ROOM
THEY CALL ME CREATURE

PROLOGUE

They call me Creature.

But I'm not. I'm a human being. I'm a person.

I was born human. I lived most of my life as a human. I am still a human.

I act like a person. I think like a person.

I am not a creature!

Yes, sometimes I get urges. I get such powerful cravings.

When the feeling comes over me, I can't help myself. I can't control myself.

I get so hungry. So hungry . . . as if my whole body needs to feed. And feed and feed.

As I prowl the woods, I must kill for food. I must slash and tear and chew. I fill my belly and keep on feeding. I let the warm juices run down my chin.

Afterward, I force myself to look in a mirror. And I cry out in pain, in sorrow. In shame.

Creature . . . you ugly creature. . . .

I wasn't always like this. I didn't always have to

hide my face.

Now I live in the shadows. I have no friends. No one I can trust.

I am so lonely.

I am so tempted to talk to someone. So eager to tell my story to someone who will listen.

But I cannot let my guard down. No one must know. No one must ever know what I am.

That's why I force myself to look in the mirror.

I stare at my face and then I remember.

I remember. I remember.

I remember why they call me *Creature*.

CHAPTER 1

"CAW CAW CAW CAW!"

"It's okay, Mr. Crow," I said softly. I finished bandaging the bird and set it down gently in its cage.

"CAWW CAWWW!" It struggled to flutter its broken wing. "Dad, do you think it will heal?"

Dad didn't answer. He turned the page of the magazine he was reading.

"Dad? What do you think?"

He picked up a pencil and circled a sentence on the page.

"Dad?"

"Did you say something, Laura?" My father glanced up and squinted at me through his thick, black-framed glasses.

"Do you think the wing will heal?" I asked again.

"What wing?" Dad returned to the magazine and started scribbling notes in the margin.

I caught the surprise on my friend Ellen's face. She hadn't seen Dad's new faraway personality.

Far away.

That was the best way to describe my father these days. Even when we were in the same room together, he seemed to be someplace else.

Lucky, the big stray cat I'd found in the woods, bumped past me, nearly knocking over the birdcage. He began licking Dad's hand with his long tongue.

Dad jerked his hand away. "Please take the cat out. I'm trying to concentrate." He circled more sentences, pressing so hard, the pencil point broke with a sharp snap.

"Where am I supposed to put him?" I sighed. "I can't use the shed anymore since you're working in there."

Dad stared at the crow and Lucky, as if seeing them for the first time. "Why can't I live in a house, Laura? Why do I have to live in a zoo?"

"You're a vet!" I cried. "You're supposed to love animals—remember?"

Ellen forced a laugh. But I could see she was really embarrassed. She had never seen Dad and me yelling at each other. She hadn't seen Dad since . . . since he changed.

I had stopped inviting my friends over because I never knew what Dad was going to say or do. But Ellen was my best friend, and I missed hanging out with her. So I asked her to come over today. But maybe it was a big mistake.

I picked up the cage in one hand and Lucky in

the other. I took them both down the hall to my room and shut the door.

I swung my camera around my neck. "Come on, Ellen," I said. "Let's get to the woods."

Our house sits on the edge of a quiet country road. Our back lawn is deep and lush and ends at the woods. So I've always considered the woods and the little streams that flow through it part of my back-yard.

That's where I feel the happiest. It's so beautiful in the woods, so peaceful and filled with life.

In the mornings before I go to school, I stand in the center of our lawn and stare out at tall, leafy trees that seem to stretch on forever. Then I breathe in the morning scent of fresh pine. I love that smell.

I checked out my camera, making sure I had put in a new film cartridge.

Ellen brushed back her straight, black hair. She loves her hair. She's always pushing it back, pulling it to the side, sweeping her hands through it.

I'm totally jealous of her hair. Mine is long, and red-brown. It's totally unmanageable.

Ellen's eyes flashed. "Are we going into the woods because of your science project? Or because you want to see that boy you met there last week?"

I let out a groan. "Because of my project," I said. "Life isn't only about boys, you know."

"Well, you're the one who was talking about him all morning. 'I wonder if I'll see him again. I wonder

where he lives. I wonder if he has a girlfriend. . . .'"
She laughed.

"Okay. Okay." I had to admit it. I had been thinking about Joe a lot since I ran into him by Luker Pond.

"It's just that boys don't usually notice me," I said. "And he seemed so nice. And when I told him about my science project, he seemed really interested."

"Then we have two projects," Ellen stated. "The science project and the boy project! Let's go."

"We just have to find Georgie," I said.

"You're going into the woods?" Dad frowned at me. "You need other interests, Laura. Why don't you go to the movies?"

I sighed. Dad has loved the woods his whole life. That's where I get it from. Since I was little, he and I always roamed the woods for hours and hours, exploring, talking, laughing. We could always talk about *anything*.

Now he spent his time locked up in the little shed in our backyard. And he was always silent or grouchy.

"I have to work on my science project," I said. I followed Ellen through the back door.

She's tall and skinny and all legs, like a deer. With her big, dark eyes and sort of innocent, round face, Ellen reminds me of a delicate, graceful doe.

If she's a doe, I'm a fox. My red-brown hair is kind of like fox fur. I'm short and quick, and I have wide-apart brown eyes and a foxy smile.

I'm always comparing all the kids I know to animals. I guess it's because I love animals so much.

Ellen and I stepped out into a cool, crisp spring day. A string of puffy clouds floated low over the trees. The air smelled fresh and sweet.

"Sorry about Dad," I said to Ellen. "He's so different ever since he left his job at the animal hospital. I'm kind of worried about him."

"Maybe you should call your mother. Ask her for some advice," Ellen suggested.

"I did call her. But she said I needed to be patient. She said leaving a job is a big deal, and he probably needs time to adjust."

"That makes sense," Ellen said.

I frowned. "I wish my mom was here. I really miss her. Phone calls and e-mail just aren't the same."

My mom moved to Chicago after she and Dad divorced five years ago. They gave me a choice—and I chose to live with Dad.

"Some kids might think I made a weird choice," I admitted. "But I could never live in a city. If I didn't live near the woods, I'd go crazy."

"Chicago sounds pretty exciting to me. I'd move there in a minute," Ellen said. She peered into the distance, at a large black bird flapping over the trees.

I watched it, too. Its wings beat rapidly against its body. Hard, almost frantic.

Another bird rose from the treetops. Flying toward

us. Then changing direction abruptly. Flying away. Then back toward us. Frantic. Confused.

The woods echoed with a sharp cry as another bird soared from the treetops. Then a cloud of birds rose up. A dark cloud of beating wings. Beating so hard, it sounded like thunder.

I blinked, startled. "What is going on?" I cried.

More birds flew from the woods. Hundreds of them. Flying in a tight circle. Blocking out the sun. Plunging us into darkness.

Ellen grabbed my arm. "Wow. What *is* that?" she whispered.

"I don't know," I gasped, watching the birds, a black tornado swirling, spinning above the trees. "I've never seen birds swarm like that!"

The birds screeched and cawed. Flying low then rising high, flying round and round, circling the woods, squawking louder with each turn.

I heard the snap of a twig behind me.

I turned and saw that Dad had followed us outside. Behind his thick glasses, he gazed up at the sky. His hand trembled as he pushed a lock of hair from his eyes.

"Something has them stirred up," he whispered. "Something is wrong out there, Laura. Don't go. Don't go into the woods today."

CHAPTER 2

"I—I have to go," I replied. "My project . . ."

Dad stared at the swirling black funnel cloud of shrieking birds. "Birds don't act like that unless something is terribly wrong," he said softly.

And then he took off, running full speed across the back lawn.

"Dad!" I shouted. "Dad—where are you going? Come back!"

He didn't turn around. I watched him vanish into the trees.

"What is he doing?" Ellen asked, her hands pressed to her face.

"I don't know," I said, huddling next to her. We watched the dark cloud of birds, circling, circling. Their shrill, frantic cries echoed in my head.

I raised my hands to my ears to block out the noise—and the cries suddenly stopped. The birds circled now in eerie silence. Their flapping wings slowed.

They swooped down, down to the woods. Hidden by the leafy treetops, they disappeared. The sky glowed in the sunlight again. And once again I could hear the gentle rustle of the wind.

Ellen collapsed onto the grass. "That was so totally scary. Those birds—they seemed really angry. I thought they were going to attack us. But then they just vanished."

"I've never seen anything like that before," I said, my heart pounding. "I'll bet Dad is right. Something stirred them up. But what?"

I cupped my hands around my mouth. "Dad? Where are you?"

No reply.

Ellen climbed to her feet. "Do you still want to take photos?" She brushed her hair back. "Do you think it's safe?"

I stared at the sky over the trees. The sun sparkled brightly. No birds in sight. "We'll be okay," I told her.

Georgie, my German shepherd, came trotting around the side of the house. His tail started wagging when he saw us.

He came running up to me first. He knows I'm his best friend. I grabbed his neck, and we started wrestling on the grass.

"We're bringing Georgie with us—right?" Ellen asked.

I nodded. "Of course. I wouldn't go into the woods

without him. Georgie and I have been exploring the woods together since he was a little puppy."

Ellen led the way across the grass, and I followed after her. The camera bounced against my chest as I walked. "My project is due in less than two weeks," I groaned. "And I hardly have any photos."

My science project was to study the plant and animal life at Luker Pond. I had already photographed the different kinds of plant life. Now I needed to photograph some animal life.

I thought it would be easy. But I had visited the pond every afternoon for a week, and I was having trouble finding animals.

Ellen jogged up to the woods. Her hair swung behind her like a horse's tail. Georgie and I caught up with her at the forest's edge.

She lifted her eyes to the sky above the trees. "What do you think happened?" she asked. "Do you think some big animal frightened the birds from their nests?"

"I don't know," I replied. "And why did my dad—"

I stopped short when I heard the howl.

A high, shrill cry. The sound of an animal in pain.

Georgie raised his head, tensed his back, and started to bark furiously.

The animal howled again.

I stepped into the woods and listened carefully, trying to locate the sound.

Another howl. A wail of agony.

But it wasn't coming from the woods.

I spun around. "Whoa. It's coming from the garden shed," I said, pointing.

The shed is square and wood-shingled. It stands halfway between the house and the woods. It's nearly as big as a one-car garage, with a solid wood door and a flat roof.

"What's in there?" Ellen asked. "What is crying like that?"

"I don't know," I told her. "Dad won't let me go near it."

Ellen squinted hard at the shed. The howling finally stopped. "Laura, I don't want you to take this the wrong way—but it's getting kind of creepy around your house."

I laughed.

"What kind of work is he doing in there?" She continued to stare at the shed.

I sighed. "Some kind of research, I guess. He gets too weird when I ask him about it, so I'm not exactly sure. I tried to go in and take a look last week. But he keeps the door locked."

I leaned down and petted Georgie. Then we stepped into the shade of the forest, onto a winding dirt path that curved through the tall trees.

"Why did your dad leave his job at the animal hospital?" Ellen asked. "Was he fired?"

"I don't know," I said, pushing a low branch out of the way. "He won't tell me. He hardly speaks to me anymore. I don't know what to think."

Ellen's eyes flashed. She grabbed my arm. "I know what happened, Laura." A sly grin spread over her face. "I know why he left his job. Your dad and Dr. Carpenter were going out—and she dumped him!"

"YUCK!" I exclaimed. I put my finger down my throat and pretended to puke. "That is *so* not what happened," I said. "Dad and Dr. Carpenter? No way."

Dad and Dr. Carpenter have known each other for four years, ever since she moved here to run the animal hospital. If she and Dad had some kind of romance going on, I'd know about it.

"You're wrong," I said. "They never went out on a single date or anything."

"But she comes to your house all the time," Ellen argued.

"Not anymore," I murmured.

Dr. Carpenter used to come over a few times a week. We'd all hang out together. Watch videos or play Scrabble. Dad liked to make up crazy words to try to trick Dr. C. It was a lot of fun.

I loved her visits. It was great to have someone I could talk to about stuff—friends, clothes, teachers.

"I'm telling you—she dumped him!" Ellen insisted.

Dad and Dr. Carpenter? I didn't think so.

But then why *did* Dad leave the animal hospital? Dr. Carpenter said Dad was the best vet in the world.

She wouldn't fire him—would she?

We climbed over a fallen tree, blanketed with thick green and yellow fungus. We were almost to the pond.

"Let's talk about this fabulous birthday party I'm throwing for you," I said. I wanted to change the subject. "I need a list. Who do you want me to invite?"

"Only boys," Ellen replied. She grinned.

"You're joking, right?" I said.

"Why don't you invite that guy you met, Joe?" Ellen suggested. "I'd really like to meet him."

"Hey!" I said sharply. "I saw him first!"

I turned and saw Georgie examining a pile of dead leaves. Sniffing hard, he started to paw furiously at the leaf pile.

"Georgie—get away from there!" I shouted. "Georgie—no!"

Ellen made a disgusted face. "Whoa. What is he doing?"

Ellen doesn't really like being outdoors that much. She doesn't like dirt, bugs, or forest animals. She'd much rather be home, reading a book or writing in her diary. She's a great writer, and she's the editor of our school newspaper.

But because she's such a good friend, she goes into the woods with me to keep me company.

"Georgie—get away from there!" I shouted.

The dog ignored me. Grunting, he buried his head in the fat pile of brown leaves—and pulled our something in his teeth.

"What *is* that?" Ellen cried. She pressed her hands to the sides of her face. "What has he got?"

"Let me see it, Georgie," I said, stepping toward him, reaching out my hand. "Drop. Drop it, boy. What have you got?"

I edged closer. "What is it, boy? What do you have there?"

The dog let out a grunt. Then his jaw snapped open, and the object dropped to the ground.

Ellen and I stared down at it—and we both began to scream.

"It's—it's a finger!" I cried. "A human finger!"

CHAPTER 3

Georgie barked at it, his tail wagging furiously. Then he took off, heading home.

"Oh, gross," Ellen moaned, shutting her eyes. "Is it really a finger? I'm going to be totally sick."

I stepped up to it and poked it with my shoe. I squatted down to see it better.

"Yes, it's a finger," I said weakly. My stomach lurched. I studied it. "But . . . maybe it's not from a person."

Ellen had her hands over her face, and she had turned away. "Wh-what do you mean?"

"Well . . . the skin is kind of leathery. And the fingernail is pointed. And it's so hairy. . . ."

"SHUT UP!" Ellen screamed. "Don't talk about it anymore! Let's just get away from it." She started back to the path. But I didn't get up. I stared at the finger more closely.

"Strange," I murmured. "It's really ragged at the end. It looks like it was torn off."

"Just shut up about it," Ellen said. "I feel sick. Really."

"Here. Catch!" I shouted. I pretended to toss it to her.

She screamed and ducked, even though I didn't have anything in my hand. "Not funny, Laura," she muttered. "Hey—why don't you take a photo of it? For your science project."

"I'm supposed to photograph whole animals," I said. "Not just parts."

But I should take it home, I thought. Show it to Dad. Maybe he knew what kind of animal had fingers like this.

I didn't want to freak Ellen out. So while she wasn't looking, I picked up the finger. I kept it hidden in my palm so she wouldn't see it.

Ellen and I wandered through the woods. White moths fluttered over Luker Pond. High in a tree, I heard the *knock-knock-knock* of a woodpecker. Yes! Excellent! I *needed* that woodpecker! I raised the camera to my eye and searched the tree for it.

"I've got to go," Ellen said. "What time is it, anyway?"

I studied the trees through the camera viewfinder. "Close to three, I think."

"Oh, wow. I've *really* got to go," Ellen said. "I promised Stevie Palmer I'd play tennis with him at three." She jumped over a flat stone and started to jog away.

Stevie Palmer—blond hair, blue eyes, great athlete—Ellen's latest crush.

"And don't forget to invite Stevie to my party!" she shouted.

"No, wait!" I cried, lowering the camera. "Who else should I invite? Who else?"

She turned back, pulling her hair behind her shoulder. "Invite *everybody*!" she yelled. Then she disappeared behind a stand of evergreen shrubs.

I wish she didn't have to go, I thought, circling the pond. I was alone in the woods, and for the first time in my life I felt tense about it.

I'll feel better once I take some photographs, I decided. I had taken only three or four. I desperately needed to find some animals—or my project was going to be completely lame.

I stepped up to the edge of the pond. Come on, animals. Where are you hiding?

I was so desperate, I snapped a picture of the white moths fluttering above the water.

I'll sit down and wait, I decided. Maybe if I'm really still, a deer will come to drink.

I sat down. And waited. I held my camera in my lap and listened to the whisper of the trees. One of my favorite sounds.

A minute later I heard another sound, this time behind me. It was the snap of a twig.

I turned around but didn't see anything.

I stood up. And heard the heavy scrape of hooves.

Was it a deer?

The sounds stopped.

I turned and took a few steps forward.

Behind me, I heard the footsteps again.

I stopped. And once more the footsteps stopped.

I shuddered as a tingle of fear ran down my back.

I'm never frightened in the woods. Never. Even when I'm by myself.

But today was different.

I pictured the circling birds . . . the ugly finger in the grass . . . I heard my dad's warning to stay away. . . .

And now something was trailing me. Something was creeping up behind me.

"Dad?" I called.

No answer.

I listened hard. I heard the excited chitter of birds in a high tree limb. The whisper of wind. The creak of a branch.

Holding my breath, I took another step. Another.

I was listening for the footsteps. And I heard them. The heavy thud of shoes or hooves.

With a gasp, I spun around quickly.

"Wh-who's there?" I cried.

CHAPTER 4

A boy stepped out from the trees. He gazed at me shyly, then lowered his dark eyes. He was short and kind of chubby. He had long, black tangles of hair, very shiny, nearly as long as Ellen's.

"Joe—hi!" I called. I breathed a sigh of relief.

"Hey, it's you!" he said, trotting up to me.

I smiled at him. "I heard something following me. I—I didn't know what to think."

Pink circles appeared on his cheeks. "It's only me," he said softly.

He's so shy, I realized. And really cute.

He wore baggy denim cutoffs and a black T-shirt. A long silver chain dangled around his neck. In his right hand he carried a fishing pole.

He pointed to my camera. "Snap anything today?"

"No, I . . ." I glanced down and suddenly realized I was holding the disgusting finger. If Joe sees it, he'll think I'm totally weird, I decided.

"I heard a woodpecker in that tree over there," I said, pointing.

When Joe turned to the tree, I let the finger fall from my hand. He turned back—and I stamped my shoe down over it.

"I'm desperate," I said. "Where are the animals? Are they all on strike?"

"Maybe we could drag some over," Joe said. "You know. Go to a pet store or something. Get some hamsters or turtles and bring them to the pond."

"I don't think so," I said, laughing. "But keep thinking."

We stepped up to the pond. Joe kicked a stone into the water. His long hair fluttered in the wind.

"Catch anything today?" I asked. The last time I met Joe in the woods, I found him sitting on a flat rock, fishing in a stream. He told me he loved to fish, but he never ate what he caught. He always threw the fish back. That made me like him even more.

"No. No luck today," he said. "I'll try again tomorrow."

"So how are things at Wilberne Academy?" I asked. I admit it. I had a little bit of a sneer on my face.

He turned to me. "You're making fun of me because I go to a private school, aren't you!"

"No way!" I insisted. "It's just . . . well . . . the guys I know from Wilberne are such snobs. And you don't seem like that."

He snickered. "Hey, thanks. I think."

I decided I'd invite Joe to Ellen's birthday party. The idea made my heart start to pound. I realized I was suddenly nervous.

Go ahead, Laura. Just invite him, I told myself. Don't make a big deal about it. Be bold—like Ellen.

I took a deep breath. "Uh . . . Joe?"

Two chattering birds interrupted. They were so loud, right above our heads. I turned in time to see them take off, chirping together as they flew.

They were joined by three or four other chattering birds. What a racket! They formed a ragged V and flew out of sight.

Joe shook his head. "What's *their* problem?"

We laughed together. I liked the way Joe's eyes narrowed into little moon slivers when he laughed. He reminded me of a bear—a little, friendly bear you see in cartoons.

I decided to try again. "Uh . . . I'm giving a party for my friend . . ." I started.

I didn't have a chance to finish.

Everything seemed to explode at once. Trees shook. Animals cried out. Birds cawed and squawked.

The sky blackened as birds took off, flapping their wings wildly. The grass bent as field mice stampeded past our feet.

"Wh-what's happening?" I cried.

Joe spun around, his eyes wide with fright and confusion.

The sky grew even blacker, as if night had fallen.

A shrill, chittering squeal rang out, echoing off the trees. And over the whistlelike cries came the furious flapping of wings.

"Bats!" Joe cried.

Yes. Bats—hundreds of bats—swarmed above us, squealing, swooping high, then darting into the trees.

"But—but—" I sputtered. "Bats don't fly in the daylight!"

I gasped as a bat swooped over my head. I felt its dry, sharp wing scrape against my face, felt a blast of hot wind off its body.

"Get down, Laura!" Joe grabbed me by the shoulders and pushed me to the ground.

"Get down! Cover your head! They're ATTACK-ING!"

"Cover your head! Cover your head!"

Those were the last words I heard. The flapping wings drowned out Joe's screams. The shrill bat cries seemed to pierce my eardrums.

I pressed myself into a tight ball and covered my head with both hands. "Ohhh." I let out a terrified moan as bat wings slapped my back and shoulders.

This can't be happening! I thought, shuddering. Bats don't come out during the day.

What is going on?

I felt the beating of wings against my hands. Felt a sharp tug on my scalp.

"Leave me alone!" I screamed, frantically brushing two bats from my hair.

All around me—all *over* me—the beating wings, the scrape of talons, and the cries . . . the shrill siren cries.

No—please—no, I silently prayed. Go away. Go away!

I tried to stay curled in a tight ball. But each slap of a bat wing, each thud of a bat slamming into me, each scratch of a bat talon against my clothing made me squirm in horror.

"Joe—are you okay?" I shouted. "Joe—?"

No answer.

And then the shrill squeals began to fade. The sound of beating wings rose up, away from me.

"Joe?" I cried, still afraid to open my eyes. "Joe? Why don't you answer me?"

CHAPTER 5

"Joe?"

Bat wings flapped in the distance now. The shrill cries faded and died.

Trembling, still hunched into a tight ball, I slowly opened my eyes. And raised my head.

And screamed again.

Beside me, Joe was hunched on his knees, battling two large bats.

One bat had its talons stuck in Joe's thick hair. It batted its wings furiously, shrieking, struggling to pull free.

The other bat clung to the neck of Joe's T-shirt. Its outspread wings blocked Joe's face from view.

But I could hear his desperate cries.

He swiped at the bats with both hands.

The bats shrieked and flapped.

Joe toppled onto his back. He wrapped a hand around the bat at his throat. Squeezed until the bat grew silent.

The curled talons loosened. Joe heaved the bat into the trees.

The other bat clung to his hair.

I stood frozen in horror, watching Joe struggle. Then I finally managed to move. I dived to the ground—and reached for the flapping bat.

"NO!" Joe screamed. "GET AWAY!" Then he rolled over in the dirt. Grabbed the bat with both hands. And carefully pried it from his hair.

The bat squawked and squealed.

Joe heaved it aside. Before I could say anything, he leaped to his feet and started to run.

"Joe—" I called. "Stop!"

He stopped on the far side of a small clearing. His face was bright red. He was gasping for breath.

"Don't go. My house is right over there," I said. "My dad is a doctor. I mean, he's a vet. But he knows about bats. Let him take a look at your cuts and scratches."

"No," Joe said, shaking his head. His hands clutched the sides of his hair. "I—I mean, no thanks."

"Is your head cut? Did they scratch you?" I asked.

"I think I'm okay," he insisted. "Anyway, my mother is home. She'll take me to the doctor."

"No—wait," I said. "If you're cut, you should see someone right now. Come with me. My dad will—"

"No. I'm okay. Really." He turned away. And still

holding his head, he started to run. Just before he disappeared into the thickening woods, he called, "See you soon."

"Wait!" I shouted. I forced the words out. "I want to invite you to a party! Joe!"

But he was gone.

I sighed. I stood there staring after him. I could hear the flap of bat wings in the distance.

My whole body itched. I could still feel their talons scratching my clothes, could still feel the air off their fluttering wings.

Something got them riled up, I thought. Like the birds earlier this afternoon.

Something in these woods frightened them. Something made them act totally weird.

But what?

A few minutes later I stepped out of the woods, into our backyard. The shed door was shut tight. Dad had returned. I could hear him banging around inside.

I was desperate to tell him about the bat attack. If I had been scratched or bitten I would have, but I wasn't. Plus, I knew when he was in the shed, he didn't want to be disturbed. So I went inside to start dinner.

Usually Dad and I took turns making dinner, or we'd make up new recipes together, and it was fun. Sometimes Dr. Carpenter would join in. I really missed her. I realized now that Dr. C. had sort of become my fill-in mom.

I pulled a chicken from the refrigerator, dug my hand into the chicken, and started to pull out the gunky stuff inside.

Through the kitchen window, I could see the woods. Quiet now. The trees swaying softly, darkening as the sun went down.

The phone rang. I jerked my hand out of the chicken and tried to wipe the guts off on a dish towel.

Then I picked up the phone. "Hello?"

It was Ellen. "Laura—where have you been? I've been calling you for half an hour."

"In the woods," I said. "It was so weird, Ellen. I—"

"Don't invite Stevie to my birthday party," she interrupted.

"Excuse me?"

"Erase him from the list," she said. "What a creep. Just because I'm half an hour late for our tennis match, he throws a fit. Then he tried to slam the ball down my throat all afternoon."

"Ellen—" I started.

"Can I help it if I beat him in three straight sets? He is *so* not mature, Laura. And when I offered to give him tennis lessons, he called me a bunch of babyish names and stomped away."

I laughed.

"Just cross him off the list. Okay?" Ellen snapped.

"No problem," I said. "Hey—you just missed Joe. He was in the woods."

"Oh, wow," she muttered. "I really wanted to

meet him. Did you invite him to the party?"

"I—I tried," I said. "But—"

"Oh, I've got to go," Ellen interrupted. "My brothers are fighting upstairs, and I'm in charge."

She clicked off before I could say another word.

I set the phone down and stuck my hand back in the chicken.

A short while later dinner was ready. I'd made a green salad, baked potatoes, and string beans to go with the chicken.

I carried everything to the table, then glanced at the clock. Nearly seven, and still no Dad.

What was he doing? Did he completely lose track of the time?

I stared out the kitchen window at the shed. I didn't want dinner to get cold. And I was so eager to tell Dad about the strange bat attack and the creepy finger I found.

I pulled open the back door, cupped my hands around my mouth, and called to him.

No reply.

Two robins lifted their heads and stared at me. I started to jog across the grass, and they flew away.

"Hey—Dad?" I called, stepping up to the shed door. A sharp, chemical smell floated out from the shed. Like the smell in a doctor's office. I heard a soft, whimpering noise coming from inside.

I tried the door. To my surprise, it wasn't locked.

"Dad?" I pushed the door open just a crack.

I glimpsed a lot of equipment, stacked to the ceiling. What was Dad holding between his hands? What was making those noises?

A small pink animal.

He gripped the animal in one hand—and was about to give it an injection with an enormous hypodermic needle.

"Dad? What are you doing?" I called.

He spun around, and his expression turned to rage. "Get out!" he screamed. "Out! Get out of here! Don't ever open that door!"

I backed away with a gasp and pulled the door shut. I'd never seen him become so furious.

My legs trembled as I stepped away from the door.

Why did he yell at me like that?

Why was he acting this way?

My eyes filled with tears.

In the past few weeks my father had become a complete stranger to me.

I felt so alone. So totally alone—and frightened of my own father.

Dad and I ate in silence for a while. He kept his eyes on his plate and shoveled down his food quickly, as if trying to get dinner over with.

The only sounds were the clink of our silverware and the raspy *caw caw caw* of the injured crow in my bedroom.

"I'm sorry." Dad finally raised his eyes to me. "I didn't mean to shout at you."

I took a deep breath. "Why *did* you scream like that?" I asked.

He scratched his graying hair, studying me. "I'm doing very important work," he said. "And I can't have any interruptions. The timing is so important."

Dad stood up to clear the table. "I know I've been very tense lately. I know I haven't been paying much attention to you. But things are going to get better. I promise." Dad smiled for the first time in weeks. "How about a game of Scrabble?"

Dad and I moved into the living room and set up

the Scrabble board. He started making up crazy words, and I did, too. And suddenly everything seemed back to normal again.

So I thought it would be okay to ask him a question. "Dad, exactly what kind of work are you doing?"

He swallowed. His cheek twitched. "I can't talk about it."

"Why not? Don't you trust me, Dad?"

"I can't talk about it. Until it is completed, I can't discuss it with anyone." He sighed.

"But—" I started to protest.

He pulled off his glasses and placed them down on the table. "No more questions, okay? There's nothing more to say," he said softly.

"I'm not a baby," I said, my voice trembling. "If you're doing some kind of secret work, you can trust me."

"I'm sorry, Laura. I really can't discuss it with you."

Dad leaned back in his chair. He closed his eyes as if he was suddenly exhausted. Then he opened them. "Want to finish this game?" he asked.

I nodded, even though it was the last thing I wanted to do.

When we finished playing, Dad helped me put the game away. "Laura, it might be a good idea if you lived with your mother for a while," he said. He kept his eyes down on the Scrabble box.

I grabbed my chest as if I'd been stabbed.

Those words hurt so much.

"You—you want to send me away?" I choked out.

"It might be best."

"I have to move away because . . . because I asked you what you're doing in the shed?" I said, trying to force back the tears.

"You'll understand someday," he said quietly. He pulled his glasses back on. "It's for your own good."

"No!" I screamed. "No! How can it be for my own good? You know I don't want to live in Chicago. I have to be near the woods. And what about my school? And all my friends? I can't just leave them because you have some kind of stupid secret!"

"Laura—" Dad raised a hand to silence me. "I'm your father. I have to do what's best for you. Believe me, I don't want to send you away. I love you more than anything, but . . ."

I pressed my hand over my mouth to hold back a sob.

I can't believe he is saying this, I thought, unable to stop my whole body from trembling.

"Okay, okay," I finally choked out. "I won't go near the shed. I promise. And I won't ask any more questions. No more questions about your work."

Dad squinted at me. "You promise?"

"Promise," I said.

But there was no way I was keeping that promise!

I'm going to learn his secret, I decided. I'm going to find out what's the big deal. What's so secret that he'd send his own daughter away?

I'm going to find out the truth.

CHAPTER 7

I went to bed a little after eleven. But I couldn't fall asleep.

I was too hurt to sleep. Too hurt and frightened and angry—all at the same time.

I reached for the phone on my night table and called Ellen. "Hello." Her voice was groggy with sleep.

"Did I wake you?" I asked.

"It's okay." She yawned. "What's wrong? You sound terrible."

I told her about what Dad had said to me. "I can't sleep," I whispered. "Every time I shut my eyes, a new horror scene appears in my mind. I keep picturing my dad in his white lab coat. Holding a helpless little animal in one hand and a huge hypodermic needle in the other. Injecting little animals with strange chemicals. Making them whimper and howl."

"But your dad is a vet," Ellen said. "He gives shots to animals all the time."

I stared up at the shadows on my bedroom ceiling, my mind spinning. "But it's different now," I said. "He won't tell me what he's doing. What kind of experiments would have to be a secret—from his own daughter?"

"I don't know. But your dad wouldn't hurt a fly. He could never torture an animal. It's impossible."

"Ellen, he lost his job at the animal hospital. Maybe it was because he was doing something wrong," I said.

"You don't know that," she argued. I knew she was trying to calm me down. But nothing she said made me feel better.

I finally let her go back to sleep. Then I closed my eyes and fell asleep, too—but not for long.

A low rumbling sound floated in through my open bedroom window and woke me up.

I glanced at my clock radio. A little before two in the morning.

Rubbing my eyes, I crept to the window and gazed out at the woods. Darting lights flickered through the trees.

I forced back a yawn and stared hard. The lights swept slowly back and forth, floating eerily like ghosts. A shiver ran down my back.

There are no roads in the woods. And no other houses for nearly a mile. Who could be out there?

I'd better wake up Dad, I thought. I turned away from the window.

No. I changed my mind. I'm not going to wake him up. I don't really want to talk to him now.

But I had to find out who was out in the woods. I pulled on the jeans and tank top I'd worn during the day. A few seconds later I opened the kitchen door and stepped outside.

Clouds drifted across the sliver of a moon. A shifting wind made the grass bend first one way, then the other. Like ocean waves, I thought. It was a warm breeze, but it sent a chill down my back.

I carefully shut the door, listening for its soft click, making sure it was closed. Then I trotted across the lawn toward the woods.

I searched the trees for the lights. But they had vanished. The rumbling sound had also stopped.

"Weird," I muttered.

I stopped halfway across the yard and listened. Silence now. Silence . . .

Except for a low cry.

A sad whimper.

I turned. The cries were coming from the shed.

The shed. I had to see what was inside it. This was the perfect time.

Dad kept a padlock on the door. But I knew where he hid the key. I crept back into the kitchen and pulled the key from the little cup where Mom used to keep her Sweet'n Low packets.

Then I sneaked back outside. I felt a chill of fear as I stepped up to the shed. I could hear the animals inside, groaning, crying. It sounded as if they were pleading with me to rescue them.

"I'm coming," I whispered.

But I wheeled away from the door when I heard another sound.

A low growl. And then the pounding *thud* of heavy footsteps.

Running. Running rapidly toward me.

I was too startled to move. I froze as the big creature appeared from around the side of the shed.

It took a powerful leap. Leaped high. Caught me at the shoulders.

And knocked me hard to the ground.

CHAPTER 8

"Georgie!" I cried. "Get off! Get off me!"

Tail wagging furiously, the big dog pinned me to the ground and licked my face. His hot breath steamed my cheeks. I was laughing too hard to roll away from him.

"Georgie—stop!" I pleaded. "Are you lonely out here? Is that the problem?"

Finally I pushed him away. I sat up and wiped the thick slobber off my cheeks.

A light washed over me. I turned to the window and saw the kitchen lights on. The back door swung open. Dad poked his head out. He held his pajama bottoms up with one hand and squinted into the yard. He didn't have his glasses on.

"Laura?" Dad called, his voice clogged with sleep. "What are you doing out here in the middle of the night?"

"There were lights," I said. "In the woods. And I heard some kind of rumbling sound. I—I wanted to see what it was."

Dad scratched his forehead. His graying hair was sticking out all over his head. "You were probably dreaming," he said, frowning.

"No. It was real," I insisted. "The lights were moving around the trees, and—"

"Come inside," he said. He squinted at me. "You weren't trying to sneak into the shed, were you?"

"No. Of course not," I lied. I had the padlock key wrapped tightly in my fist.

For a moment his stare turned cold. I felt as if his eyes were stabbing me. "Come inside," he repeated. "I don't want to hear about lights in the trees. I'm tired."

I sighed and slumped into the house. I could see there was no point in trying to talk to him.

Once Dad went upstairs I slipped the key back into its normal place. I glanced out the kitchen window and stared at the shed. I could still hear the mournful cries. Suddenly I knew where I could find some answers.

The animal hospital.

I'll go see Dr. Carpenter at the animal hospital tomorrow, I decided. I know she and Dad aren't talking, but that doesn't mean I can't talk to her.

She'll tell me the truth about Dad. I know she will.

• • •

After school the next day I loaded up my back-pack, pushed my way through a crowd of kids, and ran out the front door of the school building.

It was about a two-mile walk to the animal hospital, and I wanted to get there before Dr. Carpenter left for the day.

The animal hospital was tucked in a cul-de-sac at the other side of the woods. It was an enormous two-story white stucco building with a steeply sloping red roof.

It had started as a small, square building and had quickly grown. Now it had endless wings, annexes, and research labs, stretching in all directions into the woods.

Inside, it looked more like an old hotel than a hospital. The long halls twisted and turned and seemed to stretch for miles. The doors were made of black oak and creaked when you opened them. The walls were painted dark green. A crystal chandelier hung over the waiting room, which was furnished with old brown leather armchairs and sofas.

Since it didn't look like an animal hospital, it was always surprising to hear the barks and yowls and chirps of the patients.

I had seen the operating rooms a few times when I visited Dad. They were white and bright and sparkling clean. And the research labs were also very modern and medical looking.

As I stepped into the waiting room, a flood of memories swept over me. I remembered so many visits here. And several really upsetting scenes. . . .

I remembered an adorable white-and-brown cocker spaniel puppy that had been hit by a car. And a bright red-and-blue macaw that had an ear of corn stuck in its throat. And two huge yellow dogs who started a snarling, raging fight in the waiting room, clawing each other until the carpet was puddled with blood.

The waiting room was empty now. I glanced at the clock above the reception desk: a little after four-thirty. A young woman sat behind the desk, shuffling through folders.

I asked to see Dr. Carpenter and told her my name. She picked up the phone, pushed a few buttons, and muttered into the receiver.

A few seconds later Dr. Carpenter came sweeping into the room, her white lab coat flying behind her. "Laura! How nice to see you!" she cried and wrapped me in a hug. "How are you? I've missed you so much!"

I hugged her back, taking in her pretty blond hair, her bright green eyes that always seemed to catch the light, and her warm smile. I missed her, too.

I remembered sometimes when I was angry at Mom, I secretly wished that Dr. Carpenter was my mother instead.

I glanced behind her, where a quarter, a dime,

and a penny, mounted on black velvet and set in a small silver picture frame, hung on the wall. It made me smile. It reminded me of Dr. C.'s first day at the animal hospital, four years ago.

Georgie had swallowed some change I had dropped on the kitchen floor, and he got really sick. Dr. Carpenter operated, and it was a great success! She framed the change—because it was from her very first patient.

Dr. Carpenter laughed and twirled me around, as if I were still a little girl. "Laura, did you stop by just to say hi?"

I hesitated. "Well . . . no." My smile faded. "I really wanted to talk to you. I mean, if you have time."

I suddenly felt nervous. Could I really ask her to tell me the truth about Dad?

"I seem to have plenty of time," she replied. She gestured around the empty waiting room. "I've been spending more and more time in the research lab. Kind of frustrating. But it's important."

She put a hand on my shoulder and guided me through the door, down a long hall with closed doors on both sides. Her office stood at the end of the hall. She gestured for me to take a seat in a low blue arm-chair in front of her desk.

The desk was glass, clean and uncluttered except for one stack of papers and folders, and a telephone. The walls were covered with framed photos of animals, some of the pets she had cared for.

Dr. Carpenter slid gracefully into the desk chair and swept her blond hair back over her shoulders. Then she leaned across the glass desk and smiled at me.

"This is such a surprise," she said. "I'm so happy that you came to see me. What did you want to talk about, Laura? Is it boy trouble? Something you can't discuss with your father?"

I laughed. I'm not sure why. The laugh just burst out.

"Do you get to talk to your mother much?" Dr. Carpenter asked. Elbows on the desk, she rested her head in her hands, studying me with those intense green eyes. "How is she doing?"

I shrugged. "She calls once a week. And I visit her a lot," I said. "But she's so far away. It's not like having a mom who's always there for you. . . ." My voice trailed off.

Dr. Carpenter frowned. "I know what you mean. Well, how is Ellen? Who is she in love with this week?" Dr. Carpenter laughed.

"Last week it was Steve, the tennis player. This week—I'm not sure." I laughed, too.

"So what are you and your dad up to these days? You two still making up Scrabble words? Still taking long walks in the woods?"

I took a deep breath. "We don't really play Scrabble all that much. We hardly do anything together lately."

My throat suddenly felt so dry. I coughed. "He's— I don't know—different lately."

Dr. Carpenter's eyebrows went up. "Different? What do you mean? How is he different?"

"Well . . . he's very quiet and . . . angry. He hardly talks to me. He—he spends a lot of time alone, working in the shed."

"Hmmm. That doesn't sound like your dad at all. What is he working on?" Dr. Carpenter asked.

"I don't know. He won't tell me," I replied.

Dr. Carpenter reached across the desk and squeezed my hand. "Laura, he's probably just out of sorts. Leaving a job isn't easy. You have to give him time."

I swallowed hard. "I . . . wanted to ask you about that. Why . . . why *did* my dad leave?"

Dr. Carpenter released my hand. She leaned back in her chair and sighed.

"Please tell me," I pleaded. "Why did my dad leave the animal hospital?"

CHAPTER 9

"I had to let him go," Dr. Carpenter said finally.

I gasped. "You mean—you fired him?"

She sat up straight. Her cheeks reddened. "Well . . . that's not really the right word. I had to let him go because—"

"Why?" I interrupted. "Why?"

She swallowed. "It's hard to explain, Laura. We . . . had different goals. We wanted to take our research in different directions."

I let out a deep breath. Different goals, I thought. That seemed okay.

Suddenly I felt all the tension leave my body. It was good to have someone to talk to. I knew coming here was the right thing to do.

I sat back in my chair. "What kind of work is Dad—" I started to ask another question, but the phone rang.

"Sorry," she said, making a face at the phone. She picked up the receiver and talked for two or three minutes. "No, you shouldn't bathe him," she kept saying. "Keep the fur dry. I know, I know. You'll have to put up with the smell. No. You shouldn't bathe him."

After a few more minutes she hung up the phone and stood up. "I'm sorry, Laura. I'd better get back to work. But come back anytime. Really. I mean it. I've missed you."

We said our goodbyes and I left.

Outside, heavy clouds had rolled over the sun, and the air had turned cold. Wisps of fog floated low to the ground.

Visiting Dr. Carpenter was a good idea. But I still felt so confused. I wasn't any closer to finding out why Dad was acting so strange.

When I reached home, I headed to the shed. I put my ear to the door. Quiet. Dad wasn't in there. I yanked hard on the lock.

"You won't get it open that way."

I jumped back in surprise as Joe jogged out from the woods.

He grinned at me. "I think a key would work better."

I laughed. I was glad to see him. He looked really cute in baggy denim shorts and a faded red T-shirt.

This time I'm definitely going to invite him to the birthday party, I decided. "What are you doing here?" I asked.

He shrugged. "I was exploring, you know. I spotted

the back of the house from the woods, but I didn't know it was yours."

He grinned and swept back his long hair with both hands. "You should have come to the pond today. I saw a whole family of deer there."

I rolled my eyes. "Of course. The deer come when I'm not there. They don't want me to get an A."

We both turned when we heard a growl coming from the trees.

A dog's growl.

Georgie loped to the edge of the clearing. He stopped a few feet from us and raised his head, big, brown eyes studying us suspiciously.

"Hey—where'd you come from, boy?" Joe asked.

"Georgie!" I called. "What were you doing in the woods?"

Georgie's tail began to wag. He lowered his head again and trotted up to us. Dead leaves clung to the fur on his side.

I reached to pull them off. Then I tried to hug him, but he pulled away. "Georgie, what's wrong?" I asked. "Aren't you glad to see me?"

Georgie bumped up to Joe and sniffed his khaki shorts, making loud snuffling sounds.

Joe laughed and jumped back. "Hey, stop! That tickles! You have a crazy dog, Laura!"

I bent down. "Georgie, what's wrong? Come over to me."

He pressed his wet snout against my arm and

sniffed hard. Then he began to sniff the legs of my jeans.

To my surprise, he let out an angry growl.

His back stiffened. He backed up, glaring angrily at Joe and me. Then he pulled back his lips and bared his teeth.

"Georgie—are you crazy? What's wrong, boy?" I cried. I turned to Joe. "He's the most gentle dog in the world. Really."

Joe took a step back. "Someone forgot to tell him that!"

"Easy, boy," I said to Georgie, still crouched down. "Easy now. What's wrong, boy?" I asked softly, soothingly.

The dog gnashed his teeth and began to snarl. Frightening, harsh growls from deep in his throat.

He lowered his head, eyes wild now, glaring up at us.

"Easy, boy . . ." I whispered. My legs suddenly felt rubbery and weak. "Georgie . . . it's me. . . . It's me. . . ."

Baring his teeth, Georgie opened his mouth in a terrifying growl. His fur bristled. His whole body tensed—and he leaped to attack.

CHAPTER 10

I didn't back away. I didn't move. I tried not to show how afraid I was.

Georgie stopped inches from me, snapping his jaws.

"Easy . . . easy," I whispered. "Good dog. You're a good dog."

Looking up, I glimpsed Joe, his face tight with fear. He had backed away to the edge of the clearing.

"Laura . . ." he called. "Get up. Get away from him."

The dog snarled furiously. His sides heaved in and out as he breathed, wheezing noisily. White drool ran down the front of his open snout.

"Good dog . . . good boy . . . Georgie, it's me. . . . It's me. . . ."

I couldn't crouch there any longer. My legs were trembling too hard. I couldn't hold myself up.

With a cry, I toppled backward. I landed hard. Sitting on the grass. I was practically eye to eye with the snarling creature.

His jagged teeth were inches from my face. Fat globs of drool ran down his open mouth and splattered on the grass.

"Please—" I cried. I raised both hands as if to shield myself from the attack.

Joe came rushing forward. "Get away! GET! GET!" he shouted. He swung both arms wildly and screamed at the top of his lungs.

To my surprise, Georgie stopped snarling. He gazed up at Joe and uttered a pained whimper. He appeared to deflate. All of his muscles went soft.

As I stared in surprise, the dog lowered his head and turned away from us. His tail was tucked tightly between his legs, and his ears went flat against his head.

Whimpering, he slunk away.

"Georgie? Georgie?" I choked out. I sat on the ground, frozen. My mouth was so dry, I couldn't swallow. My whole body shuddered.

"He's never acted that way before," I said, hugging myself tightly, trying to stop myself from shaking.

Joe helped me to my feet. "That was really your dog? What was his problem?" he cried.

"I—I don't know," I said. "Maybe he—he smelled something," I choked out.

"Smelled something on *us*?" Joe asked. "Like what?"

I shook my head. My heart stopped thudding

313

against my chest. I started to feel a little more normal. "Beats me," I said. "Maybe he smelled something on my jeans."

Joe squinted at me. "Your jeans?"

"Maybe he smelled something from the animal hospital on them. I was just there. The hospital always makes Georgie nervous—ever since his operation."

I told Joe about the time Georgie swallowed the thirty-six cents.

Joe continued to study me. He didn't say anything for a long moment. He appeared to be thinking hard. "What were you doing at the animal hospital?"

I pulled a spider off the sleeve of my T-shirt. "You have to promise not to tell my dad," I said.

Joe laughed. "I don't know your dad."

"Well, you have to promise not to tell anyway," I insisted. "I just went to see someone there. Someone I could talk to. About things."

Joe nodded. He shifted his weight from one foot to the other. "Hope your dog is okay," he said finally. "I'm—I'm glad I know where you live." He started walking toward the woods. Then he broke into a run.

The party, I thought. With all the fright over Georgie, I forgot about inviting him. "Hey, Joe—" I raced after him.

"Got to hurry!" he shouted back. "My parents hate when I'm late for dinner. Catch you later!" He vanished into the trees.

I didn't even get his phone number, I thought. How stupid is that?

I heard the crunch of leaves. Yes! He's coming back, I thought. I'll ask him to the party *and* get his phone number.

I stared and waited, but Joe didn't appear.

I listened. Silence now—and then a voice. A man's voice.

I walked deeper into the woods, following the sound.

Something dropped to the ground with a crash—and I gasped. I moved in closer—and saw it.

The front of a Jeep. It was painted green and brown, camouflage colors. It blended in with the trees perfectly.

An army truck, I thought.

I took a few steps closer. Now I could see the entire vehicle. It wasn't an army truck. It was a large, covered Jeep with a trailer behind it, also painted in camouflage.

The Jeep had huge tires and heavy bumpers. It was parked in the path that curved toward Luker Pond.

The trailer was nearly as big as a moving van, with the top poking up into the trees.

I stepped cautiously closer. The driver's door on the Jeep was hidden by a tree trunk, so I couldn't see if anyone was inside.

As I drew closer, I heard a heavy *thump thump*.

Startled, I flattened my back against a tree.

Thump thummmmp.

Something in the trailer was beating against the trailer's side. Or kicking it. An animal.

I gasped when I heard the cry. A pained cry.

Thump thump thummmp.

It kicked again, uttering another low cry.

I stopped and stared, listening to the creature struggle.

Why was this vehicle out here in the middle of the woods?

And why was there an animal howling inside it?

CHAPTER 11

I circled around the back of the trailer—and saw two men. Both wore blue denim overalls and pale blue workshirts. They were sitting on a large rock, chatting and chewing away on long submarine sandwiches.

One of them swatted a horsefly on top of his head. His head was shaved, completely bald. The other man was very fat and had a blue baseball cap pulled down over long, straggly coppery hair.

I started to walk up to them. I wanted to ask what they had in the truck.

But then I saw their rifles, propped against a tree trunk behind them.

I pulled back. A chill ran down my spine. It wasn't hunting season. Why did they have rifles?

THUMMMMP.

The thing in the truck gave a powerful kick.

I don't like this, I decided. I ducked behind a fat tree trunk before they saw me. I pressed against the rough bark and listened to their conversation.

"Why are we catching these things?" the bald one said.

"Beats me. Maybe the boss is starting a zoo," his partner replied.

I held my breath, listening.

"Finish eating," the fat one said. "We've got to get this thing out of here before he kicks a hole in the trailer."

"If anyone sees us, it'll be a little hard to explain," his partner agreed.

"Hey, you'd look good in prison gray!" the other one said, laughing.

Prison! They were doing something illegal.

They climbed to their feet.

Please open the trailer, I thought. Open it so I can see what's inside. I peeked out from behind the tree to watch them.

They didn't open the trailer. They picked up their rifles and tossed them into the Jeep. Then they climbed inside and drove away.

I waited until they were out of sight. Then I took off for home.

My mind whirled with everything that I had seen in the woods these past few days. The birds, the bats, the ugly finger, the flickering lights—and now these men.

The lights must have come from the truck. That much I could figure out. And the men could have upset the bats and the birds.

I've got to talk to Dad, I thought. I've got to tell him about those men and the rifles.

I ran all the way to the backyard. I started shouting halfway across the lawn. "Dad? Are you home? Dad?"

I charged into the house.

"Dad?"

No reply.

No note on the fridge.

I wheeled around and tore back outside to the shed. I pounded on the door with my fist. "Dad? It's me! Open up!"

Silence.

"Dad?"

I grabbed the door handle and started to pull.

"Oh!" I let out a gasp when I heard a loud *click*. Right over my head.

I looked up—and stared at a camera. A little black camera over the door. The kind of security camera they have in banks and stores.

It clicked again.

This is sick, I thought. So sick. I can't believe my dad put a camera up there. He has totally lost it.

I forced back a sob and backed away from the shed door.

I can't take this anymore, I thought. I have to see what's inside.

I ran back to the house. I found the key in the little

cup in the kitchen and carried it outside.

I stopped at the shed door.

Should I really do this? The key shook in my trembling hand. I backed away from the door.

Click.

A wave of disgust washed over me as the camera took my picture again and again.

I pulled open the padlock. Took a deep breath.

And stepped inside the shed.

CHAPTER 12

"Whew!" The sharp aroma of alcohol and other chemicals stung my nostrils. I clicked on the ceiling light. And glanced around.

Where were the animals? The back wall had metal cages stacked to the ceiling. But the cages were all empty, most of the doors hanging open.

I crossed to the worktable. One side was cluttered with jars and bottles. An endless, clear tube, filled with a bright red liquid, snaked like a Crazy Straw over the table and emptied into a large bottle.

Hypodermic needles lay scattered on the rest of the table. Long ones and short ones. Some empty. Others filled with a pink fluid.

An electrical generator hummed quietly in one corner. Metal dishes were stacked on top of it. An open tool kit bulged with wrenches and pliers. Next to that stood my father's desk, and behind it, cartons of books and papers, stacked three high, against the wall.

My eyes darted from one side of the room to the other. Nothing unusual here.

I walked over to the desk and saw a blue binder in the center. A desk lamp was aimed down at it. I leaned over the desk and studied the binder.

Did this have Dad's secret in it? Was this the record of what Dad was working on?

My hand trembled as I opened it. The pages were filled with typed formulas in blue and red ink.

After a long paragraph the word *FAILURE* had been typed in large letters. After another long paragraph the word DIED had been typed in red.

"The animals don't respond." This was underlined on the next page.

And then I read these chilling words: *"If we kill them, we will learn more. How many can we kill?"*

"Oooh," I moaned. Those words made me feel dizzy.

Dad was killing animals. This was too much. It was too much for me to handle.

I backed out of the shed. I closed the door and snapped the lock.

"I have to get away from here," I said out loud.

I had to go somewhere quiet and peaceful. Somewhere I could think.

A hummingbird buzzed above a tall reed that swayed over the pond. I raised my camera to my eye. The hummingbird darted to the water.

Click. I snapped the shutter. Then I lowered the camera around my neck and watched the hummingbird flit across the water.

Clouds drifted over the lowering sun, casting deep evening shadows through the trees. Every few minutes I felt cold raindrops on my head and shoulders.

But I didn't care. I *had* to come to the woods. I had to be here, where I felt at home. At peace. In the gentle quiet, surrounded by trees, the water shimmering darkly in front of me, I could catch my breath and think.

I turned and saw the tall, fat fern leaves shake on the other side of the pond. Must be an animal in there, I decided. I raised my camera. Come on, I silently urged. Show yourself. I need to finish my project.

I held my breath as a raccoon poked out from the fern leaves. Yes!

I didn't wait for him to come all the way to the water. I clicked once. Twice.

Gotcha.

My mood started to lift.

But then I heard voices behind me, from the other side of the path. And a loud *thunk thunk.*

The raccoon darted away. I spun around. Took a few steps toward the sounds. And saw the camouflaged Jeep and its trailer.

The two men walked along the path up ahead of

the trailer. Their rifles rested against their shoulders.

I placed my hands around my camera. Then slowly raised it to my face.

I'll take a few pictures of them, I decided. And show them to Dr. Carpenter.

I stepped out onto the path. Aimed it at the two men. And clicked off two quick shots.

The snap of the shutter echoed in the quiet woods.

The men spun around quickly. One of them pointed. "Hey—!" he called.

I knew I couldn't outrun them. I had to talk to them. "Hi," I said, trying to sound calm. "What's going on?" I motioned to the Jeep and trailer.

Thunk thunk thunnnnnk.

The men glanced at one another and didn't answer.

The fat one tugged at his cap and studied me. "You live around here? How come you're in the woods?" he asked. He had a hoarse, raspy voice, as if he had a sore throat or maybe smoked too much.

"It's not a good time to be in the woods," his partner said coldly. He had silvery gray eyes that reminded me of ice.

"I'm . . . working on a science project," I said. My hand trembled as I raised the camera to show them.

They both glared at the camera. "What are you taking pictures of?" the bald one asked.

"Plants and animals," I replied.

Thummmp thunnk.

"What kind of animals?" the bald one asked, frowning.

"Animals that use the pond," I said. "You know. Chipmunks . . . rabbits . . . raccoons . . ."

They both nodded.

I stared at the rifles on their shoulders. They knew what I was looking at, but they didn't say anything.

"You explore the woods a lot?" the one in the baseball cap asked finally.

I nodded. "Yeah. Sometimes."

"See anything strange?" he asked.

"No. Not really," I replied. I was dying to ask them what they were doing. And what they had in the trailer.

But before I could get the question out, they raised their rifles to their waists. And then they came at me, eyes so cold, expressions so hard.

Gripping their rifles, they moved quickly. Walking heavily toward me.

No chance to run.

"What—what are you going to do?" I whispered.

CHAPTER 13

"You'd better give us the camera," the bald one said, narrowing his eyes at me.

"Excuse me?" I gaped at him.

"We'd better have that film," he said. "If you don't mind."

"I *do* mind!" I cried.

But his partner moved fast. He grabbed the camera and tugged it off my neck.

"Hey—give me that!" I shouted. "I need that! That's mine!" I made a grab for it—and missed.

He snapped open the camera and pulled out the film cartridge. He yanked the film from the cartridge, exposing it to the sunlight. Ruining it.

Then he handed the camera back.

"You have no right to do that." I scowled angrily.

They turned and walked to the Jeep, carrying their rifles at their waists.

"What's in the trailer?" I shouted. "What's kicking so hard in there?"

They exchanged glances. The bald one swung his rifle onto his shoulder.

"It's a deer," his partner said.

"Yeah, it's a deer," the bald one repeated, his silvery eyes flashing. "We've got a sick deer in there."

"But—the rifles—" I blurted out.

"Tranquilizer guns," the one in the cap said.

"We're taking this deer to be treated," the bald one said. "He's in pretty bad shape. Something bad going on here."

"You should stay out of the woods for a while," his partner warned. "Yeah. And don't take pictures. It's dangerous."

Was he threatening me?

I watched them climb into the Jeep. The bald one started the engine. The Jeep roared and sent a cloud of black exhaust up to the treetops. Then it rumbled away, the trailer bouncing heavily behind it.

I stood in the path, waiting to calm down. I clenched and unclenched my fists at my sides.

"Those two creeps are liars," I said out loud.

That wasn't a sick deer in that trailer. How could a sick deer kick that hard if it was tranquilized?

Those men were definitely lying.

I jumped over a jagged, white rock and started along the path to home. I had walked only a few steps when I saw a little creature, half-hidden by a thick tuft of grass.

It looked like a newborn pig. It had tiny, round

black eyes and a cute pink snout.

It can't be a baby pig, I thought. There aren't any pigs in these woods. I leaned down to get a closer look. Are you a wild pig? You must be some kind of runt!

The little creature let out a squeak—and jumped into my hand.

I cried out in surprise. I nearly dropped it.

It sat in my palm, staring up at me with those cute, little black eyes.

"Wow. You're a friendly guy," I said to it. I raised my palm to study it. "I'm glad you're not afraid of me. I wish I had something to feed you."

It tilted its round head to one side, as if it understood me. It squeaked again, twitched its pink snout, and opened its mouth. I was startled to see two rows of sharp, pointed teeth.

I really have to photograph this guy, I thought. But I don't have any film. I think I'll bring him home with me and take his picture there.

He jumped again. Onto my shoulder.

A second later I felt a sharp stab of pain in my neck.

"Owwww!" I uttered a shocked cry as the creature clamped its teeth into my throat.

"Hey—OWWWW!" I gripped its back and struggled to pull it off me.

But the pain made me stop.

The pain . . . the pain . . .

It shot down my whole body.

The teeth were so deep—and shut so tightly—if I pulled the creature away, I'd tear a hole in my throat!

"Noooo!" I moaned, gripping the animal, squeezing it, struggling to remove it.

Warm liquid trickled down my neck. My blood!

I heard a lapping sound. Sucking and lapping.

The pain throbbed and pulsed.

The blood flowed down my neck.

The pointed teeth chomped and dug in hard.

The lapping and smacking sounds grew more rapid. Frantic.

He's drinking . . . I realized.

Drinking my blood.

CHAPTER 14

Gripping the tiny pig, I could feel it start to swell up. Its belly inflated, and I could feel liquid sloshing around inside.

My blood!

I opened my mouth in a scream of horror. "NOOOOOOO!"

The creature drank furiously, sucking hard, its teeth cutting my skin.

I screamed again. Again.

I dropped to my knees. I started to feel weak . . . so weak.

And then I heard a shout. The snap of twigs.

Dad stepped out from the trees, his eyes wild, his face twisted in fear.

He spotted me down on the ground. And then his mouth dropped open in surprise as he saw the creature at my throat.

"Hold still! Hold still!" he screamed.

He dived down beside me. Dropped to the

ground. Reached both hands for the creature.

"Don't pull it!" I shrieked. "It'll rip a hole—"

Dad clenched his teeth as he struggled to pry the little animal's jaws apart. His face darkened to red. "Yessss!" he cried finally.

He stumbled back. I saw the creature leap from his hand and scramble into the tall grass.

The pain still throbbed in my throat. I touched my neck and felt the warm blood trickling down my skin.

"Are you okay? Laura? Are you okay?" Dad kept repeating. He leaned over me and pushed my hand away so he could see the wound.

"I . . . don't know," I whispered.

"Here." Dad pulled a handkerchief from his back pocket and handed it to me. "Press this against your neck. It will stop the bleeding."

I held the handkerchief against my neck, and Dad helped pull me to my feet.

"Whoa," I murmured, shaking my head. I felt dizzy, kind of light-headed. "What happened? What *was* that?"

Dad shook his head. "I didn't really get a good look at it," he said. "I was so busy prying its jaws apart. . . . And then it ran off. How do you feel? Are you okay?"

"Okay, I guess. The pain is starting to fade." I let out a deep breath. "But it was so weird," I said, picturing the little animal jumping into my hand, then lunging for my neck. "It didn't just bite me. It was sucking my blood." I shuddered. "It was sucking my blood like a vampire."

"Let me see your neck." Dad took the wadded-up handkerchief and studied the wound.

"I don't like the way that looks." His brow tightened with worry. "We have to get to Dr. Davis right now."

Dr. Davis took us into his office immediately. He is a short, pudgy, egg-shaped man with a tiny head. He reminds me of an ostrich.

"Laura—what happened?" he asked, leading me to the examining table.

"Something bit her," Dad said. "A baby chipmunk, maybe. But I'm not sure. It was hard to tell because whatever it was, it had lost all its fur."

I stared over the doctor's shoulder at Dad. Why did he lie? No way that was a chipmunk. Why didn't he tell Dr. Davis that it was a strange little pig?

Dr. Davis examined the wound. "It could have been a diseased animal. Maybe rabid," he said softly. "Did it look rabid?" the doctor asked.

"I'm sorry," Dad answered. "It ran off. I just don't know."

"Rabies shots are very painful," Dr. Davis said. "I'll rush your blood sample to the lab before we start with shots. I'll have the results by tomorrow morning at the very latest. In the meantime, I'll give you a prescription for strong antibiotics. Start taking them right away."

Rabies. My stomach tightened. Please let the blood tests be okay, I thought. I watched Dr. Davis prepare a needle and thread to stitch up the wound.

I closed my eyes and pictured the animal that bit me. I saw its pink body. Its little piglike snout. It was not a chipmunk, I thought. It was definitely not a chipmunk.

A short while later Dad and I crossed the parking lot to the car. "How does it look?" I asked. "Do I look like Frankenstein now?"

Dad ran his fingers gently over my neck. "It should heal without much of a scar," he replied. "It might itch after a while. Try not to scratch it, okay?"

"Yeah, sure," I muttered.

"Do you have any symptoms at all?" Dad asked as we reached the car. "Do you feel at all strange or sick?"

I shook my head. "No, I feel okay."

I climbed into the car and waited for him to slide behind the wheel. Dr. Davis had given me some painkillers, but my throat still ached.

"Dad, why did you tell Dr. Davis it was a chipmunk?" I asked. "It didn't look like a chipmunk."

Dad started the engine and backed out of the parking space. "I didn't see it very well. And without its fur, it was hard to tell what it was."

"But it looked like a pig," I said. "It had a snout. It didn't look like chipmunk at all. Why didn't you say it looked like a pig?"

Dad turned to me. "It was simpler, Laura. That's all. It doesn't really matter. We'll get your blood tests and find out what to do next."

I swallowed and stared out the window. We drove for a while in silence. "I hate to say it, but I'm a little afraid to go back in the woods," I confessed.

"Don't worry about that," Dad said. "You won't be back in the woods for a long while."

My mouth dropped open in surprise. "Excuse me? Why not?"

"Why not?" Dad raised his eyebrows. "You're the one seeing vampire pigs! Do *you* think the woods are safe right now?"

"But—but—" I started to protest.

"But what, Laura?" Dad shook his head. "We don't know what bit you. Whatever it was, it could be rabid. And we know it's dangerous. Aren't those enough reasons?"

I could see there was no point in arguing. I turned away from Dad and stared out the window the rest of the way home.

As soon as we reached our house, I ran up to my room and slammed the door. I dropped facedown on my bed and buried my face in the pillow.

I *have* to go into the woods, I thought. He can't keep me out. He can't!

A short while later I heard Dad's voice downstairs. He was talking to someone on the phone. I climbed out of bed and pulled my door open a crack.

"She seems to be fine," he said.

Who was he talking to? Dr. Davis?

"By tomorrow. We'll have the blood tests in the morning," Dad said.

Not Dr. Davis.

I walked to the top of the stairs. I could hear Dad so clearly now. I could hear what he said next—the cruelest, most hurtful words I'd ever heard in my life.

"Can you take Laura for a while? A trip to Chicago right now would help. I really have to get her out of here."

CHAPTER 15

I called Ellen right away. And in a trembling voice begged her to come over.

She and Stevie Palmer had made up, and she was supposed to go biking with him and a couple of other guys. But she said she'd tell them to go without her.

A few minutes later she showed up. I pulled her up to my room. "Laura, what's wrong?" she asked, dropping onto the edge of my bed. "You sounded so weird on the phone."

"It's Dad. He's sending me away!" I cried. "I—I heard him on the phone. With Mom. He asked if Mom could take me. He—he said he had to get me out of here."

Ellen jumped to her feet. "I don't believe it." She shook her head. "He can't send you away just like that. What's wrong with him?"

"I—I don't know," I stammered. "Maybe it was because of the animal that attacked me." I told Ellen about the little pig. Then I showed her my neck.

"Oh, gross." She gasped. "Does it hurt?"

"No, but Dad said I can't go into the woods anymore. He thinks it's too dangerous," I said, running my fingers over the raw stitches. "But then he called Mom and . . . and . . ." A sob burst from my throat.

"How could he do that?" I wailed. "He just wants to get rid of me. He called my mom without even talking to me about it. How could he, Ellen? He doesn't even care about me anymore."

Ellen hurried across the room and hugged me. "Of course he cares about you," she said. "He was upset that you were attacked. He just wants you to be safe. That's why he called your mom. But he's not serious. He'd never send you away."

"He's serious," I insisted. "He's very serious, Ellen. He wants to get rid of me."

I took a deep breath—and a new thought came to me. One that sent a shiver down my spine. "I know why he's doing this. He checked the film in his camera on the shed. He saw that I was in there."

"Whoa. Slow down." Ellen raised a hand. "Your father has a camera on the shed now?"

I nodded.

"And you went inside? What was in there?" She asked.

"His instruments and stuff. That's all," I told her. I didn't want to talk about the journal I had found. I didn't know if my father was killing animals or not. And I didn't want to say anything to Ellen until I was sure.

337

"What about the animals? What about the one we heard howling?" she asked.

"There weren't any animals inside. I don't know what happened to them," I said.

I plopped down on my bed. "I'm not going to Chicago. I'm not!" I declared.

Ellen's chin trembled. "I sure hope not," she said softly. I could see she was really upset, too. But then a smile crossed her face. "At least, not until after my birthday party!"

We both laughed.

She always knows how to make me laugh.

"I have to make him change his mind," I said. "And the only way I can do that is to find out what is making him act so strange. If only—"

I stopped when I heard a sharp cry from outside.

We both turned to the open window.

"What was that?" Ellen asked.

A horrifying howl rang out. A shrill cry of pain.

And then I heard a different sound.

An animal screech.

I dived for the window and peered out into the evening darkness.

A hunched figure darted toward the woods. I could see it loping away on four legs. It was about the size of a large dog.

As it reached the edge of the woods, it stopped— and I gasped. It stood up. Stood on two legs—and charged into the trees.

My eyes searched the backyard—
And on the ground . . .
. . . on the ground . . .
Lying on his side on the ground . . .
"Georgie!" I screamed. "Oh, no! Georgie!"

CHAPTER 16

Ellen and I flew out of my bedroom and down the stairs. I pushed open the kitchen door and tore across the grass.

"Georgie! Are you okay?" I cried.

The poor dog lay on his side whimpering. His legs twitched. His chest heaved up and down.

"Georgie? Georgie?"

I dropped beside him. I started to pet his head. His eyes rolled crazily. His tongue fell limply from his mouth.

"Ohhhh. Look. His leg," Ellen moaned. "Ohhhhh. Sick."

I followed her gaze. Georgie's leg . . . oh . . . Georgie's leg . . .

The creature had practically chewed it off.

The fur had been ripped away. Chunks of flesh had been torn off. Blood flowed onto the grass. I could see veins pulsing in the chewed-up mess, and a white bone poked out.

My breath caught in my chest. I couldn't stop myself. I started to gag. I could feel my dinner lurch up to my throat, and I struggled to choke it back.

I forced myself to turn away from the horrifying wound. "Georgie," I whispered, petting his head softly. "You'll be okay. You'll be okay."

The dog whimpered softly, too weak to raise his head from the grass.

I looked up to see Ellen running, bringing my dad, pointing furiously to Georgie. "He was attacked!" I shouted to Dad. "His leg—it's pretty bad."

Dad's mouth dropped open when he saw the chewed-up leg. "He's losing a lot of blood. I'll slow the bleeding." Dad took off his T-shirt and shredded it.

"Laura, go in the house and get the bandages," he said as he wrapped Georgie's leg in a strip from his T-shirt. "We'd better get him to a vet—fast. He's going to need surgery on this leg."

Dad and I carried poor Georgie to the van and set him down gently on the backseat. He stared at us with those big, dark eyes and didn't move. We were covered in blood.

"I'll call you later," I told Ellen. I climbed into the van beside Dad.

"Hope he's okay," Ellen said, shaking her head sadly. Her eyes glistened with tears. "Call me!"

As Dad backed the van down the driveway,

Georgie whimpered softly behind us.

"I think I saw the animal that attacked Georgie," I said.

"What was it?" Dad kept his eyes on the road.

"Well, I'm not really sure. It was too dark to see clearly. But it was about Georgie's size—" I told him.

"Well, that could be anything," Dad interrupted.

"I know," I said. "But here's the weird thing. It was running on four legs. And then it stopped and stood up, and ran into the woods on two legs."

Dad swallowed. "Two legs?" He didn't take his eyes off the road.

"Yes. Isn't that strange?"

Dad didn't reply.

I glanced out the window. Most of the houses we passed were dark. Georgie cried softly in the backseat.

"Hey, wait!" I cried. "This isn't the way to the animal hospital! Dad—turn around!"

"I'm not going to the animal hospital," Dad said softly, still avoiding my stare.

"But—but—" I sputtered.

"There's a good place in Walker Falls," he said. "I know the doctors there. They will—"

"Walker Falls? But that's two towns away!" I shrieked.

"It's a good place," Dad insisted. "They're experts at this kind of surgery."

"But, Dad—"

Finally he turned to me. To my shock, his eyes were cold. His expression remained hard. "Don't argue with me, Laura. I know what I'm doing."

"Okay. Fine." I sighed. I turned away from him and stared out the window.

We drove the rest of the way in silence.

Dad won't go near the animal hospital, I realized. Even in an emergency like this one.

Why won't he go there? I wondered.

What did he do that he can no longer face Dr. Carpenter?

What horrible thing did he do?

CHAPTER 17

We had to leave Georgie in the hospital. The vet cleaned and stitched up the wound. But he wasn't sure if Georgie's leg could be saved. We'd have to wait and see.

When we got home, I couldn't sleep. I tossed and turned all night, thinking about Georgie, thinking about the weird animal that attacked him. So many strange things were going on in the woods.

I had to find out what was going on there. And I couldn't do it from Chicago.

My whole life suddenly seemed out of control. I was afraid now of the thing I loved most—the woods. And I was angry with Dad. Angry because he didn't trust me. Or confide in me. Angry because he wanted to send me away.

I was afraid of him, too, I realized. I didn't know my own father anymore. I was afraid of what he might do next.

After school I hurried to the animal hospital. Dr.

Carpenter greeted me in the waiting room. She looked really stressed. She had dark rings under her eyes, and her blond hair was unbrushed, falling in damp tangles.

Before I had a chance to say hi, she spotted the wound on my throat. "Laura, what happened? Did Georgie bite you?"

"No. I—I was bitten by a—" I didn't know what to say. I didn't know what had bitten me.

"What was it?" Dr. Carpenter asked.

"Well, it looked like a little pig. With really sharp teeth." I let out a nervous laugh. "I know it sounds crazy. . . ."

"Where was this little pig?" Dr. Carpenter asked. "Where were you when you got bitten?"

"In the woods," I told her.

"A little pig with sharp teeth running around in the woods. It does sound crazy, doesn't it?" Dr. Carpenter frowned. "What does your dad think?"

I let out a sigh. "I don't know. He told Dr. Davis it was a chipmunk. He just said that because it was simpler than trying to explain what it really looked like."

"Oh. Did your Dad see it, too?" she asked.

"I think so," I answered.

Dr. Carpenter leaned close to me and studied the wound carefully. She smoothed her fingers gently around the stitches. "That's nasty," she muttered. She raised her eyes to me. "Did your doctor give you a rabies shot? Or any kind of antibiotic?"

"We got my blood test results this morning. I don't need a rabies shot," I said. "He did give me antibiotics." And then I gasped. "Oh, no. Dad picked up the pills. But he forgot to give them to me."

Dr. Carpenter put her arm around my shoulder. "Don't worry. The wound doesn't look infected. But it is a little swollen. I think I should give you an injection to stop the swelling."

I had forgotten that Dr. Carpenter was a medical doctor as well as a vet. "Okay, but I guess I should check with my dad first," I said.

"Tell you what," Dr. Carpenter said. "I'll call your dad right now and ask his permission. Okay?"

"Well . . . yeah," I replied. "Thank you, Dr. Carpenter."

She disappeared for a few minutes, leaving me in the waiting room. When she returned, she had a smile on her face. "He apologized for forgetting the pills, Laura. He said it would be a good idea to give you the injection right away."

"Okay. Great," I said. I was trying to sound brave. I *hate* shots!

She led the way into the lab. Then she pulled some bottles from a cabinet and prepared the injection.

"How . . . how did my dad sound when you spoke to him?" I asked her.

"Fine." She glanced up at me. "Well, maybe a little

tired. Why? Is he not feeling well?"

"No. No. He's okay. Sort of," I said.

"Is he still upset about leaving the animal hospital?" she asked.

"I—I don't think that's it," I said.

"What is it, Laura? What's troubling you?" Dr. Carpenter sat down on a stool beside me.

"I have a feeling something happened here before Dad left. Something bad." I let out a deep breath.

"Something bad?" Dr. Carpenter asked, "What would make you think that?"

I didn't want to tell her about Georgie. If I told her that Dad refused to come here, she'd feel terrible.

But I didn't have a choice.

"Georgie was attacked the other night and Dad took him to Walker Falls. He wouldn't come here," I said in a rush.

Dr. Carpenter didn't say anything. She just nodded.

"Do you know why he wouldn't come here?" I asked.

She didn't answer. Instead, she stood up, rubbed alcohol on my arm with a wad of cotton, and raised the needle.

"OUCH!" I tried not to scream as the needle punctured my skin. But I couldn't hold it in.

Dr. Carpenter frowned. "That wasn't so bad, was it?" She dabbed cotton on it. "It should help the swelling."

Then she gave me a green pill, an antibiotic, to

take. She placed the rest of the pills in a small plastic bottle and handed it to me. "Be sure to take a pill every morning."

I clutched the vial in my hand. "But—what were you going to say about my dad?" I asked.

She sighed. "Laura, if your dad doesn't want to talk about what happened, it's not my place to tell you. I think he has to be the one."

She straightened her lab coat. "Why don't you come back tomorrow? I'll check your stitches, and we can talk some more then."

"Okay," I said. I started to the door. "Thanks."

"Laura—" Dr. Carpenter called after me. "Maybe you should stay out of the woods for a while."

I stared at her. She was saying the same thing as Dad!

No way, I thought. No way am I staying out of the woods.

I had too many questions.

And no answers.

The next afternoon I sat in my backyard doing my homework. I leaned against a tree, reading my English textbook. I never mind homework if I can sit outside and do it.

"Hey! What's up?" Joe walked across the grass toward me.

"Hi!" I dropped my book onto the grass and smiled. Joe was wearing black jeans and a gray

T-shirt, and he looked really cute!

"How's your dog?" he asked.

"Still in the hospital," I said, standing up. "The vet operated on him last night. We won't know for a while if he can keep the leg or not."

Joe's eyes bulged with surprise. "Huh? Your dog is in the hospital?"

"Isn't that why you asked?" I said.

He shook his head. "The last time I saw you, your dog nearly attacked you. Remember?"

"Oh, right." So much had happened since then. I told Joe about the horrible attack on Georgie.

Joe gasped. "You mean . . . they might cut the leg off?" He twisted a knot of his long hair between his fingers. "I'm sorry," he muttered. "That's such bad news."

"I know," I said. "But here's some good news." I took a deep breath. "I'm throwing a birthday party on Saturday for my friend Ellen. Can you come?"

There. I finally said it.

Joe hesitated for a moment. "Yeah, sure," he said. "Cool."

Wait till I tell Ellen he's coming to the party! I thought. This is awesome!

"Why don't you get your camera?" he said. "Let's take a walk to the pond."

"Great!" A few seconds later Joe and I were heading to the pond.

At first I felt nervous walking in the woods. But

we didn't see anything unusual, and it was really nice spending time with Joe.

We sat by the pond and talked and talked. I didn't see any animals to photograph, but I really wasn't paying attention. Before I knew it, it was close to dinnertime.

"See you Saturday." Joe stood up and started away, then turned back. "Hope your dog comes home soon."

"Thanks," I said. I watched him walk away, pushing tall weeds out of his path.

I should have asked him where *he* lives, I thought. I'll have to remember for next time.

Then I had an idea. I'll follow him home, I decided.

I turned and trotted along the path. I could hear Joe's crunching footsteps a little up ahead.

I slowed to a walk. I didn't want him to catch me following him. That would be *so* not cool.

The path curved and Joe came into view. He was walking rapidly, tapping a long stick he had picked up on the tree trunks he passed.

The path led beneath leafy old trees that bent low over the ground. The thick leaves blocked the afternoon sunlight and made the woods as dark as evening.

I kept far behind Joe, squinting into the dim light. He was jogging now, moving quickly through the deepening shadows.

I came out at the end of the trees, but I had lost him.

I gazed down the path. No sign of him. I turned and swept my eyes along the grassy clearing to my right. No. No Joe.

A rock wall stood to my left. It was as tall as me. Had he climbed over it? Where had he gone?

"I give up," I muttered. I turned and started back toward the pond. But I stopped just short of the trees when I spotted something in the clearing.

I took a few steps closer. And realized it was some kind of shack. A small, homemade hut, no bigger than a camping tent.

"Hey—is anyone in there?" I called.

No reply.

I made my way through the tall grass and stepped up to it. The walls were constructed of evergreen branches clumped together and tied with rope and bits of string. Sticks and fat leaves had been used to fill in holes the branches didn't cover.

"Anyone in there?" I called, softer this time.

Silence.

I leaned forward and poked my head through the opening in the leafy wall. It was dark inside, but circles of sunshine washed in from the top.

My eyes stopped on one of the circles of light—and I froze. And stared.

Stared at two hairy, leathery fingers on the hut floor.

And beside them . . . beside them . . . a small pile of bones . . . animal bones. Most of them had been picked clean. But some still had chunks of meat and fur clinging to them.

And in the corner . . . piled up in the corner, I saw animal heads. Even in the dim light, I could see them so clearly. Piled on top of each other. Rabbit heads, squirrel heads, a couple of raccoon heads, eyes staring blankly, glassily at me.

"NOOOO!" I screamed without realizing it.

What kind of creature lives here? What kind of beast builds its own hut and keeps dead animals inside it?

The whole shack trembled as I pulled my head out. I spun away. The animal bones, the heads, the milky eyes lingered in my mind.

I spun away and ran. Ran across the clearing. I was halfway to the trees when I heard the roar behind me.

The roar of an engine.

I swung around—and saw the camouflaged Jeep racing across the clearing toward me, the trailer bouncing hard behind it.

"STOP!" I screamed, waving my hands.

But the Jeep picked up speed.

"STOP!" I turned and started to run.

The engine roared. The Jeep plowed over small trees and weeds as it sped after me. Behind it the trailer rocked from side to side, so hard I thought it might flip over.

They want to run me down! I realized. They're not going to stop!

I leaped over a boulder and kept running. But the Jeep was catching up. I crossed the path, lowered my head, and ran.

I didn't remember the stone wall until it was too late.

No time to climb it. No time to run to the side.

I was trapped. Trapped against the wall.

I spun around and watched the Jeep race toward me.

I'm going to be crushed, I realized. I shut my eyes, gritted my teeth, and tensed all my muscles.

And heard the scrape of tires as the Jeep went into a wild spin.

I opened my eyes to see that it had stopped inches in front of me. I stared as the driver stuck his head out the window.

He stuck his head out—and I recognized him. And gasped. "Oh, noooo. You! It's YOU!"

I didn't believe it. How could this be?

"Dad!" I cried. "Wh-what are you doing in there?"

CHAPTER 18

I ran up to the side of the Jeep. "Dad? What are you doing here?" I cried.

His glasses glinted in the afternoon sunlight. I couldn't see his eyes. He scowled at me. His face was bright red.

"Get in," he growled.

"Dad—answer my question, I said.

"Get in," he repeated angrily. "I told you to stay out of the woods."

I stared at him. His expression was so cold, so angry, I barely recognized him.

"I'm taking you home," he said. "Get in the Jeep—now."

"N-not until you explain," I insisted. "What have you got in the trailer? What are you *doing* here, Dad?"

He uttered another growl. Then he shoved open the Jeep door and jumped out.

He grabbed my arm and started to pull me. "Get

in, Laura. I don't have time for this."

"Ow! You're *hurting* me!" I cried. I tried to pull free.

He tightened his grip. And dragged me around to the other side of the Jeep.

He has totally changed, I thought. He isn't the same person. He has turned into some kind of *monster*!

He forced me into the passenger seat and slammed the door.

My whole body trembled. I hugged myself to stop the shaking.

How can this be? I thought. I'm terrified. Terrified of my own father. . . .

The week passed slowly. I didn't feel very well. I felt tired and weak, as if I had the flu. The wound on my neck ached and throbbed.

Dad didn't mention sending me off to Mom again. My stomach felt twisted in knots as I waited for him to say something about it. But he never brought it up.

I was really looking forward to Ellen's birthday party, and I spent the week planning it. I wanted it to be a lot of fun—for Ellen and for me, too. I needed something to cheer me up.

I woke up Saturday, the day of the party, and ran to the window. Yes! The weather was going to be great. It was a sunny, warm day. The air smelled fresh and sweet. The green trees of the woods glowed like emeralds. It was the perfect day for a party.

Blue is Ellen's favorite color. So after breakfast I ran outside and covered the backyard with blue streamers and dozens of blue balloons. I hauled our picnic table to the center of the lawn and covered it with a blue tablecloth.

I even had blue icing on Ellen's birthday cake!

When Ellen arrived, she couldn't believe the backyard. "It's awesome, Laura. Awesome!" she declared. She gave me a hug, then hurried off to talk to two boys who had just arrived.

Up to the last minute Ellen had kept adding people to the guest list, then changing her mind and cutting them off.

Finally I just invited everyone from our class.

I cranked up the portable CD player and brought out trays of pizza. About twenty kids had shown up. They were laughing and kidding around and eating.

Ellen, surrounded by boys, flashed me a thumbs-up. I could see she was enjoying the party.

Where is Joe? I wondered. I kept waiting for him to arrive. I was dying for Ellen to meet him.

I checked to make sure there were enough Cokes. Then I brushed some flies away from the birthday cake.

When I looked up from the food table, I saw Dad crossing the lawn, making his way into the shed. His expression was glum. He kept his head down and didn't seem to notice the kids or the party.

"Dad—do you want some pizza?" I called.

He waved his hand, signaling no. Then he disappeared into the shed, quickly closing the door behind him.

I turned back to the party. I didn't want to think about Dad now.

Yes, he had given me permission to have the party in the backyard. "Just make sure no one goes into the woods," he said sternly. "I mean it, Laura. No one."

I sighed, remembering my birthday parties when I was little. We always had a scavenger hunt in the woods. Dad always set them up. He would hide things up in trees and under rocks, and sometimes even floating in the stream.

Dad was a lot of fun in those days, I thought.

I gazed sadly at the shed. Then, shaking away my unhappy thoughts, I turned back to the party.

"Time to cut the cake, everyone!" I shouted over the music. "Hey—who wants birthday cake?"

A few kids wandered toward the food table. Some girls were dancing in the middle of the yard. A bunch of guys were tossing a Frisbee around.

"Hey, Ellen—come cut your cake!" I shouted. I searched the yard for her. "Has anyone seen Ellen?" I asked.

A few kids looked around, trying to help me find her.

"She went off with Stevie," a boy called.

"Huh? Where?" I asked.

The boy pointed to the trees. "I saw them heading into the woods."

"Oh, no," I moaned. If Dad found out that kids went into the woods, he would stop the party!

I had to bring them back—fast.

I took off running across the backyard. "I'll be right back!" I called. I made my way onto the path and started to shout as I entered the woods. "Ellen? Hey, Ellen? Stevie?"

No reply.

I followed the path through a growth of tall weeds, over a fallen log. "Ellen? Stevie? Where are you guys?"

I walked all the way to the pond, then turned around.

How could she do this to me? I asked myself angrily. Doesn't she know how much trouble she's getting me into?

I wandered in circles, calling out their names. I became angrier and angrier as I walked.

"Stevie? Ellen?" I called. My eyes searched the trees. "Are you here?"

No reply.

A bird cawed. An ugly, raw sound, as if it had something stuck in its throat.

"Hey—if you're hiding, it isn't funny!" I yelled.

I heard footsteps. Fast, running footsteps through the trees behind me.

I spun around. "Ellen? Stevie? Is that you?"

"Hunnh hunnh." Animal grunts. Very close by.

I froze. My breath caught in my throat.

"Hunnnnh." A long, low grunt.

And then a high, shrill squeal. A horrible, frightening cry—like an animal in pain.

I ran toward the sound.

My heart pounding, I raced from tree to tree, searching frantically, frightened of what I'd find.

In front of me I saw a clump of evergreen shrubs shaking. A flash of red through the greenery. Then I heard a long, loud *ripping* sound. It reminded me of a Velcro shoe being torn open.

My heart skipped a beat as I moved closer to the shrubs.

I heard a moan, soft and weak.

And then I stopped when I heard the chewing. The crack of bone breaking.

Loud chewing . . . chewing . . . chewing . . .

I couldn't stand it anymore.

I had to see what was on the other side of the shrub.

With a pounding heart, I moved around the bushes, looked down at the ground—and opened my mouth in an endless scream.

A deer was sprawled on its side in the tall grass. Its head had been torn off. The head sat straight up a few feet from the body. One eye stared blankly at me. The other eye had been yanked out.

The body had been clawed apart. Pale white bones and bright red meat poked out through the torn fur. A swarm of flies already buzzed around the opening.

"It . . . it's half-eaten," I choked out.

I stared in horror at the deer. Most of the insides had been ripped out and devoured. The fur sagged loosely, like an empty bag.

"Oh, sick," I moaned, finally turning away. "Sick."

What kind of animal did this? There were no bears in these woods. So what was big enough and strong enough—and *hungry* enough—to do this?

And what if the deer hadn't come along? I thought.

I was so close to it. Would the animal have found *me* instead? Would it have ripped me apart and devoured me?

My whole body twisted in a violent shudder. I spun away from the dead deer. And realized that Ellen and Stevie were still out here. I had to find them. I had to make sure they were okay.

I circled back around the evergreen shrubs and found a path that curved towards the pond.

I started to follow the path when I heard the sound of footsteps again. With a frightened cry, I whirled around—and saw a man coming toward me, running fast. Eyeglasses glinted in the light.

"Dad!" I shouted. "Dad—what are you—"

I didn't finish my question.

As he drew closer, I gaped in horror at him. At the red stains all down the front of his clothes.

The red . . . the bright, wet red . . .

My dad—he . . . he was covered in blood.

CHAPTER 19

"The blood," I muttered.

I took a step back, my whole body tight with fear.

My dad stood hunched in front of me, breathing hard. "You promised, Laura. You promised to stay in the backyard."

"But, Dad—" I pointed. "The blood . . . What is that blood?"

He looked down, as if seeing it for the first time. He stared at it for a long moment. "I heard you screaming," he said finally. "I . . . I dropped every-thing and ran."

The blood stained both of his hands. I saw a patch of it darkening on his chin.

"I ran into a sharp tree branch," he said. "I . . . cut my chest, I guess. I didn't stop to check. I thought you were in trouble."

We stared at each other. I couldn't take my eyes off the bright, red blood. Still wet. Still so wet.

Did I believe his story?

I wanted to believe it. I really did. But I remembered the journal in the shed. *If we kill them, we will learn more. How many can we kill?*

Did Dad kill the deer?

No . . . no . . . please—no!

He pulled off his glasses and wiped them on the side of his pants. He squinted at me. "Are you okay? The screaming . . . are you hurt?"

I shook my head. "No. A deer. I heard a deer being attacked. By some kind of animal. It scared me."

I stared at my father. He couldn't have done it. He couldn't have ripped the deer's head off like that. He couldn't have, I told myself. No way. No way. No way.

Ellen and Stevie and all the other kids were waiting for me when Dad and I returned to the backyard. Dad slipped into the house while everyone gathered around me, talking all at once, smiling, relieved.

"Laura, where did you go?" Ellen asked. "We heard you screaming and—we were so scared."

"Where did *you* go?" I demanded. "I went looking for you—"

"Stevie and I were in the garage," Ellen said. "We were looking for another Frisbee."

"Someone told me you were in the woods," I said, sighing.

"Can we cut the cake now?" a boy shouted.

Everybody laughed.

We cut the birthday cake. It was a little melted and soggy from being left outside for so long.

The party broke up early. No one was really in the mood anymore.

"I'm really sorry," I apologized to Ellen for the hundredth time as she headed away with Stevie and two other guys. "I—I shouldn't have run into the woods like that."

Ellen hugged me. "It was a great party anyway. Oh, I forgot to tell you. Joe was here."

"Huh? When?"

"He showed up right after you went into the woods. But you weren't here, so he left. He's not bad. Kind of shy. But not bad."

I was so disappointed. Why didn't he stay? Oh, well. At least Ellen had finally met him.

After Ellen and the others left, I picked up some dirty paper plates and cups and carried them into the house.

But I couldn't finish cleaning up. I was too upset. And too confused. Dr. Carpenter said I could come back and talk some more—and that's exactly what I was going to do.

Dr. Carpenter knew something about Dad. Something she didn't want to tell me. But I had to make her tell me. I had to know.

I ran out the back door, letting the screen door slam behind me. Then I jumped on my bike and began pedaling hard, heading to the animal hospital.

I hoped she would be there. I really needed her help.

A few minutes later I jumped off my bike, letting it fall to the grass. Then I ran inside the building.

No one at the reception desk. I heard a radio playing down the hall. A few dogs were barking.

"Anyone here?" I called.

No answer. So I made my way to the main office. I pulled open the door. "Dr. Carpenter?" The lights were all on. I saw a cup of coffee and a half-eaten muffin on her desk. But no sign of her.

I'm not leaving this place without answers, I told myself. I can't live with all these questions about Dad. I'm afraid of him now. I can't be afraid of my own father.

I crossed the room to the wall of file cabinets.

I glanced back at the door. No sign of Dr. Carpenter.

I hurried to the file drawers. After a few seconds I found a drawer marked EMPLOYMENT RECORDS.

Yes! I thought. I pulled it out. The drawer was stuffed full. My hand shook as I started to shuffle through the files, searching for the one about my dad.

Finally I found one with his name on it. I lifted it out—and opened it.

Empty. The file was completely empty.

Someone had removed all of his records.

The file folder fell from my hand. I bent to pick it up.

And heard a startled voice from the doorway. "Laura! What are you doing?"

CHAPTER 20

I jumped to my feet. "Dr. Carpenter!" I gasped. "I—I'm so sorry."

Her blond hair gleamed under the ceiling lights. Her green eyes narrowed, studying me. "What are you doing here, Laura? What are you looking for?"

I didn't hold back. I told her everything I was worried about.

I told her about Dad locking himself in the shed day after day. I told her about the camera over the shed door. And about the strange howls and animal cries from inside the shed. I told her about the blood. I told her I thought Dad might be killing animals.

"I—I'm so worried about him, Dr. Carpenter," I said, unable to keep my voice from trembling. "I'm worried. And I'm *afraid* of him. And . . . and he wants to send me away. Can you believe it? *Can you believe he'd actually send me away?*"

She stared at me. "Wow," she muttered. "How awful. I don't believe it, Laura. I really don't. Your father is a good man, even if he . . ."

"Even if what? What is he doing?" I cried. "Do you know? Why did he leave his job here? You have to tell me! You *have* to!"

She sighed and settled into her desk chair. She motioned for me to sit across from her. "Okay. Since you're so upset, I'll tell you what happened," she said finally. "But it isn't a happy story, Laura."

I sat stiffly with my hands cold and wet, clamped tightly together in my lap. And I listened to Dr. Carpenter's story. . . .

"Your father and I were working together on some important genetic research with animals. But I began to feel that your dad was going too far. He became obsessed. He worked on the research day and night. And after a while he wouldn't tell me things he was working on. He had a lot of secrets.

"I began to suspect that he was taking the work in a different direction. I thought maybe he was doing experiments that were cruel to the animals."

I listened carefully, trying to understand what Dr. Carpenter was telling me. "What kind of research was he doing?" I asked. "What was he trying to find out?"

"We were trying to understand how genes could be used to fight viruses. By studying the genetic patterns of the animals, we hoped to change the genes and prevent disease—not only in animals, but in people, too. Do you understand what I'm saying?" she asked.

"I think so." I nodded. "And if animals had genes that could fight viruses, then you could figure out how to create virus-fighting genes in humans," I reasoned.

"Exactly!" Dr. Carpenter exclaimed. "It would be so exciting. A medical miracle!"

She sat back in her chair. "But your father started taking the research too far. I heard horrible howls coming from his lab. He wouldn't tell me what he was doing. It was all too disturbing." She let out a deep sigh.

"Your dad and I fought about it," she continued. "We talked about him leaving, but he promised to stop.

"Then one day I was looking for some of my research notes, and they were missing. No one knew where I kept my notes. No one but your dad.

"It was terrible. How could I work with someone I couldn't trust? So I had to ask your dad to leave. It was very sad. But I had no choice."

My mind spinning, I closed my eyes to think about everything Dr. Carpenter had said. And I pictured that little, whimpering animal in the shed. The one he was injecting with the big needle.

I could see my dad plunging the big needle into the squealing animal. And I knew it was all true. . . .

I jumped up. Spun away. And ran out of the room. Out of the animal hospital. I don't even remember if I thanked Dr. Carpenter or said goodbye or anything.

I grabbed my bike and tore out of there, the horrible thoughts raging in my head, whirling like a hurricane. Into the woods. I spent an hour or so wandering among the trees. It had always calmed me to be here. But not this time.

I didn't get home till long after dinnertime. Dad was locked in his shed. I was glad. I didn't want to face him.

I wasn't hungry, but I made a sandwich and took it up to my room. I picked up the phone a couple of times to call Ellen. But each time I changed my mind.

What could I say?

I went to bed a little after eleven and fell into a dreamless sleep. I was awakened a few hours later by a long animal howl. From outside.

I sat up, rubbing my eyes, tugging my sweaty hair off the back of my neck. I climbed out of bed and made my way to the window as another long, sad howl—a howl of pain—floated up from the woods.

Wisps of black cloud snaked over the moon. The trees bent and swayed in a strong breeze.

What is going on out there? I asked myself.

I dressed quickly. Grabbed a flashlight. And tiptoed down the hall. I heard Dad snoring lightly as I passed his room.

I glanced at the kitchen clock as I headed to the back door. Nearly three A.M.

Beaming the flashlight on the ground ahead of me, I crossed the back lawn and stepped into the woods. The moon kept appearing and then disappearing behind the rolling wisps of cloud. A heavy dew made everything sparkle like silver.

OWWWOOOOOOOOOOO.

I turned at the sound of the howl, my light sweeping over the trees. I stepped off the path and made my way toward the sound.

OWOOOOOOO.

So close. The sound was so close now.

The back of my neck prickled. I suddenly felt cold all over. My hand trembled, and I nearly dropped the flashlight.

I heard a door slam. I swept my light through the trees. It washed over the Jeep and trailer.

I sucked in my breath. Forced myself to stop shaking. I moved in closer.

Hiding behind a tree, I stole a glance into the driver's window. No one there. The Jeep was empty.

I heard a heavy *thud*, followed by another long, mournful howl. From inside the trailer.

I stepped closer, moving the light from side to side.

No one around.

The men must be out hunting other animals, I figured.

What did they have in there? It definitely wasn't a deer.

I'm going to find out, I decided. I'm not leaving until I finally find out.

OWOOOOŌO.

The howl grew even louder, more desperate. Did the creature know someone was out here?

My light swept over the back of the trailer until I found a long, silvery bolt on the back door.

I took a deep breath. Lowered the light. Reached for the bolt and tugged it hard.

It slid up easily, and the back doors began to swing open.

OWOOOOOOO.

The long, sad howl greeted me, along with a sour smell.

I raised the light. Aimed it into the trailer, focusing on the animal tied up, sitting on the floor.

I opened my mouth to scream—but no sound came out.

Was it an animal? *Was* it a real, living creature?

"Ohhhhhh." A horrified moan escaped my throat. The flashlight jiggled in my hand. I gripped it in two hands to hold it steady.

And stared . . .

Stared in shock and amazement at the ugly creature gazing back at me. Its body was huge, and piglike. But it had human arms and legs. It's skin was creamy colored but lined and leathery.

And its face . . .

I raised the flashlight, and the light trembled over its face. Its face . . . so ugly . . . so strange. . . .

A pig's face. Round and bald. A snout and two long teeth curling out over its chin. Pointed pig ears. But its eyes—they were human eyes . . . and they looked so sad.

It opened its snout and howled again. It pulled and strained against the thick ropes that held it down.

Staring at me with those sad, watery eyes as if pleading, it shoved its massive body against the wall of the trailer.

Shoved it again. Again. Its fat body shook like Jell-O.

"No," I whispered. "No."

I lowered the light and backed away. I reached for the door handle. I trained my light on the creature for one more look. I shuddered.

Part pig. Part human. Did my father create this beast? Is this what he was doing in secret?

Dr. Carpenter had told the truth, I realized. Dad was doing his own research. His own terrifying experiments.

I shoved the door shut. I was reaching for the bolt when I heard voices.

I spun around and saw two men step out of the trees. The same men I had met before.

Circles of light swept the ground in front of them. Then they both raised their lights to my face. They uttered angry, surprised cries.

I raised my hands to shield my eyes.

"Did she see it? Did she?" the bald one asked.

"Yes," his partner replied.

The bald one let out a low growl. "Grab her," he ordered. "Don't let her get away."

CHAPTER 21

The flashlight fell from my hand. I spun away from the lights in my face.

"She saw too much," one of them said. "Don't let her escape."

I started to run.

OWOOOOOOO. The creature in the trailer howled and heaved himself against its side, making the trailer bounce.

I glanced back to see the two men coming after me. Their lights danced on the ground as they ran.

I ducked my head beneath a low tree branch and dived into a clump of tall weeds. I forced myself to run faster, their angry cries ringing in my ears. So close . . . they were so close behind me.

I can't outrun them, I realized. And I can't see well enough to find a good place to hide.

My feet slid out from under me on a wet patch of mud. I fell hard, landing on my back.

I heard one of the men laugh. The beams from their flashlights swept over me.

I forced myself to my feet. Grabbed a fallen tree branch—and heaved it at them blindly.

I heard it thud to the ground.

The men were silent now, running after me. Closing in.

My side ached. My back throbbed from my fall.

They're going to catch me, I realized. I can't let them. I have to get to Dr. Carpenter. I have to tell her about the pig creature. If I can get to her, maybe we can stop Dad. Together we can stop him.

I scrambled over a low mound of flat stones. Then ducked into a string of tall evergreen trees.

"Where is she?" I heard one of the men ask. "Stop running! We just want to *talk* to you!"

Liar.

I huddled in the dark safety of a broad evergreen tree. But a few seconds later I heard their footsteps crunching closer.

I lowered my head and darted into a wide clearing.

A mistake. A terrible mistake. Now I had nowhere to hide.

"There she is!" I heard one of the men say. "I've got her now."

I saw their lights moving on the other side of the evergreens.

I started to run across the tall grass. But I stumbled over something. Something big and soft.

I bent down to see what it was.

"Ohhhhh." I groaned as I realized I was leaning over the dead deer. The ripped open, half-eaten deer.

The smell of rotting flesh rose up to my nostrils, sickening me.

The torn skin hung loosely over the remaining bones.

I looked up and saw the lights moving. The men were running toward me, pushing their way through the evergreen trees.

In seconds they would see me.

Where could I hide? No trees or rocks or shrubs in the clearing. How could I hide?

I took a deep breath.

I grabbed a flap of the deer's skin. I tugged it up. It felt heavy and wet in my hands.

The sour smell washed over me. I held my breath to keep from puking.

I pulled the skin flap up as far as it would go.

And I climbed inside the deer.

CHAPTER 22

The wet deer skin flapped against my body. As I hunched down, the putrid guts squished against the knees of my jeans. Bones jabbed me in the side.

I pulled the skin tighter around me, but it was slippery and I had trouble gripping it.

Flies buzzed above me. I could feel the moist guts seeping into my clothes.

I shut my eyes and held on tight, covered by the deer skin. The back of my neck itched, but I couldn't scratch it. Something wet and gloppy fell onto my forehead.

I realized I'd been holding my breath the whole time. My chest felt about to burst. I had to breathe. The thick, sour odor made me want to scream. My stomach heaved.

I'm inside a dead deer, I thought. My whole body started to shake. Inside a dead deer . . .

Above me I heard the crunch of footsteps. Voices. "Where is she? How did we lose her?"

"She didn't go far."

I struggled to calm my stomach. I tried not to breathe in the foul smell. But I couldn't hold my breath any longer. I took in a small gulp of air—and threw up.

"Ooooo," I let out a sick moan.

The sound of the footsteps came closer. I felt a hard *thud* and realized one of the men had kicked the deer corpse.

I clamped my mouth shut to keep from crying out.

"This deer looks like it was hit by a truck."

"What a stink. Did you forget your deodorant today?"

They both laughed.

"This deer wasn't killed by a normal animal," I heard one of them say. "Do you think our friend is nearby?"

"I wouldn't be surprised. He sure gets hungry, doesn't he?"

"Well, he *is* a pig! Ha ha!"

"We'll find him soon if he leaves us a trail like this."

I shivered under the disgusting blanket of rancid skin and fur. My whole body itched. My clothes were wet with deer guts. Wet from my own vomit. A new wave of nausea washed over me.

If only they would move on and let me get out of here.

But no. I heard more muttering. Then footsteps. Calls of hello.

Someone else had joined them. I struggled to hear their words. But they had moved farther away.

And then I heard a voice clearly. "Why did you call me?"

I gasped. The deer skin slipped from my hands. I grabbed it back. Struggled to remain silent.

The voice. I recognized it. I recognized it so well.

MY DAD.

Should I get up? Should I climb out of the deer corpse and run to my dad? He may be crazy, I thought. But he isn't going to let these men harm his own daughter!

I started to pull back the deer skin, but stopped when Dad spoke. "Why did you call me? What's the problem?" he asked.

"It's your daughter," one of the men said.

"Laura? She was here?"

"She opened the trailer. She saw it. She saw the creature."

"Oh, no," Dad moaned. "Why didn't you stop her?"

"We tried. But she gave us the slip. So we called you."

"She didn't go far," the other man said.

"Well, let's find her!" my dad cried. He sounded very angry. "Get her—before she ruins everything!"

CHAPTER 23

My own dad!

I froze, gripped with horror.

My own dad wanted to catch me now. He really is crazy, I thought. He really is a monster!

I heard their voices fade as they walked away. "Split up," Dad said. "We'll find her by morning."

Then . . . silence.

I didn't move.

I shut my eyes and tried to think.

I couldn't go home. Where could I go?

My own dad . . . My own dad . . .

I had to go somewhere. I had to find help.

I pulled myself slowly out of the deer corpse. My clothes were wet and stained. I tried to wipe the thick, smelly guts off my arms, off my forehead. I pulled a disgusting glob out of my hair.

Up ahead, I heard one of the men cough. I turned away quickly and hurried off in the other direction. My legs felt stiff. My back ached. Every time I breathed, I inhaled that disgusting odor.

Where was I going? I didn't care. I just wanted to get away from those voices. Away from those men. Away from my dad.

I moved as if in a daze, as if wandering through a bad dream. A few minutes later I crept into my backyard. I hadn't even realized I was heading home.

I listened at the shed door. Silent. Then I sneaked all the way around the house, peering into the dark windows.

Dad wasn't home yet. He was still out searching for me.

Feeling shaky and sick, I stepped in through the back door and hurried to my room.

"This is my house," I said out loud. "My house."

But I was no longer safe here. Because I lived with an enemy. I lived with a *monster*!

I tore off the disgusting clothes and shoved them into my closet. Then I took a fast shower, listening hard, praying my dad wouldn't return.

The warm water felt so wonderful. I wanted to shower for hours and shampoo my hair a dozen times. But I knew I had to get out of there fast.

I pulled on fresh jeans and a sweatshirt and ran out through the front door. I expected the night darkness to hide me. But the sky was a pink-gray now. Almost morning.

I headed straight for the animal hospital.

I walked silently through the woods, alert,

looking . . . listening for Dad and the men.

The morning dew made the ground soft and muddy. The pink morning sunlight sent down shimmering patches of color.

"Oh." I stopped when I heard the rustle of bushes. Saw them shaking. I wasn't alone.

I ducked behind a tree—and gasped with relief when I saw Joe. I ran from my hiding place. Ran up to him and almost hugged him!

"Joe!" A startled laugh escaped my throat. "What are you doing up so early?"

He stopped a few feet from me. "Oh—Laura. Hi! What are *you* doing here?"

"It's—it's kind of a long story," I said. I kept glancing around nervously, afraid my dad would appear at any moment.

"I—I've been up all night," I told Joe.

"Why?" Joe asked. "Are you okay?"

"I need help," I said. "Will you help me get to the animal hospital? Some men are trying to catch me and—"

I reached up. He had something green stuck in his hair. A caterpillar. I grabbed it.

"NO!" Joe screamed. To my shock, he jerked away from me—

—*and his hair came off in my hand!*

"OHH!" we both cried out at once.

I stared at the long, shiny black hair in my hand. A wig!

I turned back to Joe. His eyes were bulging with horror.

And his head—his head was entirely bald.

With two pointed, pink PIG EARS at the top!

CHAPTER 24

No!" I gasped.

Joe's mouth dropped open—and I saw his teeth—two rows of them. One was normal . . . human, the other was a set of pointed pig teeth.

"I'm sorry—" Joe whispered. "I didn't want you to know."

"I . . . don't understand," I choked out.

Joe's expression turned angry. "You'll understand soon enough!" he cried. "I'm the creature, Laura. I'm the creature that's been upsetting all the animals in the woods. Because I'm not normal."

He let out an angry cry. "I'm a *creature*! The bats, the dogs, the birds—they've been acting strange because of me. Because I'm a freak. Because they know I don't belong!"

"But—" I struggled to form words. I couldn't think straight. I couldn't take my eyes off his round, bald head, his pig ears.

"And sometimes . . . sometimes I get so hungry," Joe said, clenching his pointed teeth. "I do terrible things. I'm sorry, Laura. Really sorry."

"The deer?" I gasped. "It was you who chewed up the deer? And attacked Georgie? And . . . and that was *your* hut with all the animal bones and heads?"

He didn't answer. He snatched the wig from my hand. "I . . . I came to the woods. I just wanted some fresh air," he said, his voice trembling. "I just wanted to live free for a while. I'm so tired of being locked up . . . hidden away . . . a prisoner."

Then Joe spun away, breathing hard, grunting like an animal—and ran off.

I stood frozen, watching him vanish into the trees. I hugged myself, thinking hard. Trying to make sense of everything.

How did he become a creature like that? Did Dad do that to him?

Was my dad experimenting on humans, too?

I felt sick. Dizzy.

"Dr. Carpenter." I uttered her name out loud. I needed Dr. Carpenter to help me sort this all out.

The sun was still low over the trees as I pulled open the front door to the animal hospital. The reception room was dark. No one behind the desk.

I glanced at the wall clock. Only seven-thirty. Most of the staff wouldn't be here this early.

I heard the whimper of animals down the long hall. A cat cried. It sounded so human—like a baby.

"Is anyone here?" I shouted. "Dr. Carpenter? It's me—Laura!"

No reply.

Maybe she's in one of the research labs, I thought. I knew she sometimes came in early before the patients started arriving.

I started down the long hall toward the lab. Only a few of the ceiling lights were on. The endless hall with its faded walls, closed doors, and long shadows seemed creepy in the dim light. The old floors creaked under my feet. Animals whimpered and howled.

"Is—is anyone here?" I called. "Dr. Carpenter?"

I pulled open a door. I thought it led to a lab. But it was filled with animal cages and cartons of pet food.

I stopped when I thought I heard footsteps. "Dr. Carpenter?"

No. The sounds vanished. A dog barked. The floor creaked.

I turned a corner into another long hall of doors. "Hello!" I called. "Anyone?"

I pulled open another door. An empty lab.

I knew the research lab was somewhere here in the back. But which door?

I tried the next door. A shrill howl greeted me. Other animals cried out in the darkness. Cages rattled and shook.

I clicked on the light—and gasped. "No!"

I stood frozen in the doorway, gaping at the cages that lined the back of the lab. A wall of cages with animals inside . . . not animals . . .

Creatures.

Ugly creatures. All of them. Poodles with pointed pig ears, cats with pig snouts, monkeys, furless monkeys, covered in pink pigskin.

But the worst, the most hideous, were the creatures in the tall cages. Pigs with *human* bodies, *human* arms and legs. Pigs the size of children, standing on two legs. Pigs with long, dark human hair growing out of their heads.

The pig creatures grabbed the bars of their cages with human hands.

No. Some of them had *pig hooves* at the ends of their arms.

I stepped inside the room and stared at a creature with a short, stubby pig body—and long, brown hair falling over its face. A pig face—with human lips!

They opened their snouts wide and grunted and cried. They banged hooves against the cage bars.

I wandered closer as if hypnotized. What were these creatures? Why were they here?

A giant pig with human legs and arms and human ears banged its head against the bars, too big for its cage. Beside it I saw a tiny pig creature. A pig *with a long, horse tail*!

The tiny creature was sick on its side, lying in a

puddle of yellow vomit. I bent down to see him better—

And felt a strong hand grab my hair.

The giant pig creature!

Grunting loudly, he shoved his arms through the cage bars—and grabbed my head with two hands.

Unnnh . . . unnnh . . . unnnnh . . .

He rubbed his hot, wet hands over my face. Then lowered them to my neck—and began to squeeze.

CHAPTER 25

"Unnnh." I let out a choked groan. I struggled to pry the big hands off me.

But the creature was too strong. He pulled me up against the cage. His breath stank. His hands tightened around my throat.

The animals were bleating and crying, shaking their cages, jumping up and down. So loud . . . so loud my ears rang.

But as my breath was choked off, the sounds began to fade. The lights began to dim.

Just as my body started to sag, I heard a shout.

And then another angry shout. And the big hands slid off my neck. The grunting creature pulled its arms back into the cage.

I could breathe again. Rubbing my aching throat, I sucked in breath after breath.

And then I turned and saw Dr. Carpenter hurrying across the room. Her face twisted in shock. "What are you doing here?"

She didn't wait for me to answer. She put an arm around my shoulder tenderly and examined my neck. "Are you okay, dear? Can you breathe? That big guy can be dangerous."

"I . . . I . . ." My throat ached so badly, I could barely whisper. "Those creatures . . ." I finally said, waving my hand to the cages. "Did my dad make them all?"

Dr. Carpenter narrowed her eyes at me. "You shouldn't be here, Laura."

"But—but—" I sputtered.

"You should have listened to him," Dr. Carpenter said. "You should have stayed out of the woods."

She sighed. "And now he'll be coming here after you, won't he? He'll be coming to stop my work. He already rounded up some of the creatures that escaped from my lab. He's been scouting the woods, searching for them."

"I—I don't understand!" I cried. "Please—"

"Well . . . I can't let him stop me," Dr. Carpenter said angrily. "Not until I've found a cure."

I blinked. "A cure?" I asked. "A cure for what?"

She didn't seem to hear me. Her eyes were on the cages now. "These poor creatures are all failures," she said, shaking her head. "Look at them. Look what I've done to them. Poor things . . . But I have to succeed. I have to."

She turned back to me, her green eyes glowing. "Maybe you can help, Laura."

I felt a chill roll down my back. "Huh? Me?"

She grabbed my shoulder and brought her face close to mine. "You wouldn't mind sacrificing, would you? Would you, Laura? If it would save a life?"

"S-sacrifice?"

I realized I was trembling in terror. What was Dr. Carpenter saying? I couldn't understand her.

"Are these my dad's creatures?" I asked. "Are you trying to cure them? Are you going to make them normal again?"

Dr. Carpenter took a step back from me. She studied my face for a moment, then shook her head. "No, Laura. They're not your father's creatures. They're mine."

"Yours?" my voice shook. "What do you mean?"

"You'll understand soon." She took my arm. "I've been preparing you," she said. "That shot I gave you—it wasn't for your neck wound. The shot was to prepare you . . . for the gene transfer."

"Noooo!" I let out a scream and tore free from her grasp.

Then I spun away and lurched for the door.

Pounding their cages, the creatures began to bleat and howl. I glanced back and saw Dr. Carpenter chasing after me.

"OWWWW!" I cried out as I ran into a tall cage by the door. The cage clattered onto its side. And dozens of bats flapped out, chittering and whistling.

The bats swooped up to the ceiling, then down,

fluttering back and forth across the lab.

As Dr. Carpenter struggled with them, I ducked out the door. Into the long, dark hall.

My shoes pounded on the faded rug, the floor creaking and squeaking as I ran. I could still hear the flapping of the bats—and Dr. Carpenter's shrill cries as she came after me.

Panting hard, I wheeled around a corner—and ran into somebody.

"Oh—!" A hard collision. I caught my balance quickly.

And stared at Joe. He had put his black wig back on. He gaped at me in shock.

"Huh? You're here?" I cried. "You've got to help me Joe! Help me get away from her! She's crazy!"

To my surprise, Joe grabbed me around the waist. And pushed me against the wall.

"I've got her!" he shouted. "Here she is! I've got her, Mom!"

CHAPTER 26

"Huh? What are you *saying*, Joe?" I shrieked.

Joe didn't answer me. He kept me pinned against the wall. I struggled against him. Struggled to push free. But I wasn't strong enough.

Dr. Carpenter hurried up to us. "Good," she muttered. They grabbed my arms and pulled me into another lab. Then they shoved me into a tall cage. Dr. Carpenter slammed the cage door shut and locked it.

I turned and saw two ugly pig creatures behind me in the cage. One had long, blond hair with a pig face covered with brown speckles. The other one had sharp black horns sprouting from its pig head. It looked as if it were the combination of a pig and a ram.

"Please—let me out!" I wailed. "Please—!"

The speckled pig creature lurched forward and poked me in the side with a sharp hoof.

My heart pounded as the other one raised furry paws and ran one through my hair as if brushing it.

"Please—let me out."

The horned creature brought its face close to mine. It bared its teeth—as sharp as razors.

"It's—it's going to bite me." I backed away from the beast. Pressed myself into a corner of the cage. "Please—let me out."

"I'm sorry, Laura," she said. "But we can't have you running away again. We need you too badly."

"Need me? For what?" My voice came out high and shrill.

Bats fluttered in and out of the room. I gazed frantically around the lab. Cages were stacked high along the back wall. The cages were filled with squealing pigs.

In the center of the room stood a wall of electronic equipment. I saw three or four computer monitors. Several blinking control panels. Two metal cones were attached at either end. On a shiny metal table, syringes gleamed under the lab lights.

The pig creature with the horns grunted at me, baring its pointed teeth, licking its snout with a long pink tongue. The other one swiped at me with its hoof.

"You can't keep me here!" I cried. I charged at the bars and gripped the door, struggling to shove it open. It wouldn't budge.

"It won't take long," Dr. Carpenter replied. "It will all be over by the time your dad comes looking for you."

She was pushing buttons and spinning dials on the control panel. "Joe, bring down that pig on top. Cage number forty."

Joe hurried to obey. He opened the cage and lifted out a small pink-and-white pig. Holding it tightly in both hands, he carried it to Dr. Carpenter. She lifted the pig's head into one of the metal cones and began strapping it in.

Lights flashed on the control panel.

Two bats swooped into the lab, then soared back out.

"You lied to me!" I screamed. "You said my dad was doing the cruel experiments."

"I had to lie. I had no choice," Dr. Carpenter said. "Four years ago, right before we moved here, I found a way to change genes using electric shock. I was so close to creating a gene that could fight off viruses. So close. But then we had the terrible accident."

She turned and gazed at Joe. He had finished strapping the pig under the cone. Now he held the pig's leg while Dr. Carpenter inserted a syringe filled with a yellow liquid. The pig let out a sharp squeal as the needle penetrated its skin.

"During one of the cell transfers, Joe pricked himself with a syringe filled with pig cells. He stumbled back in surprise—stumbled directly into the path of the electric current," Dr. Carpenter continued. "His cells combined with pig cells."

She patted his cheek. "My poor little boy . . . he . . .

he hasn't been the same. He . . ." Tears formed in her eyes.

"We moved here so I'd have a safe place to live," Joe said. "No one would ask about me here. No one knew me here. And Mom could continue her research. To change me back."

"Joe, I—I—thought you were my friend," I stammered.

"I don't have friends anymore, Laura," he said softly. "I have to hide in the house most of the time. Until the hunger starts. That deep hunger for fresh meat. Then I have to hunt the woods. . . ." His voice trailed off.

"Joe," Dr. Carpenter sobbed. "I'm sorry. So sorry."

"You'll change me back, Mom," Joe said soothingly. "I know you will."

Dr. Carpenter turned to me. "I've been spending all my time trying to find a way to reverse the process. That's what all these animals are for. To help me change Joe back to normal."

"But, my dad—" I started.

"Your dad didn't approve of my experiments. He didn't know about Joe. I kept him hidden. But he didn't approve of the way I was treating the animals. He said I was going against the laws of nature. He tried to make me stop. The animals were dying. But I couldn't stop. I found that if I dissected them, I could learn what went wrong. I had to kill more—until I found the cure."

If we kill them, we can learn more. How many can we kill? The words from the binder in Dad's shed exploded in my mind. "Those were *your* notes in the shed!" I gasped.

My heart sank. I should have trusted my father. He'd never hurt an animal. I should have believed in him. My dad could never hurt a living thing.

Dr. Carpenter turned to Joe. "Enough talk. We haven't much time. Help me get Laura hooked up to the other transfer cone. Then we'll inject her."

"No!" I screamed, pushing away the two pig creatures. "No! Please!"

"I haven't had a human to experiment on in some time," Dr. Carpenter said, unlocking the cage door. "But now you're here. Wouldn't you like to be the one who helps me turn Joe back to normal?"

"No!" I screamed. "Please! Please!"

She grabbed me with both hands and tugged me from the cage. Then she shoved me under the metal cone.

I tried to kick free. But she was too strong. She pinned me against the side of the machine. And pulled the cone down over my hair.

"Wait, Mom—don't!" Joe screamed. "I don't like this. I can't go through with it! Laura is my friend!"

"She's not your friend!" Dr. Carpenter snapped. She tightened a strap under my chin to hold me under the cone. "Don't you understand? Her father will destroy me before I cure you!"

"Mom—" Joe cried.

Dr. Carpenter turned to me. "The current will shoot between the two cones," she explained. "It doesn't hurt, Laura. Not at all. We'll inject you with something to help the pig's cells bind to yours. And this machine will take care of the rest. You won't even feel it."

"Noooo! Noooo! Please!" I struggled to free myself.

But I had no time.

She grabbed a syringe—and jabbed it into my arm. I screamed as the pain throbbed up my arm.

She pulled the needle out quickly, scratching herself. She blotted the blood with her lab coat. Then she reached past me to the control panel. Clutched a long handle. And threw the switch.

CHAPTER 27

I heard the crackle of electricity.

I saw Joe grab his mother around the waist and try to pull her away.

As they wrestled, the lab door swung open behind them.

"Dad!" I screamed. "Help me!"

An electrical current jolted between the two metal cones. The pig on the other side squealed and began to kick its feet.

A bat swooped into the room. It flew low over my dad, heading right for the electrical current.

Dr. Carpenter turned to face my dad. "Get out of here!" she screamed, backing away from him. "You've done enough!"

Dad kept coming, his eyes narrowed angrily on her, his fists knotted at his sides.

The bat swooped past my head.

Dr. Carpenter took another step back. "You can't

stop me!" she screamed at my father. "You can't! I'm warning you—"

But he didn't stop. He came after her. Step by step. His hands clamped into fists.

Backing her up . . . Backing her up . . .

And then she let out a high shriek as she stumbled—and fell back—into the electrical current.

I screamed, too, as I saw the bat swoop into the stream of electricity.

ZZZAAAAAP.

The whole room sizzled and crackled.

I saw Dr. Carpenter and the bat outlined in bright yellow.

I saw the bat explode in the crackling current. Its guts sprayed Dr. Carpenter as she shrieked in terror.

And then I shut my eyes. It was too horrible. Too ugly.

Too terrifying.

CHAPTER 28

I didn't open my eyes until I felt the metal cone being lifted off my head. Dad pulled me out into the hall.

He hugged me tightly. I gazed up at him, still dazed.

"It's okay now, Laura," Dad said softly. "It's all over. My work is done. We've stopped her. I've been gathering evidence. Working so hard."

"But, Dad—" I choked out. "The creatures in the shed. The binder you stole from her . . ."

"I tried to stop her research. I knew her experiments were wrong," he said. "That's why she fired me. But I took her notes. I've been trying to cure the animals she changed."

He guided me gently down the hall and led me out of the building. "Where are they?" I asked, glancing back at the animal hospital. "Where are Joe and Dr. Carpenter?"

"They ran while I was freeing you. But don't

worry. They won't get far. We'll find them."

Dad and I were home a few minutes later. I followed him into the kitchen.

He picked up an envelope from the kitchen counter and ripped it in half.

"What's that?" I asked.

"Your plane ticket to Chicago." He tossed the pieces into the trash. "I never wanted to send you away," he said. "But I was so scared. I knew how vicious those creatures could be. I only wanted to protect you."

He shook his head. "In the woods last night you shouldn't have run. I only wanted to protect you, Laura."

I rushed forward to hug him. We hugged for a long time.

Then my eyes drifted to the kitchen window. I gazed into the woods. I thought about Joe. Would I ever see him again? I wondered.

And would the woods return to normal now?

Would *anything* ever be normal again?

That night I was so tired. But I couldn't fall asleep.

I lay in bed, staring at the pale half-moon outside my window. It looked like a smile. A grin in the dark.

I had finally started to drift off. My eyes were just closing—when I heard a fluttering sound.

Something flapping against the window glass.

I sat up, alert.

What *was* that? A bat?

Yes. A bat floating outside the window, beating its wings against the glass.

"Huh?" I crept out of bed. I made my way to the window.

Thump thump.

The wings bumped and scraped the glass as the bat hovered at the window.

I crept closer. Watching the flapping wings. The tiny, round body. The bat claws . . .

And the face . . .

The face . . .

Dr. Carpenter's face on the bat's body!

Flapping, bumping against the window, she stared in at me. Her face tiny now, where the bat's head should be. Her green eyes wide with horror.

And then she opened her mouth wide.

Staring at each other through the glass, we both opened our mouths—and screamed and screamed and screamed.

Check out these other scares from R.L. Stine . . .

Hc 0-06-623842-0
Pb 0-06-055547-5

Hc 0-06-028688-1
Pb 0-06-440842-6

#1: Hc 0-06-053080-4
    Pb 0-06-053082-0
#2: Hc 0-06-059616-3
    Pb 0-06-059618-X

Pb 0-06-076674-3

Beware!

The spookiest, creepiest, most bloodcurdling stories of them all are compiled in this hair-raising anthology! Beware—you're in for a scare!

Nightmare Hour
The New York Times *best-seller!*

What horror awaits a boy who has to spend Halloween in the hospital? How do you outwit a ghost that wants your skin? Why is Nightmare Inn the most frightening place to visit? Find out in *Nightmare Hour!*

Dangerous Girls and Dangerous Girls 2: The Taste of Night

Being a teenage girl can be scary enough. But when you're bitten by a vampire and have to reverse the spell before the clock runs out, life is a lot more terrifying. Blood, romance, and horror collide in these spine-tingling, heart-pounding tales of suspense.

The Nightmare Room, Books 1-2-3: The Nightmare Begins!
Three books in one!

Enter a world one step beyond the everyday, where people can forget their own lives and a simple school locker can hold more terror than a haunted house.

AVON BOOKS

www.thenightmareroom.com   An Imprint of HarperCollinsPublishers

PARACHUTE PRESS

Books created and produced by
Parachute Publishing, L.L.C.